Darkness, Be My Friend

Darkness, Be My Friend

John Marsden

Houghton Mifflin Company
Boston

All rights reserved. For information about permission to reproduce
selections from this book, write to Permissions, Houghton Mifflin
Company, 215 Park Avenue South, New York, New York 10003.

First published in 1996 by Pan Macmillan Australia Pty Limited,
St. Martins Tower, 31 Market Street, Sydney

The text of this book is set in 12-point Transitional 521 BT.

Library of Congress Cataloging-in-Publication Data

Marsden, John, 1950–
Darkness, be my friend / by John Marsden.
p.   cm.
Sequel to: A killing frost.
Summary: As survivors of an enemy invasion of their homeland,
Ellie and her friends return to Australia as guides for soldiers from
New Zealand who plan an attack on the Wirrawee airfield.
ISBN 0-395-92274-7
[1. Survival—Fiction. 2. War—Fiction. 3. Australia—Fiction.]
I. Title
PZ7.M35145Dar   1999   98-38493
[Fic]—dc21   CIP
                                        AC

Manufactured in the United States of America

QUM 10 9 8 7 6 5

Acknowledgments

Much thanks to Charlotte and Rick Lindsay, Roos Marsden, Felicity Bell, Paul Kenny, Jill Rawnsley, Julia Watson and students of Hale School, for help so generously given.

For Neil Elliot Meiers
Born 10th January 1984
Left 29th December 1995
for another adventure

An Aussie Glossary

Aga: wood stove

Ag. bike: motor bike used on farms

anfo: ammonium nitrate (fuel oil)

B&S's: dances for young rural people

bikkies: biscuits

bitumen: asphalt, tar

blowies: blowflies

BLS: brandy lime soda

blue heeler: cattle dog

boot: car trunk

Buckley's: if you have Buckley's chance, you have no chance at all

bugger: something difficult or unpleasant

bush: uncleared Australian countryside

bush-bash: to force a path through the bush

cactus: trashed, a mess

Charolais: breed of cattle

chook: chicken

circle work: to drive a vehicle in tight circles for sport

crack a mental: to become angry

crack onto: to make a sexual advance toward someone

creche: baby-minding facility

crocodile: straight line of children walking in pairs

dag: eccentric, amusing person

dingoes: wild dogs

dobbed: told on, tattled

dreaming: Aboriginal word which expresses a close affiliation with an area of land

dunny: toilet

fair dinkum: the truth, the real thing

flat-chat: as fast as possible

the flick: the brush-off

footy: Australian Rules football

good nick: good condition

goss: to gab

graziers: farmers who have sheep or cattle

hit-out: strenuous exercise

hooning: acting wildly

hotted up: modified to go faster

hypo: hypochondriac

jillaroos: female apprentice farmers

jocks: underpants

jumper: sweater

k: kilometre

kitbags: duffel bags

Kiwis: New Zealanders

kookaburra: Australian bird

lollipop lady: crossing guard

Macquarie: a brand of dictionary

merino stud: farm that breeds Merino sheep

milkbar: small corner store, mini-mart

nappies: diapers

nick: naked, also condition

one-tonner: small tray-top truck

paid her out: teased her

perv: to look at a person in a sexual way

poddy lambs: lambs raised by hand

rapt: delighted

Ratsak: rat poison

recce: reconnaissance

ride-ons: lawn mowers that people drive

roo: kangaroo

Saladas: biscuits

sherbert: a sweet white powder eaten as candy

shout: to pay for everyone's drinks

slaters: beetles

a snack: an easy task

spur: a ridge on a mountain

sultanas: fruit that is similar to raisins

sussed out: examined, checked it out

tacker: kid

tech: school that teaches technical skills

texta: marker pen

torch: flashlight

tray: the back section of a truck — the flat part that the load sits on

uni: university

ute: utility vehicle

wethers: castrated male sheep

whinge: to whine

yakka: work

One

I didn't want to go back.

That sounds pretty casual, doesn't it? Like saying, "I don't want to go to the movie," "I think I'll give that party the flick," "I don't feel like it today."

Just one of those comments you make.

But the truth is, I felt so sick at the thought of going back that my insides liquefied. I felt like my guts would pour out of me until my stomach caved in. I could even picture it: my ribs touching my backbone.

But my insides didn't pour out. After they told us what they wanted I'd go and sit on the dunny, but nothing happened. Sitting there holding myself, wondering if I'd ever feel good again.

And it was because my life was at stake. My life. I thought there should be a long time to think about that, a lot of careful thinking, a lot of discussion. Everyone giving their opinions, heaps of counselling and stuff, then me going away and spending weeks weighing up the options.

But it wasn't like that. They pretended there was a choice, but they were just, you know, doing it to make me feel good. And OK, maybe the truth is there couldn't be a choice, because the whole thing was too important. But I didn't want to know about that. I wanted to scream at them, "Listen to me, will you! I don't care about your big plans, I just want to hide under the bed and wait until the war's over. All right? That's all I want. End of story."

And I wanted someone, anyone, to acknowledge that I was being asked to put my life on the line. That what they wanted me to do was enormous, gigantic, ginormous.

Life, to be sure, is nothing much to lose;
But young men think it is, and we were young.

That's from a poem a World War One guy wrote. A teacher in Dunedin gave it to me, and OK, I'm a young woman not a young man, but I still don't want to lose my life. I don't know much about anything but I do know that.

So, there I was, wanting weeks to think, to concentrate, to feel. To get used to the idea of going back. To get ready.

Wanting weeks and getting days. Five days to be exact. Five days between Colonel Finley asking us, and our arriving at the airfield.

If anything, I guess I felt angry. Cheated. They were treating me and my life like I was a plastic toy. Pick it up, play with it a moment, chuck it aside. Plenty more where that came from.

Colonel Finley always talked to us like we were soldiers under his command. Like there was no difference between us and his troops. But they had signed up to take risks and fight wars and shoot people. We hadn't! Seemed like only yesterday that we'd needed a lollipop lady before we could even cross the road outside school. And yes, I know, people have told me a thousand times how in some countries kids are in the army when they're eleven years old, but I didn't care about that.

"That's not how we do it," I wanted to shout at them. "We're different."

That was all that mattered to me.

Only Fi seemed to understand how I felt. Up to a point, anyway. I couldn't help thinking that she didn't see it quite the way I did. That surprised me, I've got to admit. I didn't want to look like a wimp, compared to the others. I wanted to be stronger than everyone. Fi had her own strengths; I knew that, of course, but I liked to think that I was more of a leader than her. Yet here she was saying pretty well straightaway that she'd go, while I sat there in shock, dithering, wanting to go off for a few years and think about it.

I was actually angry at her, that was the crazy thing.

Or maybe not so crazy. After all, I was angry at everyone. Might as well include her.

It started when we'd been in New Zealand almost five months. We'd escaped from a nightmare, or we thought we had. The truth is, there's no escape from some nightmares. This one followed us across the Tasman. They'd air-lifted us out of our own country after it was invaded. We'd arrived in New Zealand burnt and injured and shocked, with broken bones, and scars inside and out. We'd lost contact with our families, we'd seen friends die, we'd caused other people to die by our own deliberate actions.

We were just typical survivors of war, I guess.

And then it all started again.

It was the end of spring, moving into summer. The bushfire season. And that's appropriate because the whole thing began a bit like a bushfire. You know how it is. First you hear warnings on the radio, then you hear a rustling in the distance, like bark in a breeze, then there's white smoke, could be clouds, maybe not, can't be sure, but at last comes the smell, the never-could-be-mistaken smell of burning.

And suddenly it's on you. Suddenly there are trees exploding a hundred metres from the house and the heat's like you've opened an oven door and sat in front of it and there's the sound of roaring wind and in among the grey and white smoke you see the wild wicked flames dancing.

For us the first hint, the first warning, was a rumour going round the refugees that some of them would be dropped back into occupied areas. Either with Kiwi troops or, in some cases, on their own. Either to carry out a particular job, or to be guerillas, doing the sort of stuff we'd done around Wirrawee and Cobbler's Bay.

I must be dumb, because I didn't think they'd ask us. It never crossed my mind. Lee heard about it first. "Bet we're on their shopping list," he said. But I didn't take any notice: I think I was reading at the time. *Emma*, as I recall.

I've got to keep on trying to be honest here, because I have been, ever since I started writing stuff down, so

4

I'd better say that the reason I thought they wouldn't ask us is that we'd done so much already. God, hadn't we done enough? Hadn't we gone for it, time and time again? Hadn't we blown up a ship and wrecked Cobbler's Bay and killed a general in Wirrawee? Hadn't we had Lee shot in the leg and the other three? (I can't even say their names right now.) And hadn't we stared death right in the face and felt its cold fingers tightening its grip on the backs of our necks? What would satisfy them? Did we all have to die before they'd say, "OK, that'll do, you can have the rest of the war off"?

How much did we have to do?

It gets me so upset thinking about it.

I know there's no logic in this. I know when there's a war on they can't just say, "Look, we'll carry on without you guys for a while, you give it a miss for a year or two."

But somewhere along the line, somewhere way back in childhood, we'd been taught that life is actually fair, that you get out of it what you put in, that if you want something badly enough you can achieve it.

That's garbage. I know that now.

Suddenly at the time in my life when I most wanted things to be fair, suddenly no one was mentioning the word any more. It wasn't on our spelling list; there was no Pictionary card for it; the Macquarie went straight from "faint" to "fairy."

The New Zealanders had been good to us before this, I've got to admit. Of course that made it even harder to refuse Colonel Finley. But yes, they'd been good to us. Right from the start they'd arranged a lot of counselling and stuff. We all ended up getting that, even Homer and Lee who once upon a time wouldn't have gone to a shrink if you'd paid them. The psychologist they gave me, Andrea, I got really close to her. She became like a second mum.

And we did actually have holidays and everything. I'm not kidding, we were like heroes. Anything we asked for, they gave us. Fi and I made a sort of game of it for a few weeks, asking for everything we could think of. Then suddenly I got sick of that game.

But we went to the South Island, and skied the Remarkables, and we flew to Milford Sound and drove out through a tunnel, and we checked out Mt. Cook, then followed the east coast down and went across to Invercargill.

Andrea said I was "in denial," rushing around like a maniac because I didn't want to look at the things that had happened to us. Not that she said "like a maniac." It wouldn't be very tactful for a shrink to say that.

The funniest thing was when we were meant to go on these jetboats, near Queenstown somewhere, and we all chickened out. Like, I'm talking major cowardice. None of us had bothered to ask what jetboats were; we thought they were some little fun riverboat cruise thing. But when we got there we started to realise they were monster boats that went roaring down the river at about a hundred k's an hour, in water that was, like, five centimetres deep.

And once we realised that, none of us would go in them. We stood on the banks of the river, shivering, like a pathetic little mob of sheep waiting to be dipped, and the driver of the first boat was saying, "Come on, let's go, hockey players," and we couldn't move.

It was so embarrassing. The driver started looking at

us like, "What the hell is wrong with these people?" and finally Corporal Ahauru, who was in charge of us back then, took her aside and had a long conversation with her and I knew exactly what she was saying, exactly, down to the commas and full stops. It'd be, "They're the ones who've been in the news, those teenagers who did the attack on Cobbler's Bay, in Aussie, and they've all got major emotional problems, poor things, and I think right now they're seeing this as a little bit too threatening, a bit more than they can cope with."

Corporal Ahauru is a nurse, did I mention that before?

So we didn't go on the jetboats and the driver probably still thinks of us as cowards and frauds and at that stage not even Colonel Finley would have sent us back into a war zone.

Somewhere along the line, though, we must have got marginally better. I'm not sure how or when it happened, but I suppose after a while there were one or two good days and then, after a bit longer, nearly as many good days as bad ones. I can't speak for the others but for me it never got to be more than three good days in a row, and that only happened once. We made a few friends, and that helped, although I admit I was insanely jealous when the others started mixing with new people. It was all right for me, but not for them. I wanted them — Homer and Lee and Kevin and Fi — I wanted them all for myself.

Next thing, someone got the intelligent idea that we'd go to schools and give talks to help raise money for the war effort. We tried three times, then unanimously canned it. It was a disaster: well, three disasters.

I'm going red even now, thinking about it. We were over-confident, that was one problem. We thought it'd be a snack. That was the way we were for quite a while, going from wild over-confidence to total terror, like with the jetboats.

The first talk was at a primary school and it was a Friday afternoon and the kids were rioting even before we got there. They were in the gym, waiting for us. There'd been some mix-up about the time, so we were twenty minutes late. We could hear them yelling as we came in the gate. We thought it must still be lunchtime, judging from the noise. OK, if we'd given brilliant speeches maybe we could have turned it around, but we didn't give brilliant speeches. Lee was so soft no one heard him. Homer had more "ums" than words, Fi spoke for thirty seconds, looking like she was about to start crying the whole time, and Kevin tried to make a joke, which failed dismally and all the kids made sarcastic noises — like fake laughter and stuff — and Kevin lost his temper and told them to shut up. That was extremely embarrassing.

I'm not going to say what happened with my speech.

The second time was a bit better, because at least we prepared for it, and also it was a secondary school, but now we were too nervous to make it work properly. Lee was the best because this time he had a microphone. Homer's sentences went: "And we, um, we ah, we walked, um, to this, like, um, er, silo, I think that's where we went then, is that right, Ellie, or was that before we got Kevin back?"

The third time Kevin refused to do it at all, and Lee knocked over a jug of water when he stood up to speak.

Fi gave a great speech, but the rest of us hadn't improved much.

That's when we dumped it.

But I did meet Adam at the last school, Mt. Burns High School in Wellington, just off Adelaide Road. We were in the Year 12 (Sixth Form they call it) common room after the talks and this guy handed me the Mallowpuffs and started chatting me up. He was a prefect and he was wearing a school blazer that had so many badges I'm surprised he could stand up straight. Seems like he was the local hero. Swimming, rugby, debating, he'd done it all. Lots of boys in New Zealand wear shorts to school. They have a Seventh Form too and even some of the Seventh Formers wear shorts. It looks kind of silly, because they seem too old for it, but it gives you a good chance to perv on their legs. And Adam did have swimmer's legs. Someone told me later that he could swim a fifty-metre pool in sixty-five seconds without using his arms. I was impressed.

He used his arms on me, though. He invited me to a party that same night, and I went. It was a big mistake. It was so long since I'd been to a party that I'd forgotten how to act. I hadn't bothered to eat before I went, because I figured they'd have food there. And there was food all right: a packet of chips, a bowl of jellybeans and half-a-dozen over-ripe bananas. That's the kind of party it was. Then, to make matters worse, I had three BLS's in the first half-hour. Another big mistake. By eleven o'clock, after a few more BLS's, and more than a few slurps from Adam's beer glass, I was gone. I'd had it.

And he changed really suddenly. One minute we were just joking around like old buddies, the next he had his tongue in my mouth and was walking me backwards down the corridor to the bedrooms. I was trying to say, "Hey, what happened to beautiful old-fashioned romance? What happened to foreplay even?" but it's hard to talk with a tongue in your mouth. Sure I was kissing him back at first, but it wasn't working at all for me, I was just doing it, I don't know, because I was expected to, I suppose, he expected me to. Sort of automatically. I've never been less turned on in my life.

When we got in the bedroom he fell backwards on the bed, taking me with him. It wasn't very graceful. I felt dizzy and sick. He was tonguing my ear and all I could think was, "God, when was the last time I cleaned the wax out?" but I felt too sick and drunk to stop him, to even try to stop him. Next thing he's undoing my zip. I'm not saying I was too drunk to do anything about it, it wasn't like that, I mean that'd be rape, no, it was just that I couldn't be bothered. Oh, I tried for a minute, tried to pull my jeans back up, but in the end I thought, "Who cares, what does it matter, just get it over with and then I can go home."

I don't understand what guys get out of sex like that; not very much, I would have thought, but they obviously get something out of it or they wouldn't do it. The only good thing I can say about him was that at least he used a condom. But only because he thought he might catch something from me. I'm sure it wasn't because he wanted to protect me.

All I got out of it was a terrible feeling that I was a disgusting human being. It was so against everything I stood for, everything I believed in. The next day I felt awful. I had a terrible headache anyway, and my stomach felt like it was still doing slow spins, but worse, far worse, was the way I felt such a slut. I felt sick at myself. I couldn't talk to the others about it, couldn't talk to anyone, except about three o'clock I got the bright idea of calling Andrea, the psychologist.

She was good, like always. It took me about an hour to get it out but in the end I told her everything. I started crying as I got to the end of the story, and then I couldn't stop. I felt so ashamed. Not of crying, but of being so cheap. I was bawling into this mustard-coloured cushion in Andrea's biggest armchair and using her tissues like they were five cents a box. And they're not, of course — everything in New Zealand's so expensive. Five cents a tissue'd be more like it.

Andrea didn't say anything for ages. She's the only person I've ever met who lets you have time to think about what you want to say. She never puts pressure on you in that way. She just sits there and watches and waits.

But finally I was sitting up a bit and hiccupping and blowing my nose. She explained how I was still reacting to Robyn's death, using different things as anaesthetics, and that was all really. She had another appointment to go to, so the next thing she'd left. I did actually feel a bit better — it surprised me, but it's true. I'd never thought of any connection between Robyn's death and the way I'd acted.

But I was angry at Adam. I thought, "If I ever see him again he'll get more than wax in his mouth."

I didn't want to write about it here, and I wouldn't have, except I think maybe it's one of the reasons I ended up not putting up so much of a fight about going

11

back. I just felt awful about how I'd behaved and how I'd let myself down and everything.

Maybe I thought going back would be a way of making up for that.

I was desperate for some self-respect.

Two

It was only a day later that the bushfire started burning stronger. There'd been the rumour about using refugees as guerillas, then the next thing, the five of us were called up for medicals.

We got the full treatment, not just a physical but a mental as well. About three thousand questions, from "What did you eat for breakfast?" to "Do you still want to be a farmer when the war is over?" from "What's your favourite TV show?" to "Which is more important, honesty or loyalty?"

We got weighed, measured, pinched and probed, inspected and injected. My bad knee and my bad vertebrae. My eyesight and hearing and reflexes and blood pressure.

At lunch, munching on Saladas and cheese, breathing on the celery to warm it because it had just come out of the fridge, I said to Homer: "What do you think that was all about?"

"I don't know," he said slowly. "It's like they're checking

us out. Seeing if we're in good shape again. Maybe the holiday'll be over soon."

That's the first time I took it a bit more seriously. But only for a minute or two. I'd almost forgotten that rumour, and Lee's comment about the shopping list. I said to Homer, "We're still a bunch of wrecks. They won't want us to do anything for ages yet."

I believed that too. Secretly I thought they'd never ask us to do anything again.

What was next? Another interview with Colonel Finley, I think. That was quite unusual. He was a busy man. But at five o'clock on a Saturday afternoon he rang Homer and asked if we could come for a meeting.

You don't say no to Colonel Finley so we cancelled our plans for a wild Saturday night — in other words we turned off the TV — and went to see him. It was quite some meeting. There were six officers, two Australian and four from New Zealand. They weren't even introduced to us, which seemed a bit rude. Everyone was too busy, I suppose. But one of them had so much gold braid on his uniform that he could have melted it down, sold it, and retired on the proceeds.

It was amazing we all fitted into Colonel Finley's little office, with its nice old-fashioned pictures on the walls and the clouds of blue pipe smoke. Maybe it was bigger than it looked. It must have been, because it always looked tiny. Somehow we all found chairs. I perched on the edge of Fi's. We sat there for half an hour getting grilled about a whole lot of stuff. They had maps of the Wirrawee district and Cobbler's Bay and Stratton, but they wanted all kinds of other information, down to details like the size of the trees in Barker Street and the condition of the four-wheel-drive track going into Baloney Creek.

The questions came thick and fast and everything should have gone fine, but somehow it didn't. We know most of that country pretty well, or we thought we did, but the officers wouldn't have been too impressed. The five of us managed to disagree on every second answer. Homer and I managed to disagree on every answer.

"There's a service station on the corner of Maldon Street and West Street."

"Maldon and West? No, there isn't!"

"Well, what is there then?"

"I can't remember, but it's definitely not a service station. Which service station do you reckon's there?"

"You know, that old one, Bob Burchett or whatever his name is."

"Bob Burchett? That's on the corner of Maldon and Honey, and it's Bill Burchett, not Bob."

"Kevin, I'm right, aren't I? It's Maldon and West."

It was like that most of the time and when we got back to our quarters Homer wouldn't even speak to me.

Sunday a guy dropped in after lunch for no reason that any of us could quite work out. His name was Iain Pearce, he was in his mid-twenties, he was obviously something military—you could tell by the way he walked—but he was wearing jeans and a grey Nike T-shirt, and he just sat there chatting away like a new neighbour who'd come in for a cup of coffee. He had one of those honest uncomplicated faces, steady eyes, and a very straight black moustache. Kevin liked him at first sight, so for a while they did most of the talking.

14

And most of it was guy talk: rugby and cars and computers. It wasn't too interesting but I didn't have the energy to move, so I sat there half-listening, trying not to yawn. Fi was even ruder: she was reading a magazine called *Contact*, a newsletter for refugees like us who'd escaped to New Zealand. So she ignored them completely. Lee joined in a bit, but not Homer. Homer was still sulking, so when he talked it was in mumbles and grunts.

Gradually, though, Iain turned on the charm. I think he must have done a PR course or something, because after he'd talked to Kevin for a while he went to work on the rest of us. I quite enjoyed watching him do it. First he asked Fi about the music she liked and, because Fi loves music, she couldn't resist that. Then he found out that Fi and Lee and I had gone to a new New Zealand movie called *The Crossing*, which he hadn't seen but he knew the guy who did the special effects — maybe I should have worked out from that what kind of work Iain was in — so we told him a bit about the film. And somehow a few minutes later the subject was pig farming and Homer, who's always been mad about pigs, was talking nonstop about how he wanted to build up a herd of Poland Chinas, a breed I'd never heard of.

An hour later Iain had gone and we still didn't have a clue why he'd come in the first place.

The fire was raging now, only we didn't know it.

We knew it the next day, though. Oh boy, did we know it. The Monday. Black Monday. Fi and I had been for a run at about three in the afternoon. We went through the pine trees and along an old track to a hill that I always liked. There wasn't anything much up there, nothing spectacular, but it was a nice round smooth soft hill where the grass was always wet and green, and the fences were exactly the same as a couple of our older ones at home: dry stone walls with a single strand of barbed wire on top.

It's a hard run up there but easy coming back, except that Fi always cheats, cutting off the corners at every bend. I make it tough for myself by sticking to the track. I can still beat Fi, even when she cheats, but she doesn't really try; she mainly comes to keep me company.

OK, be honest, she comes because I bully her into it.

Anyway, this particular Monday we got back about half past three, a quarter to four, and there they all were: Colonel Finley, Homer, Lee and Kevin. They were standing in a circle, like mourners at a funeral, and the expressions on their faces were like mourners at a funeral too.

When I found out what Colonel Finley wanted I realised they were at a funeral.

Ours.

Fi and I walked up to them quite innocently. I had my hands on my hips, I remember that. We were hot and red-faced and panting, but I soon forgot my lack of oxygen and my heaving chest and my sweaty top. Before I could ask what was happening Homer told me.

"We're going back," he said.

That's Homer. If you want to understand Homer, and sometimes I don't know why you'd bother, those three words tell you everything you need to know. "We're going back." Even as I write them again now I can feel myself starting to scowl and grind my teeth. The thing about Homer is that he'd know exactly how angry it'd make me when he said that, but he couldn't stop himself. He'd say it to prove to himself that he was the Man, no one was going to tell him what to do. And of course the "no one" he was worried about was me. All our lives we'd been competing. Even now, at this critical moment, he wasn't going to give me the satisfaction of letting me think I had any say.

Our lives at stake, and Homer still wanted to make the decisions for us.

So there I was, my blood draining away through my feet, flooding out so fast I thought I would faint. I was churned up with anger at Homer, shock at what he had said, and sheer stark total terror. I felt for a minute like it was Fi and me against the four males. Funny, I knew exactly what Homer meant when he said "We're going back," I didn't have to ask. I knew he wasn't talking about going back to the pool for another swim, or going back to the cinema on Customhouse Quay.

In the end all I could do was walk past them and into the house. Colonel Finley was trying to talk to me: I think he was mad at Homer for jumping the gun like that, but I wouldn't listen, just kept walking. I assumed Fi was right behind me; it was only when I reached the bathroom that I realised she wasn't. That got me even madder: I swung right round and charged straight out again. They were still standing there, in their little huddle, Fi with them now.

I screeched to a halt and screeched at them, "What the hell is this all about?"

"Look," Colonel Finley said, in his very patient voice that he hardly ever used, "I think we'd better go inside and have a chat."

Three cups of coffee later he'd finally gone and we were left to our argument. And did we have a doozey. I ranted and raved and screamed. It was stupid really, because deep down I knew we had to go. I suppose maybe, looking back, I wasn't screaming at them; I was screaming at everything: at life, at the unfairness of it. Above all, with the fear that I might be killed, that what I saw happen to Robyn might happen to me.

But there were two compelling reasons for us to go. Two reasons that meant we didn't have a choice. One reason was the one that mattered to Colonel Finley: the sabotage they planned for Wirrawee. Sabotage that was getting more important every day now that Cobbler's Bay was back in action and Wirrawee was used more and more heavily as the centre for the whole district. Little Wirrawee, on the map at last. We were going to try to put it off the map. And with the New Zealand Air Force losing out badly in the sky, bombing was getting too dangerous. There were hardly any bombing missions any more. Guerilla activity was seen as the best hope. "Cost effective" were Colonel Finley's cool dry words.

The second reason was the one that was racing a-round our minds, whizzing like go-karts. It didn't matter much to Colonel Finley, but it meant everything to us.

Our families, families, families. That was the argument that suffocated everything else. It drew us all back home. And I mean the five of us. At one stage Colonel Finley suggested we didn't all have to go: a couple could stay behind. He didn't name anyone in particular, and we didn't ask. We unanimously rejected any talk of splitting the group. We needed each other too much.

For a few days I almost hated my parents for being locked up in Wirrawee Showgrounds.

If they hadn't been there, if they'd been safe in New Zealand, for example, would I still have agreed to go back?

It was a horrible question and one I'm glad I didn't have to answer. But all the same, I think I knew deep down what the answer would be.

Sometimes there's really only one answer.

So, would I have gone back?

Yes.

Three

Funny, I write this stuff, I quite enjoy it. I don't know, it's probably good for me or something. I remember Andrea hinting that once, but I don't care about that, I've just gradually grown to like it. So I sit here and rattle off page after page. Sometimes it seems like an effort; sometimes it flows like water. My record for a day is nearly ten pages.

But that one word at the end of the last bit, just that one word: it took me a whole day to write that.

Anyway, I'm not going to say any more about it.

They wouldn't tell us much about what they wanted us to do, but I gradually realised we would start by going into Hell, our beautiful natural hideout, so well hidden from the rest of the world. I had to mark places on a map where I thought a helicopter could land on our property, so I figured a chopper ride would be part of the deal. We knew we had to guide some New Zealand soldiers: that was our main function. But that was all we knew.

The day before we left, though, I got taken to Colonel Finley's office. On my own this time. Then he told me in detail what I'd have to do: how from the moment we landed sixteen other people would be depending totally on me. But I wasn't allowed to tell anyone where we were going. Not until we'd taken off from Wellington.

The other thing Colonel Finley said really annoyed me. Infuriated me. He started in on this speech about how we had to be ready to take orders when we got there; we had to realise that we would be under the command of professional soldiers. We couldn't go off half-cocked, or start "doing our own thing," as he called it. It reminded me of Major Harvey, so that put me off right away, but I also thought it was an insult to my intelligence. I wondered why he wasn't giving this lecture to the others.

So I told him.

"Colonel Finley, I know all this. We're not idiots. We're not going over there to play games."

He seemed a bit taken aback. I don't think his own soldiers spoke to him like that.

"Of course, Ellie, I didn't mean to suggest that..."

The interview didn't go much longer. I think he was glad to get me out of his office.

Surprise surprise, who should be at the airport but Iain Pearce. Captain Iain Pearce that is, as we soon found out. And eleven others like him. Not totally like him, seeing four of them were women. But they did have a sameness about them. As I got to know some of them better I learned that of course they were all different. OK, sure, I know everyone's different, but this bunch did look alike, dress alike, sound alike. They'd all gone through the same training programme, I suppose. Or maybe they were picked in the first place because they fitted the mould that the army wanted. They were so correct about everything: that bugged me a bit. Everything they said was correct, they never slopped around saying the first thing that came into their minds, they never said anything that we would be offended by, they only swore when the radio wouldn't work or they cut themselves shaving. You couldn't help feeling that they'd all go to the toilet at the same time, and the same stuff would come out, if you know what I mean.

We stood on the tarmac at the RNZAF base, shivering. A dozen professional saboteurs and five amateur guides. A dozen soldiers, highly trained, carrying everything from automatic weapons to Band-Aids, and keyed up for action. And five pale-faced kids, scared from their tonsils through their large intestines all the way down to their toes.

God, we were scared. Even Homer was scared. It had happened too fast, that was the problem. But if we'd had six months it wouldn't have made any difference. Matter of fact it might have been worse.

Kevin stood on his own, near the tail of the aircraft. He'd been chucking all night. I knew, because I'd been up all night myself. I hadn't slept for four nights, but last night had been the worst. Fi leant against me, looking out at the beautiful free ocean. Homer was talking to two of the soldiers. He was trying to hang tough, to look like them, but I wasn't fooled. Lee sat on his backpack with a stick in his hand, jabbing at the bitumen.

Fi turned to me suddenly and to my surprise said, "Are you OK about this now?"

"No."

"But we've got no choice."

"I know."

For four days, after our big argument, we'd avoided talking about it. We'd tiptoed around each other and talked about things like how many jocks to take, or which was the best flavour chocolate.

"I don't want to go either," Fi said.

"You didn't put up much of a fight."

She shrugged. "It's out of our control. I felt like if Colonel Finley thought it was important, we had to do it."

"Yeah, of course. I'm just taking longer to get used to the idea, that's all. It's not exactly that I don't want to go, it's more that I don't like the way we were given no choice. I mean Homer saying 'We're going back'; it's so typical of him. Honestly, he is infuriating."

"What do you think it'll be like?"

"I don't know. It's scary, isn't it, to think how much things might have changed. They're talking about Wirrawee like it's a major city. New York, Tokyo, London and Wirrawee."

"It won't be that big. It's just the airfield really."

Several newspapers had run stories on the development of a big new military airfield at Wirrawee.

"That's all we know. There could be heaps more happening. The whole countryside'll probably be crawling with soldiers."

"You're just trying to scare yourself."

"Mmm, and it's not too difficult."

"Ellie, have you really changed a lot, or is this just a stage you're going through?" But she laughed as she said it.

"Of course I've changed. What do you think?" But I didn't laugh.

"You've always had the guts to do things. You're not allowed to stop. We'd all give up then."

"I never had guts, Fi. I just did things because there was no choice. Like what you said about going back. Exactly the same."

Iain Pearce, Captain Iain Pearce, strode over to where we were talking. He marched all the time. I bet he marched to the shower in the morning.

"There's been another delay, folks. Sorry about this. It's what happens when you trust the Air Force. If you want a coffee there's a canteen at the end of the fibrolite building. But be back in forty-five, OK?"

We all went over there except Homer. And we didn't march, we slouched. Fi and I picked up our conversation as we sat clutching coffee mugs, using them to warm our hands.

"I'm more scared than I used to be," I confessed. "I'm scared of dying now. I mean I always was, but now that I've seen so much of it, I'm bloody terrified. Aren't you?"

"Yes, of course. But it's funny, I feel quite calm right at this moment. I don't understand why. I should be in a straitjacket." She peered into her coffee as if she

23

expected to find an answer there. "I think it's partly because of the soldiers," she said at last. "They're so professional about everything. I just feel we'll be like spectators this time. We can leave all the important stuff to them."

"I suppose. But so much can go wrong."

"Nothing new about that."

"Do you think we might be able to see our parents?"

"Well, Colonel Finley said he'd talk to Iain about it. He thought we'd have a good chance."

"Oh, come on, Fi! You believed that? He'd say anything to get us to go."

Fi looked so sad that I felt guilty. "Oh, do you think so? But I want to see them so badly."

"You think I don't? It's all I care about. It's all I want. If I thought I could get them out, I'd swim across the Tasman. Sharks and all."

"Then why are you being so strange about going back there now?"

"How the hell should I know? Look, I don't want to get into some big mystical scene, but I just don't feel good about it, OK? Maybe it's something to do with Robyn. That's what Andrea thinks, anyway. All I know is, I feel angry. Everything makes me angry at the moment."

Completely unexpectedly Fi said: "What did happen the night of the party with that creep Adam?"

"How did you know he was a creep?"

"Oh, Ellie! What happened to your good taste and judgement?"

That was the moment Lee and Kevin chose to come over.

"Time to go, kiddies," Kevin said.

"I'll tell you later," I said to Fi.

We walked back across the tarmac, the cold wind tugging at us, twisting my jacket around me.

"Last good cup of coffee we'll get for quite a time," Lee said.

"I know. It's awful. No TV, no nice bed, no hot baths. I can't believe we signed up for this."

"I didn't think you were going to sign up for it at one stage."

I sighed. "Oh, don't bring that up again. Fi and I have been talking about it for the last hour."

A minute earlier Fi had surprised me by her comment about Adam. Now it was Lee's turn to surprise me. He put his arm around me as we walked along. I was shocked. We hadn't touched each other in so long. We'd been as close as humans can get, but when that ended we didn't dare touch each other in case it was taken the wrong way. At least, I can only speak for myself: that's why I didn't touch Lee. I don't know for sure why he didn't touch me.

"We're going to be OK, you know, Ellie," he said. "As long as we stick together, we'll be OK."

The wind was getting colder and fiercer and I honestly don't know if it was stinging my eyes and making them water or if the tears were being pushed out by something else. But whichever it was I kept blinking till they were gone. No professional soldier was going to see me crying. Not to mention Homer.

We stood around on the tarmac for another two and a half hours. It was cold and boring and somehow, even with all the people, it was terribly lonely. Planes came and went but ours didn't go anywhere. We could see it parked near the control tower with three or four mechanics working on the engine. It was a bit unnerving, knowing it needed all this work just to get into the air. Secretly I hoped they'd put the whole trip off. We could go back to our quarters with honour intact: the failure wouldn't be our fault.

Ten o'clock New Zealand time — sorry, 2200 hours — was what Iain had calculated as our deadline: that was eight in the evening in Australia. We needed that big a margin. And sure enough, typical of our luck, it was 9.55 p.m., 2155, when a mechanic came up on a little electric motor scooter and told us the plane was ready.

I should have known not to get my hopes up.

The pressure on aircraft had been terrible, of course, with so many shot down, or grounded with missile damage. If we'd needed proof of the importance of our assignment, the fact that they'd provided a plane was enough. But it wasn't much of a plane: a little Saab jet, so old that the fabric on the seats was worn away in a lot of places. Before the war it had been used in civilian work, but now the Air Force had borrowed it. The roof was so low that some of the soldiers spent the trip with their heads bent forward.

Just as we were about to board, Colonel Finley arrived. There wasn't time for big speeches, but he shook our hands and wished us luck. It was nice of him to turn up. He'd always been pretty good to us. I mean his main interest was the war, of course, and he was only interested in us as long as we could help with the military stuff, but he'd got us good accommodation and made sure we were looked after, and he'd arranged the counselling and everything, so you couldn't have asked for more. He never seemed very warm, but there wasn't much you could do about that.

I'd been hoping till the last second that Andrea would come to see us off, even though she'd explained she had a group of patients every Friday evening at the hospital, but I still hoped a miracle would occur and she'd get there. Instead we had to settle for Colonel Finley.

Anyway, there was no time after that for much of anything. Sixty seconds later Colonel Finley had gone, they'd shut the door, and we were in the air. No stewards or hostesses on this flight: it was just sit down, get your belts on and we're out of here.

We seemed to whoosh across the Tasman so fast. The plane kept very low to stay under the radar level, but it was so dark we couldn't tell where we were. According to Iain, our being so low would slow us down because there was more air resistance, but I wouldn't have known that if he hadn't told us. It felt fast to me. We never saw the pilots, even after we landed, because they kept the door shut the whole time, but I didn't mind that. I was happy to know that they were concentrating on flying the plane.

We landed at a base in the free territory but we weren't allowed to know anything about it. Certainly not where it was. It was all maximum security. And then everything happened very fast. There was no time to get sentimental about the fact that we were back on our own soil. We had to get our packs out of the luggage compartment and race to a helicopter that was already warmed up and waiting to take off. Matter of fact it was straining to take off. It seemed to be almost off the ground when we were still a hundred metres away from it.

It was a huge helicopter, with two rotors, and, unlike the Saab, very new. It was a donation from the Americans, the pilot explained. It was only my second helicopter ride ever. The first time I'd been so sick at heart I hadn't noticed a thing, and this time I was so scared that I didn't notice much either, but one thing that did strike me right away was how much quieter this ride was than the first helicopter. We could talk quite easily.

The chopper pilot, Sam, was so different to the invisible pilots of the Saab. This guy was such a dag. He wouldn't shut up. But I liked him. He got us all to relax a bit with his stupid jokes. And, for the first time since I'd known I had to go back, he made me feel a bit like a hero again. Like I was doing something brave, something worthwhile, something special. He was a bit of a hero himself because every day he was flying into war zones and occupied territory but the way he carried on you'd think he was doing a tourist run around a tropical resort. As soon as the plane landed the lights on the airfield went off again and they didn't turn them on for the chopper. "Anyone got a torch?" Sam asked. "If these jokers paid their electricity bills we might get some lights here." He looked at me and winked. "These choppers used to be powered by electricity you know, till it got too expensive."

"Powered by electricity?" I repeated stupidly. I'm not at my best in the middle of the night.

"Yeah, it was good too, but they needed long extension

28

cords. Mate of mine flew an inch too far, the plug came out, and down he went."

At least we went up, not down, then we wheeled a-way to the north. We were on the last stage of our trip. I was still nervous, of course, but it was a different type of nervousness: instead of feeling sick and depressed I felt keyed up and was even starting to feel excited. "I'll lower the TV screens in a minute," Sam said. "Don't bump your head as you move around the cabin. Our in-flight movie tonight is *The Boy Who Could Fly*. It stars Xavier here." He nodded at the co-pilot, who just grinned. I guess he was used to Sam's chatter.

If the Saab pilots didn't talk to us because they were busy flying the plane, I don't know how the helicopter flew at all. Must have been Xavier's doing.

It was a moonless night, so I couldn't see anything. It was eerie flying like that, rushing through blackness, trusting entirely the little glowing lights on the instrument panel. Now I think it was Fi's turn to feel nervous, more nervous than me even, because she grabbed my hand after we took off, and held it all the way there. I don't know, maybe she was just excited about coming home.

I was, quite a bit.

It crept up on me gradually, this feeling that I was in the right place again, and doing the right thing. I'm an action person, no doubt about that. I'm not good at sitting around, and for a long time, apart from our tourist travels around New Zealand, I'd been sitting around.

I'd watched a lot of TV, even though most of it was, like, the fourteenth re-run of "Shortland Street." Since New Zealand got involved in the war they'd cut out every non-military import, because their balance of trade was wrecked by the military stuff they had to buy. So overseas TV shows were suddenly off the air. There were no new foreign movies at the cinemas either. Some New Zealanders thought that was too high a price to pay for helping Australia. They would have chucked us away for a new series of "The Simpsons." I must admit, I could see their point of view.

Sam was giving a fake commentary as we tore along through the night. We'd told him we didn't believe we were as low as he said, so he was out to convince us we were wrong.

"On our right we see a beautiful gum tree. Just look at those pretty little leaves. And if you look closely you'll notice the ladybird on the third twig on the fourth branch on the left-hand side."

But in between times he got serious, especially with me, because I was sitting nearest to him.

"This is your place we're landing on, is it?"

"I think so. They don't tell us much."

"It'll be nice for you to see it again."

He asked me how old I was and when I told him he shook his head.

"Are you all the same age?"

"Kevin's a bit older... like, six months."

"My God, you're young to be doing this kind of stuff."

"We didn't ask for it. We just fell into it. Anyway, in a lot of countries kids are in the army at twelve or fourteen. Or so everyone keeps telling me."

"I guess so. As far as I'm concerned you're the gutsiest bunch of people I've had in this thing. Aren't you nervous?"

"Nervous? If you had a dunny in this helicopter I'd be living in it."

That got Sam going again. "Haven't you seen our dunny? Go down the back there and lift up the hatch. You'll find a nice hole underneath it. You know how they used to call dunnies the 'long drop'? Well, our dunny sets a record for long drops."

It was a few minutes after three in the morning and suddenly Sam was silent, peering down into the darkness. "We should be in the drop zone," he said to Iain. "On the map this all shows up as clear. I'm going to come down very carefully and hope we've got a good spot. And hope no one's underneath us with a mortar.

"Get ready," he said to the rest of us. "If we have to go up we'll go bloody fast and we'll go sideways. Keep your belts on and keep your mouths shut, and stick your head between your knees if we look like hitting anything we shouldn't. Like the ground for instance."

I realised, watching Sam then, what an excellent pilot he was. He concentrated like a violinist at a concert, sensitive to every note, every subtle change in volume, every tiny variation. If a leaf from a tree had touched the helicopter I honestly think he'd have noticed it. And the co-pilot, Xavier, he had his hands on his controls too, watching Sam's slightest move. I realised when I thought about it later that he probably was doing it in case something happened to Sam—like a bullet—so he had to be ready to take over in a split second.

Terrible thought.

No one else in the helicopter moved. We all felt the tension. I don't know about the others but suddenly I wasn't thinking about what I had to do after we landed;

I was concentrating every fibre on just getting this great roaring thing down on the ground. If we could have spent an hour or two putting it down it would have been cool: Sam could have lowered it at an inch a minute. But there was the constant fear of bullets. He had to balance the fear of hitting a tree or a power line with the fear of getting shot at. If we were landing in the remotest part of our property, we should be pretty safe from bullets and power lines, but no one knew for sure. All our knowledge, and Colonel Finley's, came from way back. There could have been a brand-new military camp below us. We could be setting down in the middle of the parade ground.

Then there was a heavy bump from the right-hand side. I yelped, Fi squealed, and we weren't the only ones. But the instant he'd felt the bump Sam had the left-hand side down as well. He held the chopper there, rocking slightly from side to side. Quite calmly he said over his shoulder: "We're down, but we're on a slope. Take care getting out."

There was no panic. Iain went first, followed by half the soldiers, then us five, then the rest. Sam winked at me again as I went past: "Good luck," he said. I tried to find a grin to give him but couldn't: now it wasn't so much that I was scared, there was just too much to think about. I was suddenly aware of how much responsibility would be mine once I got out of the aircraft.

I dropped out of the hatch. Arms caught me and helped me down into the darkness. Someone turned me around so I was facing to the left. A voice yelled in my ear, "Walk fifty metres; watch the rough ground." I stumbled away into the noisy night. The fumes of aviation fuel had blown away all other smells. I kept going, arms outstretched, until someone else grabbed me and I stopped and waited, letting my eyes get used to the darkness. Gradually I became aware of a lot of movement right beside me and I realised it was the packs being passed along from the helicopter. I cursed, annoyed that I'd forgotten to help with them. Already, back on my own soil, my sense of independence was returning. The last thing I wanted was to be treated like a helpless child. But when I tried to join the line of people passing packs I think I just got in the way and muddled things up. A sudden blare of engine noise from the helicopter and a rush of wind told me Sam was leaving. I felt scared and lonely again, but everything was happening too fast to allow time for luxuries like feelings.

A hand tapped me hard on the shoulder and at the same time another hand guided my arm to a pack. I was getting really annoyed at being so helpless but tantrums were a luxury too, so I lifted the pack onto my back. "This way," someone whispered. Already the sound of the helicopter had faded away and the night was returning to its normal sweet quiet self. It was a relief to be able to whisper again. I was getting my night sight too, so it was easy to fall into line behind a big broad back and follow it. I knew why we were doing this: Iain explained when we were in the Saab that our first move must be away from the drop site, in case of soldiers converging on us. Once we were well away we would worry about where we were.

We walked fast for fifteen minutes. The sudden exercise, coming after so much sitting around, was a shock to my system. I was soon panting and blowing. My nose started running too, which was a nuisance as I couldn't reach my handkerchief. I had no idea who was behind me or who was in front, except that I knew it was a woman in front. It took ages for me to get my second wind—in fact I've never been sure that there's such a thing as second wind—but after a while I got in a bit of a routine and started to travel more easily.

Then, bump, my nose hit the soldier in front. We'd stopped. I moved forward a little, feeling important. This would be my cue. Sure enough Iain was already looking for me. "Good on you, Ellie," he whispered. "You know where we are yet?"

"No, I'll have to take a look around."

"OK, you do that. Kay'll go with you. I'll just check the troops."

As everyone gathered around him, Kay and I moved off into the darkness. I strained my eyes looking for landmarks. There was no way of knowing where we were. If Sam had been a centimetre out with his calculations we could be several k's from where we'd been heading. The ground we were on was still rough and broken. We were going downhill most of the time: that suggested the eastern boundary, near the foothills. There were plenty of sheep droppings, which probably meant one of the three big paddocks along that edge of the property, but with new owners there was no telling what they might have allowed. The sheep could be running wild in the bush.

"Anything?" Kay muttered.

I shook my head and we pressed on. I was hoping Kay, with her army training, could lead me back to the others eventually. The further we got away from them the less confident I was of finding them again.

I felt the ground getting spongy. I knelt and pressed it with my fingers. It was damp all right. I felt a sense of great relief. I hadn't wanted to let these people down. I hadn't wanted to look a fool. A lot of pride was tied up in this. But I still had to make sure. I said to Kay: "We'll walk a hundred metres this way, and we should hit the corner of a paddock."

Often now when I want to give myself a boost, to feel good, I think back to that moment when I led Kay straight to the intersection of two fences, in pitch blackness, at 4.45 a.m., after being dropped in the middle of nowhere by a helicopter. I tried to look completely casual about it, as though I'd always known it'd be there, and I tried not to look too smug when Kay said: "My God, you really do know your way around."

We hurried back to the others. We didn't have any trouble finding them.

"How'd you go?" Iain asked.

He always sounded so unflappable. It didn't matter that we were in the middle of a war zone, a thousand k's from New Zealand and possibly lost. He sounded like he was asking how I'd got on in the hundred metres at the school sports.

"We're not where we aimed for. But we're in quite a good spot. About a k and a half from the track. It's a bit of a bush-bash to get to it. There's no way there'll be any soldiers around here though. It's the wildest part of the property."

I was all set to lead them straight off into the bush but Iain pulled out his thin little flashlight and made me show him on the map where we were. I think he wanted to reassure himself that I knew what I was talking about. But Kay helped when she said: "She knows the place backwards, Iain. She bent down, touched the ground, then told me exactly where the fence was."

I realised that to Kay, who was from Auckland, it must have seemed like magic. She probably hadn't even noticed the spongy grass under her feet. Of course I knew every spring on the place — well, you have to — so once I'd felt that dampness on a downhill slope surrounded by rough ground I knew we had to be in a corner of Nellie's, our biggest paddock on the eastern side.

I kept it to myself though. True magicians never give away their secrets.

Iain, being ultra-cautious, got a compass bearing, although the map he had wasn't accurate enough really, but as soon as he'd finished we were ready to go. I swung my pack on my back and, full of energy at last, took the only position I'm really comfortable with: the lead. And away we went.

It only took ten minutes before they had to ask me to slow down. I was proud of that, too. I was charged up all right. My mood had changed completely. Fi, behind Iain, who was behind me, was shocked. As we stood waiting for the others to catch up she said: "Ellie, they ought to drug test you."

I shrugged and laughed. "Being back home, that's my drug."

I have to admit, though, it was a tough bush-bash. For all my sudden confidence I missed the stockyard, probably by less than a hundred metres, but I did miss it. When we came out of the bush we hit the fence between Nellie's and Burnt Hut, the next paddock, instead of the stockyard. That meant we'd overshot the spur, so my little mistake added about twenty minutes to the trek. I didn't say anything to anyone, because there was no way they would have known, and why make myself look bad? I just gritted my teeth, swung to the left, and led them up the fenceline.

We hit the track at about 5.30. Daylight was too close for us to be able to have a break. Iain just grunted "good girl," when he saw the red-brown dirt in the dim light, then quickly detailed two soldiers to go ahead of the others, in case of enemy activity. He didn't want me to go but I told him they'd need me. I knew the road better than anyone. I knew where it curved, where it dipped, where enemy troops might be camping or resting if they were out on patrol.

Anyway, the odds of them being up in this country were about one in a thousand.

It wasn't like I'd lost my fear in these couple of hours. It was just that I'd been able to push it down. It was still in me somewhere. But there wasn't room or time for it at the moment.

So the three of us slogged on. We kept climbing. I'd forgotten how much of war was like this. So much hard yakka, grunting up and down mountains, carrying weights that felt like every textbook I'd ever owned had been plonked in my backpack, and then some. Trying to remember that every bush, every tree, could contain death. Relaxing for a minute or two, letting your mind wander, daydreaming, then suddenly thinking, "Oh my God, I haven't been concentrating; that daydream could have cost me my life."

Ploughing on hour after hour, day after day sometimes, just so at the end of it you could kill someone or be killed.

Well, we ploughed on, until by 9 a.m. we were standing on the top of Tailor's Stitch.

Four

So much had happened, since the first time we'd stood there as a group, the seven of us, Homer, Fi, Robyn, Lee, Corrie, Kevin and me. And later, Chris. Two, and possibly three, of that group would never stand there again.

But the rest of us had returned.

And suddenly it seemed very important that we had returned. Sure, now we were hiding in the shadows. The first time we had stood in the open, relaxed, laughing, fooling around, feeling we were at home, this was our land. We'd never questioned that. Took it for granted.

Now we took nothing for granted. Especially our lives.

The five of us who were left, the five survivors, stood in a group, using a clump of old wizened twisted gum trees as cover. We ignored the Kiwis for a minute and stared down into Hell. No one said anything. The only sounds were the normal bush sounds: the whispering of leaves, the moaning of crows, the faraway scream of a parrot. I don't know what the others were thinking but I was thinking that this was where I belonged, this was my dreaming. I'd become a gum tree, a rock, a parrot myself. I'd resisted coming back here but now that I was here I never wanted to leave it again.

On my right Iain said: "That is a wild place."

Ursula, who was also a Captain, and who was second-in-charge to Iain, said: "I've done a lot of tramping in New Zealand, but this is as wild as anything I've seen."

"Tramping" sounded so funny to me, but all the Kiwis used it.

"And can you really get us down in there?" Iain asked me.

"Sure thing," Homer answered. "No trouble at all."

"I didn't even feel my lips move," I thought, but I didn't say anything. It wasn't the right time to start another fight with Homer, Big Man I-always-have-to-be-Leader Homer. Instead I said to Iain: "If we go along the ridge, towards Wombegonoo there's a way in."

It seemed like we were earning our keep. This was why they'd brought us. This was the best hiding place for a hundred k's in any direction. And we were the only people in the world who knew about it.

We shouldered our packs again and, keeping off the ridge, staying below the tree-line, made our way towards the hidden path that led down into Hell. It was terribly difficult walking that way because the sides of Tailor's Stitch are so steep and every second step started a miniature landslide. But we had no choice. In broad daylight we were completely exposed on the top. Walking like this was just one of the many prices to be paid for allowing invaders into our country.

When we got to Wombegonoo we pointed out the tree to Iain. The problem was that there was no cover between us and the tree. A sheet of rock, quite smooth, bare as a bitumen playground, stretched from the summit of Wombegonoo to the old gum tree. I think we five, if we'd been on our own, would have gone for it. We were so used to feeling safe up here. But Iain didn't like the risk. He decided we'd have to wait till dark.

So suddenly, after all the tension and fear and excitement, there was nothing much. We set up a bit of a camp on the western side of the ridge and, because it looked like being a hot day, we hung a few tent-flies for shade, down in among the scrub where aircraft couldn't see them. Iain posted three sentries and everyone else, including me — especially me — went to sleep.

Boy, did I sleep. I can't think of any reason I would have slept so well and so long. I mean, sure, I hadn't slept for nearly a week, but you'd think I'd have been even worse now that I was back in the heart of danger. Maybe I was having a reaction to all the stress of the night. But whatever, I slept more than four hours, which I never do normally. Not in the daytime.

After that, after I woke, there was just a lot of sitting around. It got pretty boring. Some of the soldiers, and Kevin and Homer, were playing cards. One was reading a book he'd borrowed from Fi — I don't think they were allowed to bring books and stuff like that themselves, they were meant to travel light — and a couple were talking about rugby, which I've noticed New Zealanders do quite a lot. Just before we left, the New Zealand Government announced the suspension of all rugby for the duration of the war, because all the young guys had been conscripted. Even in World War Two they hadn't cancelled rugby. So they were all whingeing about that.

It was like a school camp in some ways. You could almost forget that we were in the middle of a war zone.

The day dragged on. I was anxious to get down into Hell. It was home to me now, in some ways. Home in Hell. What did that say about me? Who lived in Hell? I knew the answer to that. The devil and the tortured souls. Which one was I? Most times I thought I knew the answer to that, too. But sometimes I felt like I had become a devil. The things we'd done made me shudder, made me sick. I'd talked about them to Andrea, and that helped. A little. She kept saying, "Talking always helps." It was like a motto to her. But I don't think even she understood exactly what it was like. How could she? It doesn't matter how much training you've had, you're not going to suddenly become an expert in helping teenagers who've killed people. There aren't a huge number of cases around for you to practise on.

All this stuff had made such a difference. It wrecked my relationship with Lee, for a start. I still looked at him longingly sometimes, wanting to get back what we'd enjoyed so much, wanting to hold him in my arms again, to feel the excitement, his and mine — because his excitement was one of the things that excited me — and wanting the wonderful warm feeling of being naked together. It had been so different with Adam. Nothing but aggression and selfishness and grog. It didn't feel like he loved me. It was more like he hated me, wanted to attack me. Even in the old days, at school in Wirrawee, I'd noticed that a lot of boys who made a big deal about their girlfriends and their great sex lives seemed

41

to have almost a hatred for girls. All at the same time. It was weird. But I felt the same thing in Adam.

Lee was never like that. I was the one who'd stuffed him around. He'd always been generous with me. Like at the airport in New Zealand, walking back to the waiting area after we'd had our coffee. Somehow with all the terrible things happening around us I'd become dead inside, in the loving part of me anyway. I couldn't feel anything for him. I couldn't feel anything for anyone, except Fi, and my parents. Oh, and Andrea. But it was my parents I longed for mostly. I wanted to be a little girl again and cuddle into them, wriggling in between them like I'd done in their bed when I was three or four, snug and warm in the safest place in the world.

Instead I had Hell.

I went for a walk that afternoon. Again I had to fight Iain to get permission. I didn't like that, having to ask permission to walk around my own land. It reminded me too much of life with Major Harvey. Of course it was a lot different with Iain. He was relaxed and friendly and easy to talk to. But I still had to persuade him that it was OK.

"There's no chance of enemy soldiers up here, Iain."

"Well, the chances are minimal, yes."

"And I'm not going to get lost. I know this area like the back of my hand."

"New Zealand Search and Rescue spend most of their time saving experienced trampers."

"I'll be careful, I promise. No bungee jumping, caving, rock rolling. Trust me."

When he eventually did agree and I went for my walk

I spent the first fifteen minutes fuming about the conversation. It was annoying being so sure of something but then having to convince someone else. At home my parents had always trusted my judgement. That had been one of the big shocks when I got to school, finding that things were a bit different there. It depended, of course. Depended on the teacher. At Wirrawee Primary, for instance, if we hurt ourselves we'd go to the staff room and borrow the first-aid kit and fix ourselves up. Then this new Principal came when I was in Grade 3. I was sitting outside the staff room with the first-aid box, and I was digging a splinter out of my finger with the needle. The new Principal came past, asked me what I was doing, then cracked a mental when I told him. He didn't only tell me off, he told the teachers off. I could hear him in the staff room, raving about legal consequences and stuff. I thought he was stupid, but after that if we got a splinter we had to ask a teacher to take it out.

You can never stay angry for too long in the bush though. At least, that's what I think. It's not that it's soothing or restful, because it's not. What it does for me is get inside my body, inside my blood, and take me over. I don't know that I can describe it any better than that. It takes me over and I become part of it and it becomes part of me and I'm not very important, or at least no more important than a tree or a rock or a spider abseiling down a long long thread of cobweb. As I wandered around, on that hot afternoon, I didn't notice anything too amazing or beautiful or mindbogglingly spectacular. I can't actually remember noticing anything out of the ordinary: just the grey-green rocks and the olive-green leaves and the reddish soil with its teeming ants. The tattered ribbons of paperbark, the crackly dry cicada shell, the smooth furrow left in the dust by a passing snake. That's all there ever is really, most of the time. No rainforest with tropical butterflies, no palm trees or Californian redwoods, no leopards or iguanas or panda bears.

Just the bush.

Iain wouldn't move over Tailor's Stitch until it was completely dark. He was right, of course: even in the dimmest light we risked our silhouettes being seen by anyone who happened to be looking in the right direction. But it was frustrating, sitting there waiting, every minute thinking, "OK, it's dark enough now, let's go," then thinking, "Oh no, there's still a streak of grey in the sky, right across the ranges, better wait a few more minutes."

Then suddenly we were all on our feet, hoisting packs, stuffing pockets, shaking hair out of our eyes. Iain called me over and told me to lead again, which pleased me a lot, although Homer pretended he didn't even notice.

And so, when everyone was ready, we began the trek, back up the steep side of the ridge, over Wombegonoo, and into my sanctuary of Hell.

Getting in and out of Hell was never easy because of the steepness and narrowness of the track. Also, it was very slippery in places where the creek flowed along it for a few metres, so that the creek and the track became the same thing. Doing it in complete darkness was really annoying. All that slipping and sliding and, just as you recovered, getting hit in the face by a branch. Then Iain, behind me, would lose his footing and crash into my back. It was like babysitting Kevin's brothers. You felt you were in a wrestling match half the time. There was no doubt about those Kiwis, though — Colonel Finley told us they'd been handpicked for their initiative and guts, and they did handle it well. Lots of jokes and stuff.

I handled it OK, I guess, but I was pretty tired. I didn't have much to say.

It was just before ten o'clock — 2200 hours — that we "landed safe and sound, at the bottom of that terrible descent."

Or, to put it another way, we found ourselves home again, in the depths of Hell.

Five

I don't know what the others did that first night. I think they all went to bed. I know Fi and I did. We put up our tent — pretty roughly — crawled into it and stayed there.

One good thing about having professional soldiers around was that we didn't have to do sentry duty. That was such a bonus. In the past we'd dragged ourselves out of warm beds and sleeping bags at all hours of the day and night, in wet weather and dry, moaning and whingeing and swearing and hating it. So far though no one had mentioned that we should do anything so uncomfortable and unpleasant. Fi and I were giggling about it that first night. We agreed that volunteering would be silly: after all, these guys were paid to do it. And they were so gung-ho, so fired up. Half of them had never been on active service before, and the rest of them hadn't done much. It would be a pity to cut them out of their fun.

"What do you think Iain wants to do in Wirrawee?" Fi whispered.

We hadn't been allowed to know any details of their actual mission. Colonel Finley explained it was for everyone's protection: if we were caught, the less we knew the better. The four words "if we were caught" had me shaking and shivering when he said them. In my sessions with Andrea the main things I'd talked about, over and over, were the time in Stratton Prison and what happened to Robyn. Talking about them helped, but gradually I'd come to accept that these terrible things were part of me forever; all I could do was find ways to cope with them. At least Colonel Finley had given us some guarantees that we should be OK. Iain had strict instructions. We were only to be used as guides, we were not allowed near any battles or "warlike activities" (Colonel Finley had shown me the first part of Iain's written orders) and we should only have to make one trip to Wirrawee, to show them the way around.

It was obvious though that they would be aiming for the airfield. Nothing else in Wirrawee was worth attacking, or nothing that we knew of anyway. Murray's Eats, the caravan that sold hot dogs in the supermarket carpark on Saturday nights, wasn't much of a target, and I think we'd made such a mess of Turner Street that it would be cactus for a long time yet.

We discussed all this. But we also knew that none of it would get us close to our families. The New Zealanders' plans wouldn't include a visit to the Showgrounds, where we believed most of the prisoners were still kept. Showbags and dolls on long cane sticks weren't on the Kiwi shopping lists. The last information Colonel Finley had given us, two weeks earlier, before we even knew about this trip, was that people were still being released on work parties as the countryside became more secure, and as the system of hostages improved.

I was just drifting off to sleep when Fi said something that had me feeling like spiders were crawling all over me. I sat up in my bag.

"What did you say?"

"I said we could sneak out of here and look for them if the Kiwis go off on their own."

"Fi! We can't! Oh my God, do you think we should?"

"Well, it's the only way we'll get to see them. There's no way Iain's going to let us look for them."

"But you were telling me back in New Zealand that Colonel Finley was going to arrange everything."

"Hmm, yes," Fi said. "But you know, I'm starting to think you might be right about Colonel Finley."

"Fi!" I was sort of laughing because it sounded funny for her to be cynical about anyone. She was normally so trusting. "I thought you liked him."

"Oh, I don't mind him," Fi agreed. "But it's true, he is only good to us when it suits him. He didn't care about us when we were hiding in that car wrecking yard. Once he found we didn't have any information, and we wouldn't go back into Cobbler's Bay, he lost interest in us pretty quickly."

"But he's got a war to win," I argued. "That takes priority."

I was really only sticking up for the Colonel because I was enjoying the argument, not because I believed much in what I was saying.

"Oh, of course. I don't expect him to bring us breakfast in bed, or lend us M16's. But if we want to do something and it doesn't get in anyone's way, I think we should do it, and not worry about what Colonel Finley thinks."

"Ask forgiveness, not permission," I said, remembering something someone said to me once.

It took Fi a second or two to work out what I meant, then she laughed.

"Yes," she said, "exactly. Gosh, Ellie, you're getting back to your old self."

"It's being here," I said, "in our own backyard again. It makes a difference. I'd forgotten."

"I missed it when we were in New Zealand," Fi said. "I even missed Hell, and all the hiking. I even missed demolishing half my own street."

"I missed everything," I said. "We have more blowies than New Zealand. I missed our blowies."

But my mind was still on what Fi had said. "Do you really think we should go looking for them? What if we got in the way of the Kiwis? We can't do anything that might wreck their plans."

"No, of course not. That's the biggest thing. But we could go out along the Wirrawee-Holloway Road for instance, and see if we can find a work group. That's in the opposite direction to Wirrawee. Even if we were caught they wouldn't know we were here with New Zealand soldiers."

"Yes, and Kevin said they send the work parties away from their own areas, so there's more chance our families'll be out there than in Wirrawee."

"Except for the people they kept back as hostages."

"When do you think Iain would want us to take him into Wirrawee?"

"Pretty soon. Maybe even tomorrow night."

"You're joking. As soon as that?"

"Sure. Why not?"

It did make sense, I thought. Why hang around here, using up food? On the other hand they'd brought heaps with them, so maybe they were planning a long stay.

"I wish they'd tell us more about their plans," I complained. "I mean I know they have to be secretive, but sometimes I feel like it's Major Harvey all over again, treating us like little kids."

"I know one thing," Fi said.

"What?"

"Who they want to take them into Wirrawee."

"Who?" But I felt my stomach go liquid again as I asked it. I didn't want it to be me, because I didn't want to get caught or hurt or killed. But I did want it to be me because it would have been such an insult to be left behind.

"You sure you can handle it?" Fi asked.

"Yes, of course! Just tell me!"

"You and Lee."

I felt such a confusion of feelings that I didn't know where to start.

"But...but I don't know if I want to go. And what about Homer? He'll go sick. How do you know, anyway?"

"I heard Iain and Ursula talking, this afternoon."

"But I didn't think they'd want me to go. I mean I'm the one who didn't want to leave New Zealand in the first place."

"Yes, that's what they were talking about. About whether you'd be, you know..."

"Whether I'd curl up in a little ball and cry when we got close to enemy soldiers."

"Well, not quite in those words, but I guess that was the general idea."

"So why do they want me to go?" I was fishing for compliments, of course.

"I suppose, your reputation. We turned you into a bit of a legend, didn't we? Plus you seemed to do OK last night, and tonight. I think that was a little test, when Iain got you to lead the way into Hell."

I was furious.

"Test? Test? Where do these turkeys get off, giving me tests? We've passed more tests than they've wiped their bums. Leading the way into Hell, whoopie-doo, big test, wow, how'd I go? Did I pass? Gee, I hope I passed. Iain and his bloody tests, what a cheek."

"Well, Ellie," said Fi, who never let me get away with much, "you must admit you were pretty difficult to get on with when they asked us to come back."

"They didn't ask us, they told us," I complained. "It's a bit different."

"I don't think they'll tell you to take them into Wirrawee," Fi said. She sure was choosing her words carefully. Did she see me as that unstable? "But I think they're hoping you will."

"What about Homer? Why don't they want to ask him?"

Again Fi paused, searching for the right words.

"I think they got the idea back in New Zealand that he was a bit irresponsible. Too much partying."

Adults often made that mistake about Homer. He had been pretty crazy when we were at school, but that was more a reaction to the way he was treated than anything else. It sounds terrible comparing people with animals, but the way teachers hassled Homer reminded me of something that Dad said about stockwork, that the quieter the drover the calmer the sheep. He had this theory that you shouldn't swear at sheep, because then they could tell that you didn't like them. He sacked a worker once because he swore too much at the sheep. I mean, he didn't tell the guy that was the reason, but it was.

"God, Homer'll totally blow his stack."

That was the end of sleep for me. Just when I needed some, too. I wriggled around for hours. I'd get comfortable for a minute or two, then decide it was too hard on my hip, or there was too much pressure on my shoulder blade, or my arm was getting pins and needles. Of course the long sleep I'd had that morning made it hard for me to sleep now. But the real problem was that I was already making the trip into Wirrawee. In my mind I was walking those dark streets, trembling at every shadow, leaping around in panic at the slightest sound.

It made me wonder if I still had the nerve for this kind of stuff.

I got up as soon as it was half-light. I'd probably slept a few hours, on and off, but I didn't feel like I had. Fi was asleep, so I dressed quietly and slipped out of the little tent to reacquaint myself with Hell.

There's nothing like the very early morning. It's the sweetness of the air, the sweet coolness; it's the bubbling of the creek which, for some strange reason, always sounds more energetic than it does later on; it's the gargling of the magpies. The first thing I did was go and look at the chook pen, even though I knew I wouldn't find any live chooks there. I was right about that. I won't go into the gruesome details, but those pathetic little feather dusters had become victims of the war themselves. I guess they starved to death. We'd rebuilt their pen so that the creek flowed through it, so they had plenty of water, but they'd eaten everything in there except the dirt and the wire.

Then I went and looked at another victim of the war.

Chris' grave was pretty much the way we'd left it. Getting a bit overgrown with weeds, though. I pulled out one, was about to pull out another, then stopped. Chris had been quite into weeds, in his own unique way. And he'd certainly been into doing things differently. I grinned and left the other weeds alone.

Walking away I started remembering again that awful trip down into Hell, carrying Chris' body, but I shook my head quickly, not wanting to think about it. At least he'd had friends to bury him. There were times when I wondered if I'd be even that lucky.

I wandered along the creek. I thought of heading to the Hermit's hut, but didn't like the idea of going through the darkness of the undergrowth. Instead I stayed out in the brightening warming sunlight and found a rock that I liked. I curled up on that, my knees to my chest, and hugged myself for a while. I couldn't believe I was back here. Watching trashy TV in New Zealand, going to disgusting parties with a disgusting person, eating too many hamburgers and chips: it all seemed a long way away suddenly. I seriously began to wonder if I should go back to New Zealand when the others went. The Kiwis had a radio—two radios in fact—so they could call up the chopper when it was time to go. Maybe when they made their call I should take a raincheck. I smiled to myself as I thought how they would react.

"But you didn't want to come in the first place!" they'd cry.

"Oh, well," I'd say, "it's good to keep changing your mind. It shows you're thinking. I'll only stop changing my mind when I'm dead. And maybe not even then."

I heard the crunch of a footstep on the rock behind me and looked around to see Ursula. I liked Ursula. She had quite long reddish hair and reddish cheeks, and a nice big mouth that smiled a lot. She'd been an aerobics instructor before she joined the army, and Iain told me she'd represented New Zealand in hurdles at a Commonwealth Games. She'd only been in the army six years, and I think it was a bit of a meteoric rise to be a Captain that quickly.

"Hi," she said, "how did you sleep?"

"Terrible. I got up before dawn. How about you?"

"Fine. Like a baby."

"I don't know why people say that. Most babies are shocking sleepers, aren't they?"

She laughed. "So they say. I keep as far away from babies as I can."

"I can't say I've had a lot of experience myself."

She sat on the next rock, a couple of metres to my left, and threw a dead leaf into the creek.

"It's nice here," she said, after a few moments.

"I know. I'm glad I'm back now."

"And it's so well hidden. Looking down from the top I just couldn't believe we'd get in. You were so clever to find it."

"It was a total accident."

"Yes, Fiona told me."

"When do you have to, you know, start doing stuff?"

"Well, that's what I wanted to talk to you about. We'd like to go into Wirrawee tonight. And if you feel up to it, we'd like you to be one of our guides."

I tried to act like I hadn't already heard.

"Who else would you take?"

"Well, please don't say anything till we've talked to the others, but we were thinking Lee might be a good choice."

"Yeah, he would be good ..." I was torn between two loyalties. "But I think you should take Homer too."

"We thought it was important to have him in charge back here."

"Ooh," I thought, "that's neat. That's very clever, but I don't think it'll be enough to satisfy Homer. I think he'll see through that."

And that's what happened. As I came back from the creek with Ursula, about ten minutes later, the first thing I saw was Homer storming off towards the track, looking like he was going to walk straight to Wirrawee and blow the whole place up by himself. He stayed away for the rest of the day. When we left that afternoon he was still sulking; in fact he seemed to be taking it out on the poor old bush. I could hear him smashing down timber which, according to Kevin, he was going to use for a store shed.

Somehow I didn't think that store shed was ever going to get built.

Six

It was a long walk. One night we'd been at a party in Wirrawee, at Josh and Susie's place, and Homer had been hitting the grog in a big way, and everyone was giving him a hard time, and he kept saying he was cold sober, and finally, at 3 a.m., he announced that to prove he was sober he'd walk home. A minute later he was heading off down the drive, with us all waving him goodbye as we fell about laughing. I was staying overnight so I had no way of knowing if he'd got home or not, but at eight in the morning the phone rang and, when Josh finally staggered out to the kitchen to answer it, it was Homer. He was so pleased with himself that I could hear his voice from Susie's room, where I was in the spare bed.

But that's the only time I'd heard of anyone walking from our properties into Wirrawee, or vice versa.

No, wait, that's not true. My grandfather had a worker

named Casey I think his name was, and he was famous for his walking. "Spring-heel Bob" they called him because he had an unusual way of bouncing on his heels. Apparently he used to walk everywhere, even to Wirrawee if he had to. I remember my grandmother saying he'd walked to Stratton once to see his girlfriend. In those days the mail was only delivered as far as the Mackenzies' place, and he walked there twice a week to get the letters.

My grandfather was too stingy to let him have a horse.

I was full of ideas for shortcuts for us to get into Wirrawee that night, but Iain wouldn't listen to any of them. He put safety above everything, which was fair enough, of course, but I thought he took it a bit far. Not only did we have to walk, we had to make all these detours to avoid houses and roads. It made Homer's famous walk look like a little after-dinner stroll. It tested my fitness, too. I'd thought I was still pretty fit when they asked me to slow down on our way up to Tailor's Stitch, but I soon realised my stamina wasn't anywhere near the soldiers'. They could have gone for a week at the same pace. No wonder their horses kept coming over and winning the Melbourne Cup. These guys could have won the Melbourne Cup on their own. They didn't need horses.

It took us all night. We weren't allowed to speak which meant my muscles could talk to me uninterrupted. They sure had plenty to say: nothing but complaints. Whinge, whinge, whinge. I don't blame them, though. They were hurting. I wished I'd done more running, back in New Zealand.

When we got close to Wirrawee we stopped for a consultation with Iain and Ursula. There would have been time to go into town for a quick look around before dawn, but they felt it wasn't worth the risk. So we scrambled into some scrubby country, not far from the ruins of the Mackenzie house, and holed up for the day.

This time there was no hope of my wandering away for another walk. Iain was adamant. I could see his point and I didn't make any fuss. I was starting to like my own company more and more, but on this trip I wasn't likely to get much of it. It was a hot day and I was pleased to be able to get my breath back and give my legs a rest. It seemed that since we'd returned we'd been going nonstop: apart from the morning in Hell, my feet had hardly touched ground.

I had another good long sleep that lasted about as long as the one two days before. Seemed like suddenly I could only sleep in daytime. I wasn't too comfortable when I woke up though. A rock had dug its way into my back and the sun was burning my face.

I struggled up and made my way over to Lee and the others. They'd started a game of miniature cricket using a pebble as a ball and a twig as a bat. I watched sourly. I was all hot and sticky and sore and uncomfortable, my legs were aching, and I wasn't in the mood for games. But gradually I got sucked in: when the pebble came my way a few times I fielded it. Eventually I took a catch and got to bat. It was quite fun. It made me sad in a way, though. This was the life we should have had. Playing silly games, mucking around, enjoying being kids for as long as we could. That was how we'd spent half our time at school. When Eric Choo broke his leg we'd turned his crutch into a bat and invented another variety of cricket: when you hit the ball you had to run around the rubbish bin and back to the wicket, using the crutch to travel. From then on when anyone came to school with a broken anything that needed a crutch we'd all cheer and start the game up again.

That's what I mean. Just silly stuff like that. We had enough years in front of us to be serious and grown-up and respectable. Why rush it?

But on the other hand we always complained when teachers and other adults treated us as kids. In fact there was nothing that annoyed me more. So it was a frustrating situation. What we needed was a two-sided badge that said "Mature" on one side and "Childish" on the other. Then at any moment we could turn it to whatever side we felt like being and the adults could treat us accordingly.

One thing did make me think, though. It wasn't exactly all these people telling me about kids in other countries being in the army when they were ten. I mean, if you listened to that stuff you'd think that babies in nappies were parachuting out of aircraft with M 16's in their little paws. No, what I did wonder about was those photos of Aboriginal kids being initiated as full adults, full members of the tribe. Because in every photo they looked to be about ten or eleven years old. And I'd always wondered about that. If they were fit to be full adults when they were ten, what was wrong with us that we weren't ready till we were twenty or twenty-one? Or in some cases even older I knew twenty-four-year-olds who were still treated like little kids. Randall McPhail, for instance. Sometimes I didn't think he was ever going to grow up. He was twenty-eight and still living with his parents, still burning around the district in his hotted-up Holden ute with stickers on the back saying things like "No ute, no circle work" or "I survived the Stratton B&S."

Every time I saw him I was like, "Grow up, Randall."

Well, that's the way he was before the war. Maybe the war had made him grow up. But it shouldn't need a war to do that.

Everything you said now had to be dated as either before the war, or after the war started. It wasn't BC or AD any more; it was BW and AW.

The thing is, I wanted a Holden ute too, and I loved B&S's, but I sort of assumed that by the time I was twenty-eight I'd have moved on to something else. I hoped I would have.

That still didn't solve my puzzle about the Aboriginal kids. Maybe it was because they had a shorter life expectancy in those days, so you had to grow up faster. Maybe now, with modern medicine and stuff, you could take longer with childhood; there wasn't such a rush to move on to the next stage. After all, that's what had happened with us. Our life expectancy had been reduced because of the war. And we'd sure grown up fast.

Eventually the soldiers and Lee got tired of cricket. They wandered off and sprawled out under trees and bushes. Iain had four people on sentry duty this time, so that soaked up a lot of the troops. I actually volunteered to do some but he thanked me politely and explained that he wanted me fresh for the walk through Wirrawee that night.

"Typical Iain," I thought cynically, "always sugarcoating everything." If he wanted you to do the washing up he'd tell you it was hand aerobics and you needed the exercise. If he didn't want you to do it, he'd tell you he wanted your hands kept dirty so they didn't shine at night. OK, slight exaggeration maybe, but I was still sure that somewhere sometime he'd done courses on how to get people to do what he wanted. It never felt quite sincere.

I saw Lee on the other side of the hill. He was sitting under a thin black wattle, an oddly shaped tree that seemed to have gone into contortions and tied itself into a knot. I had a sudden urge to be with him so I walked up there. He was scratching in the ground with a stick. He didn't look up when I got there so I just stood and watched for a while. I realised he was writing his name, then rubbing it out, then writing it again. Sometimes he'd write it plainly and sometimes ornately. Then he wrote my name. I laughed and he rubbed it out. Then he threw the stick away. I felt a bit guilty that I'd laughed, though I don't know why. I sat down beside him. Neither of us said anything for a while, then he said, "Remember that exercise we did in English once, where we had to say what we'd save?"

"Nuh."

"Oh maybe it was a different class. I think it was Mrs. Savvas in Year 8. We had to say which things we'd save if our house was burning down."

"So what did you say?"

"I can't remember them all. We had to name five things, I think. I know everyone said their photos, their photo albums. I probably said my violin. Belinda Norris said her Barbies, I remember that. We paid her out for months afterwards."

"Trust Belinda."

"Yeah. But what I was thinking about was, it's happened to us, hasn't it? Like, our houses have burnt down and we haven't saved much."

I didn't say anything. I wasn't sure where this was heading.

Lee said carefully: "Suppose when we finish showing them what they want to see in Wirrawee, I get away for an hour, and go back to my place and pick up a few things."

"Like what?"

Lee started scraping another name into the dirt, with his finger this time. I couldn't see what the name was.

"My grandfather," he said slowly. "When he was alive, there was this scroll..."

And suddenly Lee was crying. It took me a minute to realise, because he did it so quietly. He hadn't changed his position: he was still sitting there but his body was shaking. It was like—this sounds terrible but it's the only way I can describe it—it was like someone was running a low-voltage electric current through him. I couldn't see his face, but I could picture it. His teeth would be clenched and his eyes closed tight. I put my hand over his and held it; no, not just held it but kneaded it with my fingers, over and over again. But there was nothing I could really do. The tears flowed and flowed. And the strange thing was that he didn't make a single sound. Silent crying. There's something awful about that. I don't know why it seems so terrible, maybe just the feeling that he was crying without letting himself cry. And it went on and on. I thought he'd never stop. I wasn't exactly timing it, but it could have been half an hour.

When he at last seemed to have stopped I moved up a little higher so I was beside him, and I put my arm around him. We stayed together like that for a long time. I was starting to realise that my relationship with Lee might not be completely over. I still had very strong feelings where he was concerned. I just wasn't sure what those feelings were. In the past when I'd ended a relationship, that was it: I never had a thought of reviving it. It was definitely like that with Steve. But maybe being in so many isolated situations with Lee meant that different rules applied now.

The rules for everything else had changed. Why not for relationships?

Seven

Wirrawee had certainly changed, almost beyond belief. There'd been hints of it as we walked in there, but we'd kept away from the road as much as possible, so we had no real warning. From time to time I'd seen glimpses of cars and trucks, and most of them were travelling at good speeds, with headlights on full. It seemed that since the bombing raids had been reduced they felt a lot more confident.

They felt pretty confident in Wirrawee itself. I soon

found that out. It was 11.30 p.m. when we started our cautious approach to the town. Ursula and Lee and I were leading: we came over the little hill on Coachman's Lane that was always such a bugger on the fun run — it came just near the end, when you had no energy left — and to our surprise there were lights everywhere. It was party time in Wirrawee. Even New Zealand hadn't been like this, because they had electricity restrictions there, brownouts and even blackouts. Some of that was because they were getting short of electricity, some because they were scared of being bombed. They didn't want to give bombers a nice bright easy target. Their best defence against being attacked was world opinion, which was mainly on our side. But I suppose the brownouts were fair enough. Playing it safe.

The lights in Wirrawee weren't anything out of the ordinary. It was just the shock after what we were used to — and compared to what we'd been expecting. It was the fact that it all looked so ordinary, in the middle of a war. I'd thought they'd be hiding in the dark like we were used to doing.

But the streetlights were all on, and here and there a house or shop was still lit up, as though the people were staying awake to watch "Rage" or something. Around the Showground the big spotlights were definitely on: so strong they seemed to burn the air.

It was one of the weirdest feelings I've ever had, to know that my parents were probably there, so close to me, less than a k away. As close as we had been for nearly a year. Only once, when I'd been in the carpark itself, had I been any closer. Now I wished I could fly over and land beside them. Or call out, as loudly as I could, "Hello, I'm here! Hello, Mum! Hello, Dad!"

As we stood there, looking out across the town, I took Lee's hand in mine. I don't think he even noticed. His hand was trembling slightly. It felt like the fluttering wings of a gentle butterfly. At this moment I didn't even remember that these same hands had taken human life, had killed. I certainly wasn't thinking of the fact that my hands too had taken life. For that moment I was close to Lee again, as close as I'd ever been.

Away to the west was the other big change in Wirrawee. We'd heard a little about it, but it was still weird to see it there. It was the airfield. Wirrawee had always had an airfield, of course, but just a paddock with a runway and hangar, and a small brick building called the Wirrawee Aviation Club. There were never more than six or eight small planes there. Comparing it to this new military airbase was like comparing a milk bar to the Centrepoint Shopping Complex.

And this place sure was complex. The thin dirt strip, good enough for the little Cessnas, had been replaced by a long concrete runway, gleaming in the dim lights that now surrounded the whole area. A tall cyclone fence stretched away into the distance. The Wirrawee Aviation Clubhouse was just a little thing stuck on the side of a big new grey building, three storeys high. It must have been thrown up in a hurry, and probably wasn't even finished, because there was still scaffolding on one side of it. I thought I could see a couple of bulldozers in the shadows near the scaffolding.

Iain had already moved a hundred metres down the

hill and was waiting for us to catch up. Kind of reluctantly, remembering we were meant to be leading, I went down there, passed him, and took up my position. Lee and Ursula were both in front of me, on the other side of the road. In front of me on my side was a man called Tim, a very solid-looking brown guy from Nauru.

We set off. The Kiwis had a method of moving through the town, not much different to the way we'd done it. I was quite pleased about that, thinking maybe we hadn't been so amateurish after all. It was a leapfrog technique, where the first people sneaked down the street, one on each side of the road, then stopped in a good hiding spot. The second pair followed them, passed them, and went on in the same way until they too stopped in a good place, and waited for the first pair. Behind us the others were doing the same thing. Lee was on the opposite side of the street, so that if either of us wanted to warn the Kiwis about something dangerous we could do it easily: I'd tell Tim as I went past him, and Lee would tell Ursula.

We were going along Warrigle Road, not far from the Mathers', and I knew I'd have to struggle not to be affected by that. We'd spent a lot of happy times at Robyn's place: my parents and I had gone there for barbeques every few months, and one drought year, when our swimming dam dried up, I'd practically lived in their pool. But I had to be tough, tough in my mind, and sternly tell myself not to think about Robyn. "It's just for an hour or two," I pleaded with her silently. "Don't be too angry with me."

I focused my eyes on the first dark patch we were

heading for, a spot under a bush about a hundred metres along, between two pools of light from street lamps. The street was silent, nothing moving. I remembered the first time I had left somewhere safe and entered a hostile area: in the carpark at the Showground, way back. I felt then that coming out of those shadows had changed me forever.

I walked like a cat down the street towards the dark spot. I felt that this walk changed me too. It wasn't quite as crass as me saying to the enemy, "I'm back," but it was something like that. Perhaps I was saying to myself, "I'm back," or "I'm functioning again, I'm showing some guts and determination again." Whatever. I do know that my senses were very alert. I was scanning the street like I had radar behind my eyes; my ears felt super-sensitive. I could feel each little soft touch of the cool night on my face.

And because I was so hyped up, as I got halfway along the stretch of footpath something made me pause. It was a faint flutter against my skin. Just the slightest movement of air. I hesitated, then stopped. Opposite me Ursula did the same. That was the agreement, that if one person stopped, then the other would too, immediately. I felt a bit silly, thinking it was probably nothing, a false alarm, and to stop like this so early in our walk would have them thinking I was scared.

But I still just stood there, listening, quivering with tension, trying to pick up a signal, trying to decide if I was imagining things.

And I heard a distinct crunch of a footstep on gravel, close by, to my left.

There wasn't meant to be a footstep there.

Something shrank inside my stomach, something curled up to a little black ball in there, something shrivelled and died. It affected me so much I couldn't move. The strength I'd been feeling moments earlier, the rebirth of courage, if that's what it was, perished like a prune. About a metre in front of me was a letterbox in the shape of a rabbit; next to that was what looked like a set of steps, maybe three or four. From where I stood my view was blocked by a small thick ugly conifer, not much bigger than me but enough to hide whoever was there. It seemed like it'd be one of those bare frontyards with nothing much but grass, and concrete paths. I couldn't be sure of that: it was just an impression I got.

A second later a man came down the steps. He was walking quickly and confidently, but lightly. He didn't look right or left, which was lucky for me. He went along the footpath about twenty-five metres to a parked Volvo station wagon. He must have been fairly close to Lee and Tim at that point, but I wasn't sure how close because I couldn't see them at all. The man was wearing army trousers, with a plain white T-shirt and a black jacket. His feet were bare. He used a key to open the boot of the car and he took out a small brown briefcase. I was watching everything, seeing everything vividly, but all this time I still hadn't been able to move. The man locked the boot again and began to turn to come back. Now I knew I should have moved when I had the chance. My skin began to prickle all over, every inch of it. It was the weirdest feeling. Even my scalp, under my hair, was prickling. I knew my face was burning red even though, of course, I couldn't see it myself.

And I still couldn't move.

The man was walking straight towards me. I'd forgotten about Lee, forgotten about the Kiwis. The world had shrunk to him and me, the man and me. He was walking lightly still, on his way to do some work perhaps, even at this time of night.

I did move one part of me then. My eyes. I moved my eyes. Because somewhere to my right I sensed a flicker of activity. Just a flicker. But my eyes went to it. It was Ursula silently stealthily crossing the road. She was moving with long strides. It was like watching a dragonfly darting from one lilypad to another.

A sharp gleam flashed from her hand. It was a knife, catching the reflection of the streetlight.

Who knows what might have happened? When you stand still, utterly still and silent, people can walk right past you and not notice you. Even animals can. I used to trick our old dog, Millie, like that.

"Utterly still and utterly silent," I was telling myself. "That's your only chance. Not a move. Still and silent."

I screamed.

Now, thinking about it, writing about it, I can understand it a little. And "to understand is to forgive." Isn't it? That's what they say. So it must be right.

I understand that I screamed because of all the stuff we'd been through, and because I'd seen too many people killed already, and because I'd once seen Lee use a knife to kill a man, and because I'd killed people in cold blood myself. And because of Robyn. I understand all that. And there's nothing else I need to know about it, is there?

Is there?

When I think back like this, like I'm doing now,

I seem to remember my scream as a kind of guttural noise, a hacking kind of cry. Maybe it was more a sob than a scream. I guess that was the only thing I did right. It was a low, hoarse sound, not a high-decibel glass-shattering scream that brought people to their doors and set dogs barking and cats yowling. So it was our good luck that only the one enemy soldier heard it.

After I screamed, I turned and ran. I'm not proud of any of this; that must be obvious; but it's what I did. I ran straight into Iain who'd been coming up fast behind me. He handed me on to someone else, I don't know who it was, while he went swiftly forward. I collapsed onto this other guy, clinging to him, half-sobbing, trying to fall down and at the same time trying to keep to my feet. I tried not to listen to the sounds behind me, but I couldn't not hear the gurgling sobbing noises as they killed him. I don't know what they did with the body either, I think there was some discussion about whether to make it look like an accident or whether to get rid of it where it couldn't be found. It was a real problem for them because they needed to stay under cover for another twenty-four hours or more. I could hear Lee's voice as they held their whispered conversation and I hated him for staying so calm and in control when I was not.

Anyway, I don't know what they finally decided, or what they did. I don't want to know.

After some time a soldier called Bui-Tersa came and got me from the guy who'd been looking after me. She was East Timorese and probably the youngest of all the New Zealand commandos. She was a quiet dark-haired girl with quick alert eyes and a wicked sense of humour.

She'd told me her name meant Thursday's Woman; it's a Timorese custom to name children after the day of their birth. I was grateful she'd be looking after me. I knew, of course, that they would never let me go on with them after what had happened. I knew there was no question that I'd have to go back. So I didn't put up any resistance, just let her lead me quickly and quietly through the streets and out of Wirrawee into the countryside.

In the cool clear night air, with all that space around us, away from the nightmare that Wirrawee had become, I began to breathe again. I wanted to apologise to Bui-Tersa, to say sorry to all the Kiwis, but for once I knew words were a waste of breath. I didn't care what Andrea thought, this was one occasion when talking wouldn't help. So I said nothing. I just kept following Bui-Tersa meekly across the paddocks.

I soon realised where we were going, though. And a minute after I worked it out, Bui-Tersa told me anyway.

"We're going to your farm," she said. "I might leave you at the bottom of that track where we landed the other night. That's if you think you'll be all right. If you think you can get into Hell on your own..."

She paused like people do when they want you to tell them something's fine. Her voice, normally light and laughing, was now quick and crisp.

"I'll be OK."

"Well, we'll see when we get there," she said. "But if you are OK, I probably will leave you there. Iain's got a job for me back in town for tomorrow night. Will you be able to navigate us there now?"

"Yes."

That was the only conversation we had. It wasn't that she was being unfriendly, far from it. She couldn't be unfriendly to anyone. She was too nice for that. Too nice to be a guerilla, I'd privately thought since first meeting her. But I sure didn't feel like talking and, besides, I realised early on that she was in a hurry. I could understand that, too. If she was going to drop me at the bottom of the Razor's Edge and then get back to Wirrawee that night, she would have to burn some boot leather.

Before much more time had passed I was too tired to think of talking anyway. All the events of the previous few days started to catch up with me. I felt terribly terribly weary, in a way that I never had before. It was like I was a hundred years old. If someone had offered me a walking frame at that moment I think I would have clutched it with both hands.

We kept going, somehow. There wasn't any choice, that's what it boiled down to. I felt very bitter at the way I'd betrayed myself, let myself down, and failed the Kiwis so badly. I concentrated on that — not deliberately, it just happened that way — and somehow that kept my legs moving, even though they'd lost all their energy and strength ages ago. But yes, they kept going.

We got to the track at 4.45 a.m. Bui-Tersa asked me how I felt, but again I could tell what answer she was hoping for. She was itching to get back with her mates. That was fair enough. I'd have been the same in her situation.

At least, that's what I would have said before this night. Now I couldn't be so sure.

But I felt OK about going into Hell on my own

anyway. I was back in the bush, that was the thing. The change in my feelings was no more complicated than that. About the only bad things that could happen in the bush were snakebite or bushfire. Getting lost was no big deal — I could always find water, and if you had water you could survive a long time. Anyway I couldn't get lost around here — I knew the country too well. The previous night Wirrawee had felt like a disease to me, the bush felt like the cure.

So I said goodbye to Bui-Tersa. I was so tired and sick at heart over what had happened that I didn't think about what she was going back to. It never crossed my mind that I mightn't see her again.

Eight

Kevin and Homer were glad to see me and I was glad to see them. I'd forgotten Homer's tantrum and he seemed to have got over it, so we just pretended it hadn't happened. I didn't tell them much, just that I'd stuffed up.

Then I went looking for Fi.

She was asleep so I crawled into the little tent, lay beside her and went to sleep myself.

It was lunchtime before I woke. I lay in the hot tent. The sun had moved, or the Earth had. I suppose they both had. Anyway, there was no shade over the tent any more. Homer and I frequently had long arguments over whether it was better to have your tent in the morning sun or the afternoon sun. As usual we had directly opposite opinions. Homer liked the morning sun because he said it was nice to wake up to; I liked the afternoon because it meant your tent was still warm when you went to bed.

I lay there slowly baking. A couple of blowies had got in and were doing their aerial patrols at low revs above my head. Sometimes they went so slowly you thought they would stall. On the outside of the tent I could see the dark silhouettes of dozens more flies sitting patiently on the transparent green nylon. Flies on the fly. They irritated me terribly for some reason. I lost my temper with them and punched the roof of the tent fiercely, nearly putting a hole through the fabric.

"I think Ellie's awake," I heard Homer say, in his usual dry sarcastic way. "Doing your aerobics, Ellie?"

To my surprise Kevin suddenly appeared in the entrance to the tent and gave me a cup of Tang. It was an orange juice powder that he'd brought from New Zealand. Mixed with the water it gave a drink like orange cordial. It was silly really, considering our creek water was probably the freshest in the world, but he'd wanted it and he'd been willing to carry it in and we didn't have the restrictions on what we brought that the Kiwis did, so it was fair enough. And once he'd done all the hard work of carrying it in, we helped him drink it.

But it was nice of him to bring me breakfast in bed. It was his way of saying, "Whatever happened, we're still on your side." That was the kind of relationship we'd developed, the five of us, even if it did get a touch strained at times.

I knew eventually I'd have to face the music, tell

them what happened. They'd be bursting with curiosity, of course. I would have been, in their situation. So I thought grimly: "Better get it over with," and crawled out of the tent, carefully balancing my Tang. I went over to where they were sitting, in the shade down near Chris' grave.

I just told them straight out, no mucking around.

They were cool about it. I sort of knew they would be. They were about the only people in the world, along with my parents, who I could have trusted to react like that. What's the name of that song, "That's What Friends Are For"? I don't plan to get mushy in my old age, but we did have a friendship, the five of us. We could say that for certain.

The day kind of drifted after that. We were in a typical situation from this war, typical for us anyway, sitting around waiting, not having much to do, filling time in whatever boring mind-numbing ways we could. Fi and I cleaned up the campsite, then sat by the creek with our feet in the water, talking about nothing in particular.

We didn't say anything about the war. After last night I felt too guilty to want to discuss the war.

Plus sometimes it was just all too scary. There was so much to be afraid of that I didn't know where to start. Our main fear revolved around our families. When we'd been caught and taken to Stratton Prison, did the soldiers make a connection between us and our families, prisoners still at Wirrawee Showgrounds? Or were they too busy, too disorganised, too distracted by the bombing? Kevin was the only one who could give a false name. Major Harvey knew the rest of us, so we couldn't fool him. Kevin he didn't know, and Kevin had taken full advantage of the fact and said he was Chris. Harvey had known we had an extra group member, back in Hell, and Chris' parents were in Belgium, so it was a smart move by Kevin. If only we could have had the luxury of doing the same.

So Fi and I talked of shallow silly things, like clothes and boys and friends from school. It was about one per cent successful in helping me forget what had happened in Wirrawee, but it was better than sitting around brooding. Fi did my hair as we talked. To my surprise she admitted she liked one of the soldiers, a big black-haired guy named Mike who I think was Maori or Samoan. I mean, she really liked him. She didn't just think he was cute: she wanted a relationship. I'd been thinking of us as kids and them as full-on adults, which they were, of course, but Fi made me realise they weren't much older than us. Knowing Fi I didn't think she'd do much about Mike, but I started wondering if there were any who I could see myself liking in that way. A couple of them were pretty cute. Then I thought, "I'm sure they'd be interested in you, Ellie, after the way you acted last night."

So I killed that one off successfully.

We agreed that when it was dark we'd go up on to Wombegonoo. From its eastern side there was a spot where you could see Wirrawee. During the early stages of the invasion there was nothing to see at night, but now that they were using so many lights it would be different.

I was scared of what we might see but I was still anxious to go. What we were hoping for was a ginormous fireworks show. With the new airfield sitting there waiting to be blown to dust, and with the Kiwis so competent, I felt optimistic about the result. Nervous, sure, but optimistic. What I didn't want to see was a whole lot of gunfire, or planes taking off and bombing stuff, or any evidence that the enemy was fighting back. Because, of course, if that happened I was going to blame myself; I was going to think that my loss of control had caused a disaster.

So at dusk we hiked up out of Hell and took the twisting narrow track, as thin as a shoelace, to the summit. It was surprisingly cold up there, after a series of hot nights. We huddled together in a clump of bodies, just four of us now. I wondered what was happening to Lee, if he was safe, whether he was alone, what he'd be thinking. I felt even more desperately ashamed of the way I'd broken down, more ashamed about it than at any other time, even when it was happening. There was nothing I could do about it now, nothing practical I mean, and I didn't say anything to the others, but I promised myself that I would make it up to everyone somehow.

Dad told me once how he'd taken the ute into Burchett's when the windscreen was shattered by a roo that he'd hit, and he asked Bill Burchett to fix it for him.

"I can't fix it," Bill answered, "but I'll put a new one in for you."

Well, that was the position I was in. I couldn't fix what I'd done, I could only try to do something new that would be useful. I wouldn't scream the next time.

Assuming I got another chance.

So, anyway, we sat there. The bush was busy, like always. An owl landed in a tree just off to my right, then suddenly took off again with a great fluster of wings. A rattle of pebbles down the hill had us all peering nervously through the dark. It was the kind of noise that before the invasion we would hardly have noticed, but now it was enough to have us reaching for the tranquillisers. A possum screeched at another possum and leaves shook as one of them ran up a tree trunk to safety.

It's a strange time, night-time. Things that would be beautiful or cute in daytime are disturbing at night. You're never sure about anything. Your thoughts are different.

I had plenty of time to think about stuff like that because absolutely nothing happened in Wirrawee, as far as we could see. We sat there getting cold and stiff until 5.30 a.m. Of course, we did a bit of sleeping from time to time, but there was always someone awake. And nothing happened.

It wasn't too big a deal. Iain had warned us it might be like this. We knew from our own experience how many things could go wrong. Iain and Ursula had explained the contingency plans to us. If they failed on the first night they would try again the next. And again the next. After three failures they would either come back to Hell or get a message to us. If we hadn't heard from them after four nights we could assume something had gone wrong. We were to use the spare radio to make contact with Colonel Finley and arrange a pickup.

That was a situation we preferred not to think about.

Because these guys were so competent, because they smelt of success the way my mother smelt of Chanel No. 5 when she and Dad were having a big night out, we hadn't spent much time thinking about that option.

But perhaps we thought about it a little more after the second night. Because again nothing happened. Owls came and went, wild dogs howled, we saw a snake on a bare rock at around midnight, which is a rare sight even on a warm night like we had, but nothing happened in the direction of Wirrawee.

At 5.30 we trudged down into Hell again, starting to feel a little nervous, a little sick.

I felt quite a lot sick. I just couldn't stop wondering if something had gone wrong because of my screaming at the soldier. It didn't take too much imagination to think of some terrifying possibilities. In my mind I saw the Kiwis dragging the man's body away and being surprised by a passing patrol, then bodies falling as gunfire ripped the night away.

It was no good saying anything to the others, because with the best will in the world they wouldn't be able to do anything, except mumble, "Oh no, you're just imagining it, Ellie," or "Don't worry, they'll be fine."

So I lounged around all day feeling desperate.

The third night I thought I would scream again, this time with the tension and boredom of it all. I kept staring at Wirrawee wishing for an explosion, willing it to happen, certain that if I only longed for it passionately enough there would be a sudden eruption of flame and the hills would echo with the rumbles of a gigantic blast. Then wouldn't we dance! Wouldn't we just get up and hug each other and do a war dance and rush down into Hell to prepare a celebration feast for the warriors returning home.

But there was nothing.

Now we knew there was a problem.

No one said anything on our trip back into Hell. We went off to the tents and crawled into our bags and tried to catch up on lost sleep. I don't know about the others but I didn't do much sleeping. And Fi's breathing was different to the sounds she normally makes when she's asleep.

I lay there sweating for a couple of hours, then gave up. I slithered out of the tent and immediately saw Homer, who was sitting at the cold fireplace with a stick, going through the ashes over and over again in a kind of desperate, pointless way.

I went and sat next to him but neither of us said anything for at least half an hour.

When Homer did speak I got a shock. The silence had been so long I'd almost forgotten he was there.

"We'll have to go and look for them," he said.

"I know."

I'd been thinking the same thing but had been too scared to say it. It was frightening and at the same time a relief when he came right out and said it like that.

"I agree," Kevin said from his tent.

"And me," came Fi's little quiet voice.

I almost laughed; it seemed so funny to hear them join in when we hadn't even known they were listening.

"Can't a bloke have a private conversation around here any more?" Homer complained.

"Give them one more night to get back," Kevin said, ignoring Homer's comment.

"Yeah, they'll turn up tonight," I said.

"What are we going to tell Colonel Finley if they don't?" Fi asked, from our tent.

"Worry about that when it happens," Homer said.

"He'll want us to come back," Kevin said.

In my heart I knew Kevin would be secretly wishing he could go back, and that's why he'd said it, but so what? There was a time when I'd thought Kevin was a bit weak, but now I'd shown everybody my own weakness, so I couldn't criticise him. Anyway, surely the bigger the fear the greater the courage? What I mean is, if you're never scared, doing brave things isn't that impressive, but Kevin was scared a lot of the time and still did brave things, so doesn't that make him an even bigger hero?

"He's got Buckley's," Homer said.

No one had anything to say to that.

I was frustrated at sitting around doing nothing so I took a walk up the creek to the ruins of the Hermit's hut. Even a four-wheel drive couldn't have got up there and all I had was ten-toe drive, but I slogged my way through the water, my head down to keep under the trees and creepers. The hut hadn't changed, of course. Dark and cool and empty; the damp wood slowly decaying, slaters and millipedes and earwigs hiding in the moist rotting fragments. I pulled out the metal box, the box that Lee and I had found so many months ago, and slowly read through its contents again. What a strange world these people lived in! Such strict rules, such formal customs. It reminded me of books like *Emma* and *Persuasion*, even though that world of ballgowns and courting and marrying for money and position was a long way from the Hermit's world of clearing bush and battling fires and snakes and drought.

It was a long way from our world too, where the biggest question for couples was whether to put your tongue in on the first date.

Back in those days a lot of marriages were arranged by parents. The kids didn't get any choice. It made me wonder: if my mum and dad had arranged a marriage for me, who would they pick? I guessed Homer, but only because they knew him better than any other boys. And it would be a good business deal to bring our two properties together. It'd make a nice bit of real estate — and put us in a position to take on the big companies who were gradually buying up the choice properties in the Wirrawee district.

"There I was doing it again," I thought angrily. Forgetting that all those things were over now, that this country was no longer ours, that a different group of people were occupying the land. I chewed the knuckle on my index finger angrily. How had we let this happen? Where had we gone wrong? What should we have done differently?

Well, maybe we'd been a bit lazy. Not lazy in the way of lying in bed all day. We worked pretty damn hard on our place, I knew that, and just about everyone I knew worked their butts off. It's a wonder there weren't a lot of bumless people walking around the district. No, where we'd been lazy was with our minds. We didn't put our brains to work the way we put our bodies to work. When it came time to think about tough issues we headed outside to check the water levels in the tanks or put more air in the pressure pump or service the Ag.

bike. Given a choice between reading *New Weekly* and an article on politics or economics, there are no prizes for guessing what we chose. We watched cartoons instead of the "ABC News." And now we were paying the price. Somehow physical work never seemed as hard as mental work. Maybe because with physical work there was usually a limit to it. You knew the size of the hole you had to dig, or the number of sheep you had to drench, or the number of fence posts you had to cut. With mental work there was no limit. Once you started you were straight into infinite figures, and infinite figures are very big numbers.

Ms. Kawolski was my English teacher in Year 8 and in the whole year she didn't say a single thing worth remembering. In fact, I don't remember a single thing she did say, except one. Just out of the blue one morning she said, "Knowledge is power." I don't know what she was talking about: I just remember sitting there thinking, "Wow, that's pretty true actually."

Sometimes it's the mood you're in, I think. One day a teacher tells you the meaning of life and you yawn and look at your watch and try to work out how many seconds to go before the bell. Another day a teacher says something pretty obvious, or something you've heard a million times before, and you think, "Oh my God, that is so true, she's right, variety is the spice of life."

Or whatever.

Being in the Hermit's hut always put me in a deep, serious mood, where I thought about stuff I never normally thought about, although what I did next wasn't too deep or serious. I got out my pen and wrote a message to Lee on a bit of smooth, well-sanded wood that was above the window frame. I wrote, "Dear Lee, I love you and I'm coming to look for you. Meet me in the bike shed."

This was a bit of a joke, because at Wirrawee High the bike shed was where you went if you were serious. And I mean serious. The bike shed at lunchtime was X-rated. It led to a lot of jokes about riding bikes. Even with my last boyfriend, Steve, I hadn't got into the lunchtime scene in the bike shed. We were serious enough; it was just that the bike shed at lunchtime wasn't a place to go if you were worried about your reputation, and I've never wanted to chuck away my reputation. Which, of course, is another reason for being disgusted with myself about Adam in New Zealand.

So anyway, to say to someone, "Meet me in the bike shed" was like saying, "Take me, I'm yours" or "Let's do it" in our language.

After I'd written the message I sat outside the hut, in the one patch of sunlight that could sneak through all the vegetation. The sunlight kept blinking as the branches above me moved slightly in the feeble breeze. I sat there and after a while I realised that I'd never felt more alone in my life. Fi and Homer and Kevin were only a few hundred metres away, in the clearing, but it wasn't enough. I wanted to be surrounded by all the people I'd ever known and cared about. I wanted to be held and rocked by them. I'm not sure if even that would have been enough, though. Deep down inside I realised there was a part of me that would always be alone: that from birth to death, and beyond, everyone had something that was theirs and theirs alone. It was scary to realise that I had this solitary little part of me, but I think it was something to do with growing up too: the knowledge that OK, I was part of a family, part of a network of friends, but that was not the whole story. I did exist independently of the people who loved me and surrounded me. It was a lonely thought, but not necessarily a bad one.

The Hermit's hut was a strong place. I hadn't quite realised that, the other times I'd been there. Strong because it survived physically, sure, but that's not what I mean. Its strength came from the experiences of the man who had lived there. Somehow his isolation let him gradually lose his weaknesses, his softness. Just before the invasion I'd been using the back of an axe to hammer in star pickets for tree guards. Around our place the tree guards have to keep out not just rabbits, but sheep and kangaroos too. Those wimpy little tree guards made of cardboard or plastic are no good for us. We use wire netting that comes up to my armpits. So I'd been driving in the pickets for that when I mis-hit and broke the axe handle. The short part of the broken handle was stuck firmly in the head of the axe. No drama, it happens quite often and I did what I always do: chucked it in the Aga to burn away the broken wood, then fished out the steel axe-head the next morning before I fired the Aga up again.

And that was the memory that came back to me as I sat in my ragged little patch of warmth by the creek. The memory of the useless splintered wood burned away by the fire, until only the solid hard axe-head was left. I hoped that what had happened to me with the soldier in Wirrawee had burnt away the useless weak parts of me, and that what was left would be strong. Strong enough for whatever lay ahead.

Nine

We didn't have any real plan. We just knew we couldn't go back without Lee, let alone the New Zealanders. When they didn't turn up on the fourth night we called Colonel Finley on the spare radio. It was Saturday morning 5.50 our time. Colonel Finley's voice was as calm and level and controlled as ever. But I knew him well enough by now: I could hear the tension. He knew something had gone terribly wrong.

He said to wait till Wednesday and call him again. He was hoping the missing soldiers might still turn up. He said, "If they're not back by then, we'll bring you out."

But I wondered if he might have had another thought in his mind. He did say, among all the interference and static, "Sit tight, don't get involved," but he didn't say it too strongly. The soldiers were much more used to him than we were. I couldn't help thinking that if we were able to do anything, to find out what had happened for instance, or even to help the Kiwis, the Colonel wouldn't try too hard to stop us. And if something terrible happened to us in the process, well, he would be upset, of course, I don't want to make him sound like a monster, but on his balance sheet the risk would seem worth it.

So, we started taking risks.

Our first risk was to go in daylight. We knew if these guys were in trouble we couldn't wait around in Hell until there was a dark night or a nice evening or a long weekend. We were packed already — just light packs — and we moved fast along Tailor's Stitch, keeping off the ridge so we couldn't be seen against the skyline. And, by God, we did move fast. There was no time to think. Fi was leading for once, and she set a cracking pace. Kevin was next, then me, then Homer. We went at a run, the loose stones slipping and sliding under our feet. I got swiped in the face half-a-dozen times by branches that Kevin let fly as he pushed them away from him, until I lost patience and yelled at him. "Take a bit of care, will you!"

When we came to the four-wheel-drive track Fi didn't hesitate. Going downhill fast with packs on your back is no fun: your ankles twist when you land on rocks because there's no time to choose where you're going to put your foot, your thighs ache because you use them for brakes all the time, and you feel every point on your back where the pack doesn't exactly fit the curves of your body. We were panting and sweating and gasping for breath. We weren't being as careful as Iain and the New Zealanders, but no matter how far the colonists had spread we knew they would not be up here yet. Not yet, and probably not ever. I didn't blame Iain and Ursula for being so cautious, of course, but we knew the country and they didn't.

Near the bottom of the track we stopped at last. Fi led us into a little clearing that we'd used a couple of times before. We threw ourselves on the ground, quick to grab what rest we could, and struggled to get our breath.

"From here on we'll have to go carefully," I said, stating the obvious.

"You lead the next bit, Ellie," Fi said. "It's your land."

"Used to be," I said. Privately I'd been wondering if they'd ever want me to lead again.

After ten minutes' rest I took them across country, counting the dry cracked gullies as we traversed them, so I wouldn't lose track of where we were. When I figured we were about to run out of scrub, near the Leonards' place, I turned right and headed down to the road. It was a bit dangerous maybe, but we didn't have a lot of choice. To stay in bush would have meant a huge detour. We were so worried about Lee and the Kiwis that we felt we didn't have the time for detours. And we were rapidly getting tired. We'd had almost no sleep, and we were travelling at a fast pace through difficult country. I knew that this stretch of road was lined with trees, so I figured we could keep in among those and get enough cover if we were careful. Very careful.

There wasn't much traffic. Three times we had to hide when we heard vehicles. One was a semi with a load of sheep, just like in the old days. One was a car, a blue Falcon that I didn't recognise. The third was a genuine army truck, a fair dinkum troop carrier, painted olive green and khaki, and driven by a soldier. There was a tarp over the back, so we couldn't see what was in there.

The land didn't look as neglected as it had in the

autumn. For a while I'd thought it was deteriorating so badly that it might get out of control. But since then there'd been signs that it was looked after a little better. For instance, we passed one paddock with a mob of freshly shorn merino crosses, and another with a good crop of rape that was probably only a month or so off harvesting. There were a lot of weeds around, gorse and thistles and blackberry, and a big patch of St. John's Wort, but that wasn't so unusual. Life's a constant battle against weeds.

By lunchtime we were at one of the trickiest parts of the trip. The Shannons' place is only five k's from Wirrawee. There was no real cover on the road, so we had to go across paddocks again. A fringe of shade trees ran along the fenceline and we thought they would give us a bit of protection. They ended at the bottom of the hill, but the fence went on up the hill and over it, like a giant zipper. The hill still hadn't been cleared much. It was pretty scrubby with more bush up the back of it, which is why we were attracted to it, of course. We figured if we could get up there it'd be easy to get another k or two closer to town.

The lower part of the hill was all rocky, a natural little fortress. To our right was the house, an untidy collection of buildings that Mr. Shannon was never satisfied with. He'd moved at least three buildings in the last five years, but it hadn't helped at all: just made a bigger mess. One of the sheds especially, he'd moved too close to the house, so it made the house look sort of insignificant.

A lot of people lived there now, judging by the cars parked in and around the machinery shed. That was something we'd noticed, the way these people settled in much larger numbers than we had. They seemed to have four or five families in places where we'd had one. Maybe that was fair enough, I don't know. Maybe the land could cope with more people than we'd put on it. All the wasted land along the sides of roads, the long paddocks, I supposed they'd be farming those soon.

Could be a problem in a drought though, when that feed was pretty important.

We snuck along the line of shade trees very slowly and very cautiously. With every step we were watching for danger. We went one at a time, leaving a good gap between each person. I was first, weaving in among the trees and where there were no friendly trunks, staying in the shadows. All the time I was trying not to think of the last time I'd seen an enemy soldier, trying not to think whether I might fall apart again.

There didn't seem to be anyone around, though. I waited for the others at the base of the little fortress of rocks, not watching them as they slipped silently along the thin ribbon of cover, but instead scanning the paddocks and the homestead, looking for the slightest movement of anything other than sheep or rabbits or magpies or hawks.

It seemed peaceful enough.

Kevin was the first to join me, then Homer, then Fi. And still, nothing out of the ordinary.

I stood, a little cramped after crouching behind a rock the size of my desk at home. I led the others up into the jumble of granite, while Kevin kept watch at the rear, to make sure nothing happened behind us.

I walked right into a little crater, like an open-air theatre: a bowl of green surrounded by boulders.

And I walked right into maybe the biggest surprise I'd had since the war began.

In the crater was a group of children. There were as many as a dozen: I didn't have time to count. They were immersed in some game, I don't know what that was either, but something involving guns, I think, because some of the kids had sticks that they were pointing at others and a couple had rope around them, like they were the prisoners. Quite a few wore sashes: ragged strips of green across their skinny bodies. Pretend uniforms, probably. Most wore baseball caps.

I would have backed out, but they saw me straightaway. Everything froze. Everyone froze. There was a long long pause. My heart seemed to beat extra hard, so hard that I felt it wanted to come out of my chest. I stared at the children and they stared at me. Behind me Homer swore softly.

"Come away," he whispered. "Quick, before they realise."

But they had already realised, I knew that. All sorts of possibilities raced crazily through my mind, a sort of kookaburra chorus of wild thoughts. What could we do? Grab them? Hardly. There were too many of them. Bluff them? Join in their game and try to be friendly, act really innocent? The children seemed too old, too knowing, for that. Already they were backing away from us, fear on their faces. Threaten them? I saw the face of one, a little girl, start to crumple. Her mouth opened like a black hole and she began to cry. And then it was too late. They suddenly scattered, all of them screaming, running in every direction at first, but with one aim in view: to get to the house. "Come back," I heard Fi call desperately, as though they were just naughty little kids at the beach.

It was like we didn't quite realise that we were now in deadly peril because of a bunch of kids. I mean, we realised, of course, but we reacted more slowly than we would if they'd been a bunch of adults. We started running up the hill, in the opposite direction to the children, stumbling and gasping and tripping. I could hear Kevin making funny sobbing noises behind me. We ran, I don't know, maybe sixty or eighty metres up there before I stopped and turned, looking back towards the farmhouse to see what was happening.

I hoped to see nothing. Maybe the adults wouldn't believe the kids. Maybe they would be too busy. Maybe they were out working, no one even home. But I saw the worst possible sight, the exact thing that I dreaded. Some of the kids were already near the house, and they were screeching their little lungs out. As I watched, a-dults came teeming from the place like ants from a nest when you've dragged your toe across it. Even at this distance they looked angry, aggressive. I was pretty sure a couple of them were holding rifles. No doubt they kept rifles at the ready all the time in this hostile land. A moment later I knew for sure they had rifles when they saw us and a couple of them dropped to one knee and lifted the rifles to their shoulders.

"Run," I screamed at the others.

Sure the adults were a long way away, but a lucky long shot could do as much damage as a close-up easy one.

We grunted and sweated our way up the hill. The pack on my back felt like I'd grown a hunchback and it was made of lead. As we approached the crest I thought of something and although it scared me to stop I knew I had to say it. I turned and faced them. I could only see the tops of their sweaty heads.

"When we get to the top," I gasped, "keep low, don't stand up, go over the top really fast."

I was proud of myself for thinking of that. And proud that I'd taken the risk of stopping to say it. In wars people get medals for less. But Homer just grunted, "What do you think we are, stupid?" and the three of them kept coming, like they were in some terrible cross-country race.

If I needed any incentive to keep going I got it then. An angry whistling noise, like a high-pitched turbocharged cicada, whizzed past. And another, a little further away. It doesn't matter how tired you are, being shot at is very motivating. I turned and kept on grinding my way up the last little bit of the hill, making my legs pump like they had batteries. Homer and I arrived at the top together. I flung myself over the skyline but immediately turned around and crawled back so I could get a look at what was happening.

Kevin and Fi, gasping, desperate, eyes staring, came over the top and went past me. At the bottom of the hill the first adults were arriving. Four of them were already starting up the slope, but just as I got a look at them they stopped, and all at the same time, like they'd rehearsed it, they turned and began shouting at the people behind. I guessed what had happened. At least one of the people with rifles had kept firing after their friends went past. It was no wonder they'd stopped, but I was rapt. For once they'd got a taste of their own medicine.

I couldn't stay there watching. Already Fi was calling me. I got up again and ran on after them. They were rushing towards the scrub. I followed as fast as I could. The bush up there was just light timber, clumps of trees in places, lots of single trees, and tussocky yellow grass. There was some good pasture as well though, big green patches watered by springs.

Homer was leading now and he was taking us towards the only patch of thick bush. I wasn't sure that was such a good idea.

I yelled at them: "Stop! Wait!"

They weren't very keen to stop, but they did pause and look back, to see what I wanted. I caught up with them, but I was panting so hard, was so terribly frightened, that I could hardly speak.

"Wait," I said again. "If we go there, it's so obvious, that's where they'll look first."

I could see the doubt, the indecision, start to creep over their faces.

"But there's no cover anywhere else," Homer said.

"If we go in there, we're trapped."

"Well, where else then?"

"Get as far away from here as we can. They won't start a proper search straightaway. Before they do, let's make all the ground possible."

They didn't argue. There wasn't time for arguing. I took the lead again and ran through light bush, searching all the time for an idea, some hint of where to go or what to do. There was nothing obvious. It was such typical light scrub. Every hundred metres looked the same as every other hundred metres. I figured we had at least a minute, maybe two. But so what? Right now they'd be calling up helicopters and soldiers. With the airstrip so close they'd be here in no time. They could surround this whole area in half an hour, probably less. It was no good us finding somewhere that would be safe for a few minutes. We had to find somewhere that would be safe for however long the search lasted . . . a full day maybe, or two, or three.

We came to a fence and struggled over it. It was much the same kind of country, but with a small mob of horses grazing in among the trees. They looked up, startled and curious. They didn't run away like you'd expect. A couple even took a step towards us. I felt a wave of affection for them, a wave of longing to stop and rub their noses and let them nibble at my hand. Yet here we were, running like criminals through our own land, running from bullets, just so we could stay alive.

In a movie there would have been a secret cave that we could have dropped into. Or Sam and Colonel Finley would have arrived in a helicopter. Here it wasn't going to be so easy. But I was desperate. Whatever else happened I didn't want to be caught again. And that fierce fear made my mind work fast and frantically. A memory flashed into my mind, like a slide on a screen. It was something my Uncle Bob said years ago when Grandma decided to leave the farm and buy her house in Stratton. Uncle Bob, who's a builder, came down to look at the house she wanted. I followed him around as he checked it out. He kept looking up all the time. "What are you looking at, Uncle Bob?" I asked. He glanced at me. "People never look above their own line of sight," he said. "If the builder's done a snow job on this place you can tell by looking up high. He'll be smart enough to have it looking OK at eye level."

I was very impressed by this. And I think he said the same thing to Dad, because Dad said it to me a few months later when he was blocking up a possum hole.

I'd learnt from them, and when I played hide-and-seek I occasionally hid up a tree. Not once did anyone find me. In the end I gave up doing it, because it was so boring.

As I looked at the hard ground and the light scrub, the lack of undergrowth, the unvarying unyielding bush, and the grass mown short by the horses, I thought that Uncle Bob's words might give us our only hope. We were stumbling along now, getting slower and more tired.

I called back over my shoulder: "We'll have to get up trees and hide in the tops."

No one said anything and I thought maybe they hadn't heard. So I called again: "We'll have to climb trees."

This time Homer answered. "But if they see us up a tree... then we're trapped."

His voice was rasping. I knew he was close to exhaustion. We all were.

In the distance I heard a burring whirring buzzing noise. It was all too familiar.

"The choppers are coming," I yelled.

I veered to my left, towards another clump of trees. I didn't even look back to check that they were following. I just assumed they were. As we came in under the first trees I had a glimpse of the blades of a helicopter in the distance. I ran to a tree that looked easy and had a good crown as well. Thinking of the choppers I called to the others, "Pick one that's got lots of leaves on top."

I knew they'd heard because Fi took a look up and changed her mind about the tree she'd been running towards. She went to the next one instead.

I started to climb, but there weren't enough hand-holds; I gave up and, like Fi, ran to another. In front of me I could see Homer struggling with a difficult climb, Fi halfway up her new tree, and Kevin leaving one and trying a different one.

My second choice was better, but by that stage it did-n't matter. I had to make it work. I had to get to the top, because I'd run out of alternatives. Never had my pack felt heavier, never had I felt wearier or more scared, but for fear of my life I climbed. The mottled white bark was cool to the touch, the light green leaves brushed my face, the branches supported my weight. I went up and up. There were three long reaches where I had to really stretch, but I stretched. If it had dislocated my shoul-der I would have stretched.

The noise of the chopper was louder but I thought I could hear human cries away behind us. No longer was I looking to see how the others were going, no longer was I even thinking of them. All I wanted to do was get myself safe, get to the very top, hide in that comforting cubby of leaves. Fear makes you selfish. And then I was in there, feeling myself engulfed by the fresh light greenery, realising for the first time that my chest was crashing and heaving for breath. The noise of the chop-per was a roar now, probably only a hundred metres or so away. I clung to the tree for dear life. I was grateful for the green and brown camouflage clothing that nowadays we wore as a matter of course. Although the leaves were comfortingly thick, the branches were light, and with my pack on I was pretty heavy. I was scared the branches would break under me. I was scared the people in the helicopter would see me. I was scared the people on the ground would see me. I was sobbing, sort of half-trying to get my breath and half-crying all at the same time but not sure which was which. And I was choking down the sobs as much as I could, feeling that I would choke myself by doing it, that my lungs would burst, but knowing I had no choice.

Then the leaves around me were buffeted by a great wind, a tornado. The leaves went into a frenzy, my hair was blown crazily around my head, my clothes billowed, and from the ground came a storm of dust and twigs. The roar of the chopper hammered at my ears. My eyes were shut tight; partly to keep out the dust, partly in terror. I was scared that the helicopter was going to take off my head, that it was so low it would decapitate me.

The tree calmed again. The blast of air faded, but I still could hardly hear. The roar of the helicopter had deafened me. I opened my eyes cautiously, relieved that my head was still on my shoulders. I glanced down, even more cautiously, to see something more terrifying than the helicopter. Directly below my tree someone was standing.

Ten

He was wearing a black cap and a khaki shirt. I couldn't see any more of him than that. It may have been a soldier's uniform; I couldn't be sure. Not that it mattered a lot. He was the enemy, that's what it came down to. If he was a soldier he may have been a more dangerous enemy than a farmer. But there wasn't much in it. If he had a gun he was deadly. If he didn't, he was still bigger than me and he could probably call up help in seconds.

My life depended on his intelligence. If he looked up and saw me I was finished. If he didn't I might survive a little longer. In my desperation I began to measure the drop from the tree. If I moved about a metre I would get a clear drop to the ground. And if I made myself fall a little to the left instead of dropping like a stone I would land on top of him. What would that do to me? I didn't know. Probably not kill me, but I might break a lot of bones. What would it do to him? I didn't know that either, but I felt it would do him a lot of damage. In cold blood I made the decision: if he sees me I'll drop onto him. Anything would be better than being caught again. Anything would be better than being killed without putting up some sort of fight.

But would I be able to do it if the moment came? Would I really be able to do it? To throw myself out of a fifteen-metre-high tree? Could I overcome all my instincts and do such a frightening thing?

I was shuddering with the fear of all this but at the same time crazily telling myself to think about something else. Why? For the stupid reason that I was convinced he would feel telepathic thoughts from me if I kept thinking about him. That my thoughts were so powerful there was no way he could stand there and not get energy waves through his brain that would cause his head to turn, cause him slowly to tilt his head back and look up through the branches, up through the leaves, right into my eyes.

And perhaps that might have happened too, except he was suddenly distracted. A woman, wearing a yellow T-shirt and black jeans, came across the clearing to the man. I got a better view of her face. She was sweating heavily and looked scared. She was talking loudly, pointing behind her, her broad flushed face like a mirror of mine, as far as the fear went, anyway. The man came forward a few steps. He was wearing grey jeans, but I don't think it was a uniform. He said something in a low voice. I realised he too was puffing and sweating, his shirt wet across the back. But she went on talking, nineteen, twenty, twenty-one to the dozen. They started to move away a little further.

I had the feeling that maybe they were giving up already. I clung to that hope. But if that was their plan, it didn't last long. Almost at the same time I heard another man yelling something. The two of them stopped and looked across to their left. Then they turned to face the newcomer.

I had a good view of him, too. And I felt really scared. Because I knew at my first glance that now we were dealing with the professionals.

This guy was about thirty, smooth-faced, sharp-eyed, and in an officer's uniform. He was carrying two rifles and he gave one to the other man. It was an ugly black thing with a short barrel and a big magazine. He lifted his arm to point through the trees ahead, in the direction we'd been going. The big sweat patch under his arm was the only sign that he was stressed. The man and the woman slunk away in the direction he'd pointed. It was pretty obvious they'd been given their orders.

The officer stayed where he was, though. He wiped his forehead with his sweaty arm, then pulled out a cigarette from a crumpled pack in his breast pocket. He lit it with a match from one of those little books of matches that tear off and are always so hard to light. He sure had trouble. It took him three or four goes.

While he was doing it I took a quick glance at the other trees. There was no movement, no sign of Fi or the boys. I hadn't expected any, of course, but it was still a relief. I felt a huge responsibility for them. This climbing trees had been my idea: if it went wrong my life, which was in enough trouble already, would be wrecked forever. And I don't mean because I would die. I mean because my friends would die and I would have caused it.

The smoke from the cigarette curled up around my tree.

Smoke curls up around the old gum tree trunk,
Silver moon makes the wet leaves glisten.

How many times had I sung that at Wirrawee Primary? The little wisps of smoke stole past me now, and the smell of tobacco replaced all the familiar bush smells. It was quite a pleasant smell. Under other circumstances I might have enjoyed it.

I blinked as a sniff of smoke got in my eye. I had to

be careful not to let it get up my nose in case it made me sneeze. What a disaster that would be. I looked down again at the man. He was squatting now, his back against the tree. How many times had I seen my father in the same position? How alike all these people were under their different clothes and different skins. But this man did something I'd never seen my father do. If I lived to be a hundred and fifty I'd never see my father do this. The man idly put the burning end of his cigarette to a piece of bark and watched casually as a stream of white smoke came from the bark.

"You bloody idiot!" I wanted to yell. "Put that cigarette out."

I nearly climbed down from the tree and grabbed it from his hand. Already there were all the signs that we were in the middle of a long dry spell; already the fire danger was serious. And here was this idiot playing with matches. Didn't he know any better, at his age? Any rural five-year-old knows it's safer playing with gelignite than matches in bushfire weather. I'd been sweating enough before this; now there was one more thing to worry about.

Another man, a very small guy in army uniform, came trotting into the clearing. The officer looked at him and then nodded at the cigarette and the bark. He said something, with a little laugh, and although I didn't know his language I knew with total certainty what he said. It was: "If we don't find them, we can always burn them out."

Now I nearly fell out of the tree in shock and fear. If these turkeys deliberately started a fire, we were in bigger trouble, more desperate trouble than ever. We'd either stay in our trees and be burned alive, or we'd jump down and be shot. I just couldn't tell if the officer was serious. If he was serious, all I could think was, "These guys have no idea what they're dealing with." I was panicking, finding it impossible to think properly any more.

The small guy trotted away again. I'm not sure what he'd wanted, but I suppose he just reported that he couldn't find us or something. I stayed where I was, of course, though I was getting stiff and achey as I cooled down from our mad run.

I wanted badly to move but it looked like being a long time before I could.

I hadn't been right about many things that day but I was right about that. I'd say it was three hours before I got a chance to move. The officer walked away out of my sight a few times, but I didn't dare move then because, for all I knew, he may have been standing on the other side of the tree where I couldn't see the ground at all. The helicopter swept past four more times, once very close again, the other times close enough. Each time I flattened myself and shrank, like a rabbit when a hawk goes overhead.

The only nice thing that happened was that the horses went past. I had time to look at them properly now. There were seven of them, and they still seemed pretty relaxed about what was happening in their home paddock. They looked well cared for, too: carrying plenty of weight—too much—and with their coats well brushed. They glowed, the way horses do when they're in good nick. They stopped for a nibble occasionally but they were soon gone.

By then every limb and every bone of my body was groaning with a terrible dull ache. I was cramping up in both legs. I was desperate for some exercise. And at last I did get a brief go. A whole group of people started coming in, a couple at a time. There might have been a dozen altogether. I couldn't see any of them but I heard their voices all right: they made enough noise.

They were reporting in, I think, or maybe planning their tactics. I didn't care what they were doing but as the first ones arrived the officer walked quickly over in their direction. And there didn't seem to be a helicopter around. I grabbed the chance to stretch each leg, then my arms, and waggle my head. I pushed my shoulders up and down, then rotated my bum a few times.

I went to stretch my legs again, but as I did I brushed a big loose piece of bark with my right shin.

I grabbed at it but too late.

"Too late," I thought in despair. And as if that wasn't enough, when I grabbed at the bark I knocked off a long piece of dead wood, and it and the bark and some twigs and leaves and more dead stuff all went floating down together, with me helplessly watching.

I was ready to scream. I was ready to jump. I sobbed out loud with the bitterness and unfairness of it all. I didn't know what to do, which way to go. I felt the most terrible sickness in the guts. The bits of rubbish fell and fell, knocking into branches on the way down and it was like I was watching my death in slow motion with me utterly unable to do a thing. And because I was so obsessed by the shower of wood I hadn't even noticed the clattering frenzied roar of the helicopter banging on my ears again. But I did notice the fresh tornado of dust and debris that went billowing through the trees as the chopper slowly scoured the treetops for the sixth time.

I guess my little waterfall of bark and wood didn't get noticed in all the storm of rubbish. That helicopter, so determined to find and kill me, saved my life.

When I realised that they weren't coming after me, that no one was standing at the bottom of the tree firing up through the leaves, I clung to the branch I was lying against and said a full-on totally religious prayer. I even wondered if somewhere in Heaven Robyn was keeping an eye on me. I wouldn't be surprised. I don't know if we're all born with a guardian angel, but I figured I probably had one now.

It was a while before I became aware again of what was happening in the clearing. For half an hour or so I didn't care what was going on. It was only gradually that I started to realise that our troubles weren't exactly over. We were in the most deadly peril still. It was late afternoon and the sun was shining through the treetops with its last burst of energy and warmth before it retired for the night. I could see no movement in the clearing but, of course, I couldn't rely on that. My limbs were sorer than ever and now I badly needed to go to the toilet. I didn't dare move, though, after what happened last time. I looked again at the other trees, trying to see Fi and Homer and Kevin, wondering how they were going in their little nests, wondering if they were as scared as I was. I wished I'd shared a tree with one of them.

From across to my left I heard a whistle, a sharp shrill sound from someone with two fingers in his mouth. I scanned the hillside opposite but couldn't see who'd made it. Then it was repeated to my right and I heard it echoed away across the plateau. It was obviously some sort of signal and it got a response because, after a while, I saw a number of people moving slowly towards a place near the clearing. I think they had a meeting, because when the breeze blew my way I heard voices. One time they seemed to be arguing, another time a voice sounded like she was giving orders. I didn't know what was going on. I couldn't hear the helicopter any more, so that was good news.

The sun took ages to go down. Typical of the time of year. The whole situation reminded me of an old flickering film, where you see glimpses of the action, then long periods of nothing but grey static. But you had to work out from watching the little bits of action what was going on. It wasn't guesswork—you had to use your brains, every bit of intelligence you had—and knowledge was power, so the more knowledge you had, the more powerful you became.

Of course, power wasn't really the big issue. This was all about earning the right to stay alive.

I watched for another hour, before it got too dark. In that time I saw only one human being. It was a woman walking slowly along in the open, looking around her. She carried a modern-looking rifle and she held it at the ready position. I would have thought she was on her own, except that just as she was almost out of sight she said something to someone . . . I think. I was almost sure that she turned a little to one side and spoke. It was difficult to tell in the dusk. Maybe she was talking to the horses, because a few minutes later they came wandering into view for the second time, moving towards better clumps of grass maybe, and stopping to graze every few metres.

And I did hear the helicopter again. For fifteen minutes, even two helicopters. Both of them were further away, except for one sweep that came close enough for me to feel again the loud chattering was almost on top of me.

I didn't see it, though. Just felt it and heard it, and that was enough. But it seemed the search was being scaled down as night came on. I guessed they would throw a cordon around the area, maybe run patrols through it, and then start the full search again at dawn.

My bladder was bursting and I didn't think I could wait much longer. As soon as it was dark I knew I had to take the risk and start down the tree. I prayed there would be no one in the clearing below, no soldiers waiting with rifles in their hands and expressions of wolfish delight on their faces. I moved as slowly and ponderously as a koala, but as quietly too, inching down, feeling cautiously for my footholds, stopping and listening after each downward move.

The scariest bit was the last three metres. I felt very vulnerable. I had absolutely no way of defending myself, and this was the time when they would find it easiest to see me. I could get shot in the back and die without even seeing the face of the person who shot me. I tried not to think about what that would feel like, but I'd imagined it often enough in the past. I figured it'd be such an impact that my whole body would go into shock: it would shut down so quickly and suddenly that I wouldn't actually feel a lot, it'd be over in seconds.

That was the only consolation I could offer myself.

When my feet touched the ground I dropped instantly and whipped around, trying to get an immediate look at the clearing. But the pack on my back hit the trunk of the tree and knocked me sideways. As well, I was suffering from not having moved properly for so many hours, so I couldn't get up again easily. The result was that I didn't get a good view at all. Instead I had to struggle to get upright. True to form, I was not the athletic jungle fighter but still the awkward koala. Nothing had changed.

When I did manage to get my balance I crouched on my haunches to take a good look at the clearing. For a few minutes I actually forgot my bladder. I wouldn't have believed it possible a moment earlier, but I guess it's just another thing fear does for you.

It was all quiet in the clearing. For about ten seconds, anyway. Then I heard a noise. It was a typical bush noise, the sound of another koala, or a possum coming down a tree at nightfall to begin its evening prowl. Only this was no possum. It had to be a human possum, a Fi or Kevin or Homer possum. But I didn't wait to see which one. There was something more important to worry about. I fumbled at the buttons of my jeans, hoping I'd be able to get them down in time.

It was a close call, but I made it.

Only then — and it took a while — did I bother to see who was coming down the tree. Whoever it was had nearly reached the ground. I just hoped I hadn't made as much noise as him or her. But I snuck over there, walking as quietly as I could. It was Homer. I went to hug him but he wasn't interested. He had his mind on the same thing I had. Only when he finished was he ready for a reunion.

Then I could hear Kevin and Fi climbing down, too. Homer and I kept our eyes on the darkness around us hoping desperately we wouldn't see some fatal movement.

Reunited, we had a quick whispered conversation. Our whispers were so quiet, so brief, that the whole conversation reminded me of butterflies, touching slightly and lightly on each leaf.

"We've got to get out of here," Fi breathed in my ear.

"I know. But there might be patrols."

"We've got to risk it," Homer said, in his low rumble. "It'll be too dangerous here tomorrow."

Kevin didn't say anything. The only other comment was mine, and it was unnecessary.

"Keep very quiet."

I didn't blame them for the looks they gave me.

Eleven

Was I breathing? I wasn't sure. I actually put my hand to my heart to check. I thought I felt something, so I resumed staring into the darkness. If only I had the eyes of a cat. If only I had high-beam headlights instead of eyes. If only I could be home, a year ago, coming in after setting up the shed for the next day's shearing and heading straight for the shower.

But this was one of those times when I had to be tough with myself. Strict and stern. I forced those soft weak thoughts out of my head and stared even harder through the night. If there was the slightest movement I wanted to see it before an enemy saw me. To my right and left Homer and Fi, and further across Kevin, were doing the same thing.

We'd worked out our plan. Take ten steps, stop, get the go-ahead from the others before moving again. It had to be a definite hand motion from the others before you went on. If they stood still, you assumed it was because they'd seen something.

So when I took my umpteenth ten steps, stopped, looked across at Fi and saw her frozen to the spot I felt my face go hot and prickly. I knew I was breathing now. I too froze, partly out of terror, partly so Homer would know there was a problem.

I didn't actually see him stop but I felt that he had.

I turned very gently and slowly so I could get a better look at what Fi had seen. It was difficult, of course, because of the darkness. I felt like I was staring so hard I might damage my eyes.

In fact I saw nothing. It was my ears that gave the clue. The crunch of feet on rough ground. I'd heard it a few times now in this war, and each time it was with the knowledge that these might be the feet bringing death. I kept thinking it should get easier, this constant staring in the face of death, but it never did.

We all stood like statues. There was nothing else to

do. We couldn't run away, and we had no weapons so we couldn't charge at them. It was a paralysing feeling. I don't know if Homer or Kevin even saw the patrol, but Fi and I did. Three shadowy figures, walking slowly past. Their heads were turning from side to side, their rifles held ready: they weren't relaxed and casual like some patrols we'd come across, at other times and in other places.

And still we stood. I think they must have reached a point which was the limit of their territory, because five minutes later back they came, as silent, as wary, as deadly as before.

When they melted into the darkness again we melted in the opposite direction. It was funny, we did it by osmosis or telepathy or something. We just all headed the same way, without a signal or word being needed.

We kept going in that direction. Same slow careful strategy. We crossed the open grassed area again. I got the biggest shock of my life when, with a sudden silent swish of their hoofs, the horses loomed up. This time they were really friendly, crowding into us, looking for sugar or oats or attention. It terrified me, and I spun around frantically, hoping no one was coming up on us and using the horses as a distraction. But no one was there.

We pushed the horses away and went on. We walked quite a distance, ten steps at a time, and I at last started to allow myself the first faint glimmer of hope. Maybe they had given up. Maybe they didn't have enough people to cover the whole area, and we'd walked right through their patrol line. Maybe...

Then I saw Homer, frozen just like Fi an hour earlier.

Again I stopped, trembling, sick with rage and fear. We couldn't keep getting away with this. Either this time or the next time or the time after, our luck would run out. I'd learned that, after our attack on Cobbler's Bay. Would this be the time we were caught or killed? Did it really matter which time it was, if it was going to happen anyway? And of course it was.

I didn't see the patrol Homer had heard, but after ten minutes he slowly and silently began to withdraw. The three of us withdrew with him.

We met back in the middle of the grassy plateau. It seemed to be the only safe place. We huddled together and again talked in the faintest whispers. Three of us talked, anyway. Fi just wept, silently. The awful relentless pressure had got to her.

The only one sure of anything was Homer, and he was only sure of one thing. He was insistent.

"We've got to get out of here," he said. "We must get out tonight. We absolutely can't be here in the morning. Or it's the end of us."

That was no great help. He was right, but he still didn't have an answer. We stood in our silent miserable huddle, not a single idea in our minds. Behind us stood the horses, in their own huddle. They didn't look too happy either. Maybe they were hurt at the way we were ignoring them.

As I recall, Kevin and I thought of it simultaneously.

"The horses," I said.

"Those bloody horses!" Kevin exclaimed suddenly.

Homer realised immediately. Fi looked puzzled, but she was still crying her silent tears and maybe finding it hard to concentrate.

"The horses?" she asked, her mouth twisting with her distress. I saw the white line of her scar.

"We ride the horses out of here," Homer whispered. "That's what you mean, isn't it?"

"At full gallop," I confirmed.

My heart was pounding with excitement and hope — and my old enemy, fear. It was an outrageous idea, wild, crazy, and maybe impossible — but we had no other ideas, no other way of escape.

And yet... There were so many problems, so many dangers. Riding at full gallop, on unknown horses, through darkness, through bush, through gunfire. One branch in our faces and we'd be lucky to escape with multiple fractures to the face and skull. One hoof in a rabbit hole and we'd fly straight into the nearest tree trunk, or land at the feet of a soldier who, in my imagination, was already raising his rifle. One tree in the wrong place and the horse would smash into it at fifty k's an hour and both he and I would be as dead as if we'd hit a concrete wall on a motorbike. No helmets, no reins, no saddle. If he shied or refused or bucked, or stopped at the sight of a soldier or the sound of gunfire...

"Let's do it," I said, but hating the sound of the sob in my voice.

There was one consolation. Fi, who knew as much about farm life as she did about the history of venetian blinds, was a great rider. She'd had lessons from Daphne Morrisett, and Daphne was the pride and joy of Wirrawee, having ridden in the Olympics three-day event. Not many of us could afford Daphne as a teacher but Fi's parents were heavily into stuff like tennis lessons, piano lessons, riding lessons. Fi turned out to be a good natural rider who won lots of ribbons at pony club. Daphne said she reminded her of herself at the same age, which was high praise.

So although the danger was terrible and real for all of us, it was perhaps a little less so for Fi. We could just worry about ourselves. We didn't have to spend a lot of energy worrying about Fi, who seemed to be falling apart quickly.

The horses nodded and danced as we came to them. It's just the way horses are. It's one of the things I've always liked about them. Their soft noses prodded and poked at our pockets. Soft, with surprising strength and hardness behind them. I was reminded again of their power.

But not powerful enough to stop a bullet.

We each chose one. Mine was a chestnut, a gelding, a bit overweight, like they all were. I let him sniff my hands for a while, giving him a chance to get used to me. I rubbed his nose and neck, then ran my hand down his flank. I could feel the tension, his quivering muscles. These were stock horses, used to work, to tricky jobs and hectic riding. The chestnut had picked up my mood and was getting charged up already.

I thought I'd better get on, and try to settle him. Homer held him at the neck while Fi helped me to mount. It was difficult without stirrups. But it was fair enough for me to go first for once because I was the shortest of the four of us and probably the weakest rider. I slithered up over his neck and got myself balanced. The horse trembled, and tried to shake his head. I don't think he'd been ridden for a long time.

"They always get excited when you get on bareback," Fi said.

Sure enough as soon as Homer and Fi let him go he moved away quickly. He kept moving sideways until I could persuade him to stop by swearing in his ear and kicking him hard. Kevin mounted the same way I did, with the help of Fi and Homer. He wasn't very graceful about it, though. For a minute he was lying across the back of the horse, trying to get himself up and facing the right way. He was on a brown gelding which went for an angry little canter with Homer still holding on to the horse's head. But when Kevin did get up and Homer let go, the horse seemed to settle down.

I was worried about the noise we were making, but what could we do?

Nothing.

Fi got Homer onto a big black mare, who immediately took him for a quick trot around the clearing. The horses were getting really excited now. That was good and bad for us. We needed them to charge at full speed but we didn't want to be thrown. Fi was the last to mount and I thought with no one to help her she'd have trouble, but she just kept talking to the horse. He was tossing his head and prancing but he seemed to be listening. She led him over to a tree stump and stepped onto it, still whispering to him. Then, with a quick easy spring, she vaulted across his back and sat easily and lightly. It was sickening.

So there we were, ready for our first, and perhaps our last, ride together. Something flashed into my mind about the Four Horsemen of the Apocalypse. Who the hell were they? I had no idea, but it seemed that maybe that's what we were: four riders galloping into an apocalypse.

With the horses barely under control we tried to choose a direction to go. The one we chose was the worst in some ways: towards Wirrawee. But again, as so often in this war, we had little choice. Behind us, towards the Shannons' place, was no good because it was downhill, and that was just too dangerous at speed and at night. To our left and right the bush was too thick. We didn't want to go riding straight into town but we were still about two and a half k's away, so we should be able to get off the horses before we found ourselves in Barker Street stopping for a red light.

Of course, we wanted to get to Wirrawee. It was just a question of how and when we got there.

Anyway, that was the least of our worries. Getting through the cordon of patrols, those armed and deadly soldiers: that was all we could think about. There was nothing else worth worrying about compared to that.

The sinking feeling in my stomach told me it was time to go. We turned our horses' heads as best we could and faced the clearer part of the plateau. I gave Fi a nervous grin but she was too busy lining her horse up, and too far away to see my expression anyway. I tried to calculate how long we'd have before we were on top of the soldiers: probably about a minute and a half; two minutes at the outside. It depended on how fast the horses were, how much their months of good grass and little exercise had slowed them down, how reluctant they would be to gallop at night through bush...and on the other hand how churned up they were getting, how springy and stoked they were. It was vital that we built up enough speed to hit the patrols at maximum revs. And then, of course, would come the big test: how the horses would react if they were fired at. I had a vague idea that police horses were put through training drills, where people burst paper bags near their heads to get them used to shocks and loud noises. Our horses gave the impression that they would go berserk if a gun went off anywhere near them.

Homer looked around at us. I heard his whispered question: "Ready?"

I nodded and croaked yes, my mouth and throat suddenly so dry that my tongue seemed to swell and fill my whole mouth. I didn't look at the others but I guessed they must have said yes too, because Homer turned and gave his horse a belt, and we were off.

It was unbelievable: the strangest feeling of my life, terrifying, and in some wild way the most exhilarating as well. My horse twisted sideways just as we started— I don't think he liked what was happening—and by the time I pulled him round and got him straight again the others were five lengths in front. And they were accelerating fast, too. The horses got the idea really quickly. Maybe they'd been longing for a good hit-out. Whatever, I was astonished at the way they started moving. Within a few seconds we were rushing through the night, the sweat already cooling on my face, the big rumps of the other horses in front of me, their tails flying, their three riders crouched low on their backs, heads down, holding on, like me, for dear life. It was absolutely the eeriest thing, and one of the eeriest things about it was the silence. Apart from the quick thudding of the hoofs and the hot breathing of the horses there was not another sound.

For the first couple of hundred metres we were in clear country. Our biggest danger there was rabbit holes. I eased my horse a little to the right as I started to make up the lost ground. Coming up fast was the sight I didn't want to see but knew I would, sooner or later. It was the dark, dark patch of bush, all shadows. I felt we were lemmings, racing to the edge of the cliff. There was no cliff — I hoped — but there were death and destruction waiting for us. We were fools to think we could gallop at full speed into that, in pitch blackness, and hope to survive. This was suicide.

And suddenly it was on us. I took a deep breath as we plunged in. It was like a ride I'd been on once at Wild World, called the Super Chiller. I'd taken a deep breath on that too. We'd been at the top of a vertical drop and the little cage we were in seemed certain to drop straight to the ground, smashing into a million pieces.

In this bush I expected we would crash into a thicket of trees and rocks and bushes and be smashed into a million pieces.

The horses tossed their heads wildly, but they didn't slow down. Horses can be pretty mad sometimes. I remember when we had the Southern Region Cross-Country Titles, and Wirrawee High School hosted them. I wasn't running but I volunteered to be an official, just so I could get out of school. I was stationed at a gate on the Murdochs' property to make sure the runners didn't miss the turn-off. Near the Murdochs' house were their stockyards and they had a young colt in there that they'd just bought. As more and more runners went past, the horse got more and more excited. He started galloping up and down in the yards, faster and faster, getting wilder and wilder. Soon he was galloping full pelt at the fence and stopping just in time. He was so worked up that I got worried about him. I ran up to the house to tell the Murdochs but, when I was still fifty metres away from the gate, the colt ran into the fence at full speed. I guess he just forgot to stop. He was dead by the time I got there. Broken neck. I'll never forget it. He was a beautiful horse. Old Tammie Murdoch was devastated. She never let runners go through her property again, although it wasn't their fault, of course.

Anyway, the horse I was on didn't slow down either. He went at it full speed. The ride stopped being exhilarating and became completely and utterly terrifying. I flattened myself along his neck but at the same time tried to keep my forehead up so I could get a bit of a look at what we were going to hit. I wanted to see it before I was splattered against it. There was plenty of noise now. To my left I could hear nothing but crashing and smashing as the other three thundered through the scrub. It sounded like not one of them had slowed down. I squealed as a low branch whipped over me, missing by a centimetre. At the same time the horse swerved wildly and I nearly came off. As the trunk of a sapling brushed my foot, I was glad then that he had swerved.

I glanced ahead again and this time screamed out loud. I felt so helpless. I was sure I was going to die. There was a mess of gum trees only a few metres away in front, medium growth stuff, no gap that I could see in the darkness. There was nothing to do but put my head down, bury it in the horse's mane and wait for the crash.

There was a crash, too. A low branch, solid and hard, thumped me across the back of my shoulders, then again on the bum. I've never been hit so hard in my life.

I clung on. The horse was blowing and steaming. Branches were thrashing against me. But I actually gave the horse a kick in the ribs to keep him going. I knew we couldn't stop. The pain in my body was terrible, like I'd been bashed on the back by a telegraph pole, but I knew the pain of a bullet would be worse. Then I was whipped by leaves and light branches. We were racing through another, thinner, clump of trees. I felt like my hair was being ripped from my scalp. I wanted to chicken out now and tell the horse to stop, but I realised he was beyond that. He was bolting and he wouldn't stop until he fell over. I was gasping with pain and shock and fear. I couldn't hear the others any more. I had no idea what was happening to them.

Then things changed again. I felt it, not so much from the fact that the leaves stopped flogging me, but because the air felt different. It was cooler. There was more of it. I dared to glance up again. To my left I thought I heard Homer or Kevin call out something. But I didn't need that. In the better light out here, in this clearer area, I could see exactly what they had seen.

There were three soldiers. They were reacting quickly. Too quickly. No doubt they'd heard us coming. They probably wouldn't have guessed exactly what was happening but the crashing of the horses had put them on their guard. Two of them were dropping to their knees and raising their rifles. The other must have preferred to stand, but she too had her rifle almost up to the firing position.

I put another desperate boot into the horse's ribs. He surged forward. He was a good horse. Fast. He would have been fantastic if he'd been given a bit of work. I reckon he might have had some thoroughbred in him. Poor beautiful chestnut gelding. It was bad luck for him, the night he met me.

I never even heard the shots. It wasn't like the other times. I did see one shot, or at least I saw a flash of flame from the soldier who was almost straight ahead of me, just slightly to my right. I don't know how many shots he got off. I do know that I deliberately set the horse at him and rode him down.

I'm trying to be unemotional about this. Sometimes I feel I've had enough of emotions, and when that happens I shut down and try not to feel anything. I don't know if it works or not, I don't know if it's good for me (Andrea would say it isn't), but I know it's all I can do.

So I rode the man down. The horse reared a little as we came at him but didn't really hesitate. He was already going too fast to stop or swerve. And the man was too slow to move. He tried to fire one extra shot. In a way he was doing the right thing — from his point of view. He knew that if he could fire that last shot he could get the horse. He did get him too, but I didn't realise that at the time. And what the man maybe didn't realise was that the horse was going so fast nothing would pull him up. It'd be like trying to stop a 25-tonne Kenworth when the brake cable's cut. For all I know the horse may have been dead before he hit the man.

120

I think he probably was. That little leap he gave just before he thundered into him was probably the moment of his death.

I closed my eyes and screamed as we hit the soldier. I didn't see his face, thank God. Then I had other things to worry about as the horse went crashing to his knees. He hit the ground so hard. Slammed into it with frightening force. As he started to go down, I still didn't realise he was dead. I thought he'd just lost his footing and was falling. But already I was trying to work out which way to go to avoid being crushed. Because as he smashed into the ground he began to roll. It was at that moment that I realised he must be dead. There was something incredibly lifeless about him. He'd suddenly become nothing more than a huge lump of dead weight. But I didn't have time to spend a lot of thought on that. He rolled to the right and I threw myself to the left. At least I didn't have to worry about getting caught in stirrups. That was one advantage to riding bareback.

The fall winded me. I lay there hurting in the stomach and gasping for breath, making little wheezing noises. I could hear gunshots away to my left, so at least one soldier was still functioning. I got some breath back — not much — and got on my hands and knees. My back and bum still hurt, too. I ignored them and knelt up. I looked to the left. The only living person I could see was Fi who was wheeling her horse around. I couldn't work out how she'd got where she was. She was back behind me and was trying to line her horse up to come in my direction although she couldn't see me. Maybe the horse had shied or something when he saw the soldiers.

I don't think anyone else could have got that horse organised. He was acting pretty crazy. But Fi, bareback, got him under control. They came racing towards me. I realised that they would be coming within ten metres of where I was kneeling.

I'd never called out to Fi for help before. Not like that. Not that desperate call for help that says, "I want you to put your life at risk for me." I hadn't ever asked her to do that before. But I was too panic-stricken to do anything else. I could still hear the gunshots every few seconds, but I don't think they were aimed at Fi. I couldn't see Homer or Kevin. But there and then all I could think about was myself. I didn't want to be left on my knees in this anonymous patch of scrub, to die. I didn't want to be left alone to die. I didn't have Robyn's courage.

So I called out, with all the breath I could find: "Fi! Fi! Help me, please!"

Even as I said it I felt guilty. I knew I was exposing Fi to a terrible risk. But I thank God she heard me. My horse had tumbled down a slope and was lying behind a fallen tree trunk, so I don't think she saw him at all.

But she heard me. She turned her horse as much as she could and got him to pull up, which was difficult. I staggered over to where she was easing the horse down and trying to persuade him to stop completely. I was looking for a stump I could use so I could get on the horse. As I did I felt, rather than saw, a movement to my right, almost behind me. I turned and in the dim light could just see a soldier. I thought that the firing had probably stopped in the last minute or so, but I hadn't been too conscious of it, yet as soon as I saw this guy I realised, "Yes, that's funny, there haven't been any shots for the last bit and, anyway, this guy's too close, couldn't have been him."

The soldier wasn't in the best shape. He was a bit like me, staggering to his feet, only the difference between us was that he had a rifle and I didn't. He was struggling to get the rifle up to his shoulder so I did realise, in the dim part of my mind that was working, that he had been hurt and was not functioning well. But, of course, you don't have to function all that well if you've got a rifle. He had his eyes on Fi and after he got her I guessed he'd get me. I knew the deadly peril in which I'd placed Fi. There was nothing I could do. The man was too far away for me to reach him. Fi had her back to him now and there was nothing she could do, either. She was about to be shot dead from behind. No way could this guy miss: even with whatever injuries he had, a sitting target at that range is hard to miss.

I screamed at Fi, although there was no point, but like so many things you do by instinct, there doesn't have to be a point. She just yelled at me: "Hurry! Hurry!" She'd decided there was no use getting excited about whatever was happening behind her. That was brave. It gave me the energy to get moving: even though I was sure we were both going to be killed. It seemed better to die doing something than to give up. So I staggered to the tree stump, at the same time looking at the soldier and holding my hands out towards him in some stupid way, as though that would stop the bullets.

And then I saw Homer.

Bloody Homer, fancy owing my life to Homer. But I do. He's not the best rider in the world but he's not bad, and somehow he'd got his horse under control. He was coming at this bloke from behind, at a million miles an hour. The soldier heard him at the last minute and started to turn. He'd already been hit once and now as soon as he heard Homer he must have realised he had no hope, because he didn't even try to do anything with his rifle, just chucked it away. And only a second later he went down under the hoofs of the horse. It's frightening to see something like that, terrible. A horse travelling at fifty k's an hour, and the weight of it, and those hoofs as hard as rocks, I think this man got a hoof in the face and I'd say he was dead before he hit the ground, but I don't know that. We didn't waste time trying to find out.

Homer's horse stumbled, and I paused, willing it to get up, terrified that it'd keep falling. Somehow it got its balance. It skewed around a bit and took a few staggering small steps, but then it was OK and Homer turned it in the direction we wanted, towards Wirrawee. I didn't stand there watching any more. I ran to the stump and, with a lot of awkward messing about, got on the horse behind Fi. It was difficult, because we still had our packs, so I had to hang on to Fi's pack, and I had to sit further back than I normally would.

Fi didn't wait too long for me to get organised. She turned the horse around and suddenly, with a lurch, we were off. It was the opposite to before because now we didn't want the horses to go flat out, but they were too excited and they still wanted to go at a mad speed. Like I said, they can be pretty crazy, horses. Not as sensible as sheep.

We followed Homer who we hoped was following

Kevin, and the horses calmed down after a while, mainly because they were stuffed, I think, from the violent exercise. Before they calmed down we had a few more hair-raising moments, ducking under branches and swerving to miss tree trunks. But at last we came to a fenceline and when we looked as far as we could to the left we could just see a gate, and at the gate waiting for us was Kevin.

Twelve

The horses were blowing hard and very distressed. They'd taken a terrible beating. Kevin's was limping, while Homer's had two legs stripped and blood running down them and a bad laceration down one side. It really needed stitches, but there was as much chance of us getting veterinary help for the poor things as there was of having breakfast at McDonald's.

We decided to leave them. We were now very close to Wirrawee and we couldn't risk the noise they would make. I didn't like to leave them in such a state, but maybe they would be looked after by their new owners when they found them in the morning. It sure had been a bad night for them when we arrived on the scene. Not only had they taken such awful punishment, but they had lost one of their friends.

I felt sorry for them, losing a friend.

So we left them there, the three of them, standing in

their little huddle again, but now looking shocked and dejected and sore. Their heads were down. I wouldn't blame them if they never trusted any humans after this. I gave Fi's horse a quick thank-you pat on the nose but I don't think it meant a lot to him.

We walked as fast as we could towards Wirrawee. We were pretty shocked and sore ourselves, but there was no time for that. We'd barely gone half a k when we heard unwelcome sounds behind us. First a gunshot, then a whistle, or maybe two whistles, blown hard and frantically and long. We listened for more sounds as we hurried on. There were none. But we knew the chase would be on now, with a vengeance.

Exhausted though we were, we walked even faster, breaking into a jog as often as we could. I was trying to work out where we would come into Wirrawee. I thought it'd be somewhere around Coachman's Lane. I didn't ask the others. I didn't dare talk. Partly because it was too dangerous but also because everyone seemed in such a fragile mood. I knew, just looking at their faces, what they were feeling. They all looked the same: staring eyes, but not focused on anything, trembling lips, terrible frowns. We weren't a pretty sight.

Our pace got faster and faster. We'd stopped walking now and were half-jogging, half-running. Another whistle came from behind, but much closer, and that really got us going. Our best hope was to get to Wirrawee as fast as possible because if we had a long chase through the bush, we would lose. We had no energy left, no speed, no stamina. In the streets of Wirrawee there was at least a chance of using our brains to get some advantage.

When we got our first glimpse of Wirrawee we acted pretty much automatically. I was nearly right about the street: it was the subdivision off Coachman's Lane: lots of little curving streets with names like Sunrise Crescent. I don't know the name of the street we ended up in. We were coming out of light scrub and approaching some houses that were recently built on big blocks of a hectare or more. There wasn't much cover. These places were so new that the trees put in by the owners were still only my height. There seemed to be lots of grass and not much else. At weekends in peacetime you'd see the owners on their little ride-ons, going round and round their blocks.

But all that grass was no use to us now, of course.

We spread out, got over the first fence one at a time, and started moving cautiously across the block. It was a cream-coloured brick-veneer house, big enough, with a gravel drive and a kids' swing in the back. The place was in darkness and luckily, being on the edge of town, there were no streetlights. But from behind came the blast of another whistle and at the same moment we saw headlights coming towards us down the street. Could have been two vehicles, could have been three.

"We've got to get out of here," Homer said.

I remembered again Lee telling me how that was the most used line in movies. I felt a sudden pang of longing to see Lee, to touch him and hold his hand. One day I'd sort out my feelings about him, but not while running out of the bush, before dawn with soldiers coming at us from two directions and our routes of escape rapidly getting cut off.

We swerved off in a new direction, to the east. At first

I thought Homer had chosen it at random but then I realised he was taking us away from the roads so that anyone chasing us would have to do it on foot. That gave us some help but not much, because we were so tired we had little energy left for being chased. It was a hot night and the sweat was running off us. To make things worse we were now going uphill, which was a real grunt.

Miraculously we all had our packs, but they slowed us down like they always did. Still, I guess the soldiers, poor things, had their rifles to carry.

We worked our way across onto a spur and struggled up to a knoll. Suddenly I realised where we were. For Wirrawee to have a lookout is a bit of a joke, because there's not an awful lot to look at. But the Rotary Club built one, years ago. And we were coming towards the back of the lookout now. I'd only been up there once and I couldn't remember a lot about it. But there was a gravel road leading to it, and a cairn made of dark-coloured rocks cemented together with a plaque on top. As a tourist attraction it was small time.

It took us another five minutes to get there, even though it wasn't far. We were going so slowly we might as well have been running on the spot. And the lookout was pretty much as I'd thought. There was the cairn, a couple of picnic tables and a gas barbeque: nothing else that I could see in the moonlight.

We were stuffed. If we'd had rifles I think we would have stopped right there and made a stand, using the guns to blaze away at them as they came up the hill. It would have been a good spot for that because we would have had cover and they'd have had none. We could have pinned them down there, then faded away into the bush.

But that wasn't going to happen. We weren't armed. We had to do something, though. It was obvious we couldn't go much further. We were at the limits of our endurance. I looked at the others and they looked at me. They were a mess: haggard, frightened, exhausted. I knew what they wanted. Another idea like the horses. For a moment I was annoyed. Why were they waiting for me to think of something? Didn't they have brains of their own?

Then, to my surprise, I did come up with an idea. It was a combination of things that led to it: the word "blaze," which was still in my mind from thinking how we could have blazed away at the enemy with guns, the memory of the officer playing with his cigarette when I'd been hiding in the tree, the memories of all the warnings I'd had as a kid about matches and fires.

Normally lighting a fire at night, in dewy grass, would be hard, but this had been a hot dry night, and the wind was getting up to quite a blast. It was a hot dry wind too blowing down the spur. If anyone was still operating the bushfire warning on the road into town they would have it on "severe." Not quite "extreme" but high e-nough considering it was early in the season.

We all carried matches, of course. It was just one of those things you always put in your packs, even if we didn't light so many cooking fires these days. When the others saw me pulling the little box out from a side pocket they got the idea fast. I crouched down, shield-ed the match with my hand, and lit it. Up here on the hill, where the water would run as fast as it fell, the

grass was crackling with dryness. It took me four matches to get it to light but when it did catch, my God, did
it go. It went up so fast I took a step back to save my
eyebrows. I looked across at the others. Kevin already
had a nice fire going, Homer was fanning a little flame
about the size of his matchbox, and Fi was still frantically looking in her pack for the matches.

But the fire I'd lit was starting to rage. I felt guilty
watching it, thinking what my father would say if he
saw me. I mean he'd understand, of course, but it definitely felt weird to be doing this. The flames flickered
and ran, like mice scattering in the machinery shed
when you walk in.

I stepped forward, through the line of flames, and
peered over the brow of the hill. There was some grey
light in the sky and I could just see some soldiers. But
I was horrified at how close they were. They were on
the spur and coming fast. Little dark dots like fleas on
a dog's tummy. I guess they knew we weren't armed.
They weren't even bothering to look up. They were
determined. I knew we'd be dead if they caught us.
After what we'd done to the soldiers in the bush I
thought there was a good chance these people would
shoot us on the spot. As I was watching, my heart fluttering with fear, one of them did see me. Either me or
the fire, or both. He looked up and gave a shout to his
friends. I couldn't hear it, but I could see him point.
Certainly he pointed straight at me. They all stopped
suddenly. Behind me Homer yelled, "Ellie, get back." I
turned around and saw why. The flames were waist-high
in most places, and they were really starting to burn.
The wind was picking up at every minute. I had a bit of

trouble finding a place to get back through the fire. When I did I ran along the spur to see what the soldiers were doing. I heard someone behind me and looked around. It was Fi. She didn't say anything, just grinned at me from her grimy sweaty face. We paused beside a big old gum tree. "There they are," I said, pointing.

They'd come on another fifty metres or so but they'd stopped again. I could see why. There was a wall of flame now, and it was moving down the hill. I don't think they had much idea of what a bushfire could do, but I knew. If I knew nothing else, I knew that. A bushfire with the wind behind it, in dry grass or scrub, it moves like a semitrailer on heat. It moves like a Santa Gertrudis bull with a BB pellet up its backside. It moves like a mob of cattle in a drought when they see you drive in with a load of hay on the back of the one-tonner. It's the most frightening thing on God's earth. Exciting, in a weird sort of way, but definitely frightening.

And suddenly it took off. There was a big blow of wind, the flames answered with a roar and doubled their height in a moment. The soldiers on the spur went back a couple of steps. I thought, "You'll need to move faster than that if you want to get out of this." For the first time I realised that they might actually get trapped. They might die in the next five or ten minutes. And to be burnt to death, what a terrible, terrible thing. I had nightmares about being burnt to death. I'd always thought that would be the worst death of all.

I hadn't wanted them to get burnt. I just wanted to put a barrier between us and them.

So I did something really dumb. How unusual. I came out from the shadows of the tree and waved to them.

131

Not like, "Hi guys, how are you going down there?" but like, "Get out, get out, go back fast." It gave Fi a shock. I heard her say, "Ellie, what are you doing?" but then I guess she realised, because she didn't say anything else. After a couple of minutes she even came out and waved at them herself, although I don't think she was too keen.

The soldiers looked confused. They were gathering on the knoll. When they saw me waving so furiously one of them actually lifted his rifle, but then I think someone said something, because he lowered it again suddenly and they all turned around and went running back down the spur. Even then I didn't know if they'd be in time. A fire can outsprint a person, no worries. And this fire was on the move. Angry hot clouds of smoke were billowing up in the air, black and grey and white. Twigs, leaves, bits of bark were going up with it. Straight down the slope below us a tree suddenly whooshed into flame. At the bottom of the hill, fifty metres below the fire, the crown of another tree exploded in flames too. When I saw that, I realised this fire was really going to go. Once they start kangaroo-hopping you know you've got a big one. I began to worry about Wirrawee. If we burned the whole town down we wouldn't be too popular. With Fi following I hurried back to the actual lookout point. Through the smoke you couldn't see much of Wirrawee, but there didn't seem to be any reaction yet. The town slept on. In a few minutes I figured there'd be some action, with a huge bushfire about to roar down on top of them. As long as they'd kept the rural firefighting trucks in good order they should be all right. There wasn't much fuel on the edge of a town for a bushfire — there was a natural fire-break this side of the road — and there should be plenty of water in the reservoir still, with winter not long over.

Homer and Kevin came to where we were standing. Their faces were split by huge grins. I've always suspected boys are secret pyromaniacs. They love lighting fires.

Mind you, Fi and I had enjoyed burning down the Wirrawee bridge last summer.

"What do you reckon?" Kevin said. "Stir them up a bit?"

"Where do you think we should go?" I asked.

Homer chipped in. "Into town," he said, to my surprise.

"Into town?"

"Yes. And I'll tell you why. Because it's the last thing they'll expect. And also because we still haven't found Lee and the Kiwis, and if you guys have any memory left you might recall it's why we came out of Hell in the first place."

I couldn't answer that logic.

"Which way?" Fi asked, meaning "Which way should we go into Wirrawee?"

"Straight down the road," Homer said. "Then cut across the footy oval, and lose ourselves around Honey Street."

We could hear the wailing of sirens in the distance now. Somehow I hadn't expected that. Having sirens on fire engines seemed to be part of the old way of life. It didn't belong in this new world. But the sirens made us realise that we'd better get out before it was our asses that were on fire. Once the whole place got mobilised they'd have the manpower to come looking for us again.

We hurried off down the dirt road, keeping low and leaving a big gap between each person. We did that kind of stuff without even needing to discuss it these days. They were just obvious basic things we did to stay alive.

At the footy oval the others turned right, across the little white fence, and one by one set off around the front of the grandstand. I couldn't help stopping to look back at the fire. It was amazing. The whole hillside was blazing from top to bottom. The roar of the flames was unbelievable. It sounded like a cyclone. There was a red reflection on all the houses on the other side of the street, as though the sun was setting. The red light, and the noise, were bringing people out of their houses. As soon as I realised that I hurried to catch the others, to warn them. I'd thought that everyone would be so distracted by the fire that we'd be able to go anywhere we wanted. In fact the streets would be very dangerous, because everyone would be outside.

We had another of our quick conferences. These seemed to get quicker all the time, maybe because we were so used to each other now, so in tune with each other's feelings, that we usually knew immediately what everyone thought. So we decided straightaway to go to the other side of the oval where we could stay well away from the houses.

We worked our way around there. It was tricky and took a while. We had to use sheds and trees for cover, and had to go right back to the fence a couple of times. When we finally got to the other side we had a choice. There was a toilet block, there was a padlocked store shed, and there was the scrub behind the buildings, beyond the fence.

We chose the toilet block. There was something comforting about being in a building again, even if it was a toilet block. Naturally the boys insisted we go in the boys' toilet. I have no idea why it was important to them but it was. Maybe they thought it'd be too girly for them in our dunny. If they only knew. There wasn't much that was girly about the stuff written on the walls in our toilets.

But as soon as we went in this one I started getting really uneasy. After only half an hour I was totally claustrophobic. We were in a trap if we stayed there. If soldiers came we had no way out. I didn't like it.

I said to the others, "Let's go."

They didn't put up any argument. I think they felt the same way. We slipped out carefully, in case anyone was watching, but it seemed clear. I guess everyone was either fighting the fire, or fighting to save their own houses.

Whoops. When I say their houses, I mean the houses they stole from us.

One thing we realised fast. The fire certainly wasn't under control. The air was black with smoke and bits of ash were floating past us. Fi was coughing as soon as we got out in the open. In the distance we could see glimmers of flame. I sneaked down to the road and saw one man hosing his house—the house he stole—but the pressure in his hose was very low, of course. Some children were standing in the street watching the fire. I couldn't see anyone else. I was nervous about what we'd

135

done but I still thought they should be able to save the town. I went back to the others and told them what I'd seen. We really didn't know what to do. If we moved we risked being caught. If we didn't move we risked being caught. We might even find the fire on top of us if the wind changed slightly.

In the end we decided to move.

"If we don't," I said, "it's too easy for them to find us here. And once they put the fire out they'll be looking for us."

"Yeah," said Kevin, "they'll sure as hell be looking for us."

So we set off again. In some ways I think this was our most dangerous journey yet. To be moving through the town while everyone was out of their houses and while everyone was hating us was incredibly risky. But I was sure we had no choice.

The smoke helped us a bit, but not much else did. We were heading for the one place we all knew well, a place we were pretty sure would be unoccupied. Wirrawee High School.

We got there by the silliest routes. It was amazing how much Wirrawee had returned to "normal" living. There were so many people now. I don't know how many houses were occupied, but it was an awful lot. I just hoped they hadn't got as far as re-opening the schools, but we didn't see many kids.

We did have to take a lot of care. Every hundred metres was different. The trip included sneaking along behind a fence in one big house, belly crawling through a garden in another, and waiting half an hour in Mr.

Potts' garage while two blokes stood outside discussing the fire—at least I think that's what they were discussing. It was almost funny at times, but so scary too. The only easy part was going along the creek bed for half a k.

We didn't reach Sherlock Road until about one in the afternoon.

Getting into the schoolgrounds wasn't too bad. There's only a couple of houses in sight of the school. No one seemed to be there but of course we couldn't take that for granted. So we took ages working our way into the place. The fire seemed to be better controlled, as far as we could tell. But that was bad news in one way—it meant they'd have time now to find us. At least the school wasn't occupied. In fact it looked like it had been deserted years ago.

We were hanging out for a rest but we still had one problem: to find a way into the building. It sounds simple, but we had to do it in a way that wasn't obvious. I mean, it was no good smashing down a door, because someone would notice that. But we got into the little quadrangle in the middle of the school and we felt better in there, at least. It was completely concealed from the road. The ferns were all dead, which was sad, and there was a lot of rubbish blowing around, but otherwise it felt a bit safer.

In the end we did have to break a window. We were ready to run, in case there were burglar alarms. But it was OK. In peacetime there had been alarms, but they didn't seem to work any more.

After we got inside we cleaned up the glass, then

found some masonite and tape and boarded up the window. We were hoping that anyone who came along would think it was an old breakage.

Fi volunteered to do sentry, which was incredibly nice of her, and at last the rest of us could get some sleep.

Thirteen

We had found maybe the one building left in Wirrawee that was pretty much untouched. A few things in the office had been ripped out but nothing else was damaged. The feeling grew on me that the place had been deserted for a long time. It wasn't exactly the dust, it wasn't the silence. It was a lack of people: you just knew as you walked down those deserted corridors that no human had been there for a long time.

I suppose it was also the smell, although I didn't realise that at the time. Everyone does have their own smell. They say blind people can recognise who's been in a room by the smell they leave behind. I know I could recognise when my father had been in the bathroom by the smell he left behind. Talk about toxic. If we'd bottled that and released it as nerve gas we'd have won this war in the first week.

Of course, with my infallible judgement I'd found the only room in the school that wasn't silent. It didn't help when I was so desperate to get some sleep. It was the sick bay, where they had two beds. I had one and Kevin the other. But there must have been a slight gap between the window and its frame, and the wind whistled and howled through the hole with a note that changed all the time. It was the eeriest noise. It sounded like wild lost creatures crying in the night, their haunting voices begging for someone to save them. Except it was like they were already dead, and they were crying from the grave. Then it would stop for a minute and I'd think, "Oh good, at last I can get some sleep," and sure enough at that moment it'd start up again. Things weren't helped, either, by the fact that the black smoke from the fire was drifting past and, although there seemed to be less of it now, it did make the whole place feel and sound like a scene out of Hell.

So I didn't get much sleep. But I guess the real reason for that was my fear. It felt so dangerous to be here in Wirrawee in broad daylight, trying to sleep. Sure I could give myself a hundred rational reasons why we'd be OK. No one had been here for ages, they'd all be busy fighting the fire, they'd think we would have gone bush...

OK, three rational reasons why we'd be OK. They were good reasons, too. But they weren't enough. I was still all tensed up, staring through the window at the hot black smoke.

I began to realise that there was one more reason I couldn't sleep. The ride with the horses through the bush, running down those soldiers, coming so close to death myself: it had only happened twelve hours before. It was like everything else in this war: there was no time to react, no chance to think about stuff, to find meaning to it, or put it in a picture that made sense.

If you don't know what something means you're in trouble.

Of course I knew what last night meant in one way: I knew I'd done those things because I wanted to stay alive. No prizes for getting that right. But I wanted an answer that told me something more. If I was going to say that my life mattered above someone else's, that it was OK for someone else to die so I could survive, I had to know that was OK. Sure it's human nature to preserve your own life at all costs. Not just human nature either. Nature full stop. I've seen what a trapped kangaroo does to dogs that get too close. But if God gave me a mind and a conscience, and an imagination that can put me inside the head of someone else, then he must want me to use those things. Not just do stuff with no thought about what it meant. I'm not a kangaroo.

So I thought — and I still think — about whether it was OK.

Another thing God gave me was a sense of responsibility. I wish he hadn't, sometimes. Thanks for nothing, God. Because having got it means I'm stuck with it, and when I do something powerful, that I think might be wrong, I can't just shrug it off. I knew that I'd killed another person, maybe more than one; it's something I did, it was mine and I owned it.

So I had to cop it. Those soldiers had died last night. And the horse. I'd again made the decision that my life was worth more than theirs. And I didn't even know these people. They were strangers to me.

Was there some plan to all this? Did I deserve to live, and did those strangers deserve to die? Was this a test I had to pass? Was I going to go on and find a cure for cancer or something? Suppose one of the soldiers was going to leave the army in ten years and find a cure for cancer, but now it would never happen because I'd killed him?

That's what I was trying to say about finding a meaning to the madness happening around me.

And instead of a meaning, all I got was the weird scream of the wind, and the choking smoke and the heat of a fire I'd started myself.

By late afternoon the fire at last seemed under control. There were ashes as far as the eye could see and the playground was sprinkled with black, like castor sugar on a sponge cake, only the wrong colour.

The smell of burning, that unmistakable charred smell, filtered into every corner, every nook and cranny. It clung to our clothes and gradually blocked out everything else: the musty smell of the school, the sweaty smell of Homer and Kevin and even Fi and me, and the sickly smell of the dead possum that had fallen through the ceiling tiles in Room A23.

As dark slowly surrounded the school we started to feel a little safer. We thought it was unlikely they'd come looking for us at night. They'd have too many problems of their own, with the damage from the fire. And you can't do much of a search in darkness anyway. They might even be scared of us, too. After all, we'd shown ourselves to be pretty desperate. I got scared of myself often enough these days, so I wouldn't blame them for being scared of me. No, I didn't think they'd come looking for us after dark.

I did my turn at sentry then went to talk to Fi. She was hard to find. It felt strange to be walking the long empty school corridors. Of course, I'd never seen it like this before, but then I guess not many people had. We were in A wing. My footsteps echoed through the building. I went past the office, the Graphics room, the dunnies, the computer room, then on past the regular classrooms. The whole world could have gone missing and I wouldn't have known. That's how empty it was. It was maybe the most alone I've ever been, because this was a building made for hundreds of students and teachers, and so it felt even more alone than the Hermit's hut.

Right down the very end I found Fi. Or rather, she found me. She was in A22. She called out as I came to the end of the corridor, otherwise I would never have known she was there. I think she was actually really depressed, the way I was close to being myself, but this time we didn't depress each other like you'd expect.

"This was my favourite room," she said.

"Why?"

It didn't look too interesting. Because the invasion had come during the school holidays the rooms were even more boring than usual. No essays or pictures on the walls, no writing on the whiteboards, no books lying around. There was an emergency evacuation plan on the bulletin board, next to the light switch, and opposite that a poster of an Emily Dickinson poem. But the poster was ripped in one corner, and someone had scribbled across the bottom with a texta. From the overhead fan a pathetic bit of pink Christmas streamer still dangled. When they celebrated Christmas in here less than a year ago, little did they know how everything was about to change.

142

"It was my English room," Fi explained.

"Who'd you have for English?"

"Mr. Rudd."

"Oh yeah, I never had him."

"He was so good! I hope he's OK now."

"I wish I'd had him for something. Everyone was always raving about his lessons. He was American, wasn't he?"

"No, Irish."

Fi, who had been lying on the floor, suddenly came to life. She jumped up and launched into an impersonation of Mr. Rudd.

"Fiona, I'm sorry we had to start without you. It occurs to me that you're always late for my classes, and I'm wondering if we can make English a little more attractive for you. Would you like to sit yourself over here? This is our corporate box. Can I take your coat? Can I get you a drink? Would you like a more comfortable chair? Here, have mine. No no, really, please don't distress yourself, it's no trouble at all."

Fi was always hopeless at doing impersonations but I laughed anyway.

"He sounds sarcastic," I complained.

"Mm, not really. I mean, I suppose he could be, but it was never nasty like it is with some teachers."

"I did have Social Studies in this room in Year 8," I said. "With Mrs. Barlow. It wasn't bad. We had that Japanese Day, where we all cooked Japanese food and did origami and stuff. That was good."

"Oh yes, I remember. And on Bastille Day we cooked French food. Mrs. Barlow was good like that. Baa-baa we called her. It was such a stupid nickname."

"Remember when we had that class barbeque in Year 9, I think it was? And the boys served the sausages all raw? I nearly turned vegetarian on the spot. And there was that food fight."

"I remember that. My mother complained to the school. I had grease and tomato sauce all over my uniform. Mr. Muir got in trouble because he couldn't control us properly."

"He was hopeless, wasn't he? Were you in that class where he started crying?"

"No, but I heard about it."

"It was terrible. I didn't know whether to laugh or feel sorry for him. It was Homer's fault too, you know. He gave him such a hard time. He never let up. All those jokes about his weight. He called him 'two-tonne' to his face a couple of times, then pretended he was talking to Davo. The day he started crying, Homer had asked him, 'Mr. Muir, do you eat to live or do you live to eat?'"

Fi looked upset. She was so gentle and nice that she couldn't bear to hear about even a teacher being given a hard time. I wished I had some of her sweetness. Half would have been enough.

It was dark in the room now but we kept talking, remembering the good and bad times that we'd had in this building, in this school.

"Do you realise we've spent more than two-thirds of our lives at school?" I said to Fi.

"Have we? Gosh. Well I would have spent two-thirds of that time wishing I was somewhere else. And now I'd give anything to be back here, playing Theatre Sports in English."

"Did you play Theatre Sports? No wonder you liked it. We never did anything that much fun. Just boring old spelling tests and language. The only good stuff was when we had to give talks. And Bryony told us about her sister thinking sheep droppings were sultanas and how she'd tried to eat them. And one day we had to bring in our favourite pictures and talk about why we liked them. And it was amazing because Homer brought in this painting of waterlilies and he talked about how when he felt stressed he'd go and sit in front of this painting and stare at it for half an hour and it calmed him down. Everyone was in total shock. It was the only time I saw Homer take a break from the tough-guy role at school. No one else brought in a painting at all; they just had photos of their footy teams and stuff."

"That's what I thought you meant when you said 'favourite pictures,'" Fi said.

"Mmm, I just brought in a boring old photo of me showing Mirrimbah Buckley Park."

"What's Mirrimbah Buckley Park?" Fi asked.

"In the old days we had a merino stud," I explained. "My grandparents started it and Dad took it over. But in the end Dad thought it was too much. It was so much work and the competition was unbelievable. People were doing the most amazing things to get publicity. Putting on big sales and flying clients in for them. Dad couldn't be bothered with that scene. We couldn't afford it, anyway. Plus Dad wanted to diversify more. He sold the stud to the Lucases. But while we still had it I used to show the sheep sometimes, and Mirrimbah Buckley Park was our best ram ever. He got first at the Stratton Merino Show, Open Rams, and third at the

National Merino titles. We got a fortune for him. Grandma was so mad at Dad for selling him but Dad had already decided to sell the stud, only he hadn't told Grandma. When he did tell her it was like global warming. Grandma wouldn't talk to Dad for months. I could see her point. They worked so hard to develop the stud and then Dad takes over and breaks it up.

"The funny thing is that we've still had to get into the publicity circus with the Charolais, so you never win."

I realised Fi wasn't listening. She was staring out the window.

"What's wrong?" I asked.

"I saw something move out there," she said.

Fourteen

We hit the floor at the same time. I lay with my face in the dust of the carpet. My heart was thumping so strongly it almost lifted me off the ground. I didn't spend long thinking about that, though. Fi was already wriggling across the room towards the door, and I followed. We got out into the corridor, then, bent double so we'd be below the windows, we ran swiftly and silently back towards the sick bay. I knew Homer was on sentry and I thought Kevin would be on one of the beds, having a snooze.

I had time to feel annoyed at Homer. I thought he should have seen whoever was out there. The arrangement we'd made for the sentry was that he or she would stay in the reception area where you could get a good view of three sides of the school grounds. But you had to keep peeping out around the partition to see the fourth side. I couldn't help wondering if Homer had been a bit slack on the job.

It turned out I'd underestimated him. As we ran up the corridor we met the two boys coming to find us, bent as low as we were.

"What did you see?" Homer whispered urgently, as we met.

"Just one person, I think," Fi said. "I'm not even sure it was a person."

"I only saw one," Homer said. "But it was a person all right. Sneaking around the canteen."

We were crouched on the floor of the corridor. You could feel the fear in all of us. Because we were in a group, a circle, the fear seemed to concentrate in the middle of the group. It was like a solid thing that you could reach out and touch.

"We'd better go down the other end," Kevin said. "See if anyone's there."

"But even if there is," Homer said, "we can't get out without making a noise. We boarded that window up, remember, and they've all got security locks on them."

Suddenly I realised what a trap we'd made for ourselves. I prickled all over.

"Let's go up there anyway," I whispered. "If we think no one's around that end we might just have to knock a window out and make a run for it."

I felt it was better for us to be doing something than crouching there in terror.

Still bent over, we hurried to the other end of the

147

building. It was completely dark outside now. That was our only advantage. But if they had the place surrounded, it wasn't much of an advantage.

To get to the end we had to go into the staff room. It felt funny doing that. It still seemed like forbidden territory. There were two swinging doors that we pushed open carefully, then we scuttled around the table tennis tables to the windows. There seemed to be no moon now, and it was so black outside that we couldn't see much at all.

"What do you think?" Homer muttered to me.

"I don't know. We've got to have a go though, not just stay here and wait for them."

"But they mightn't even know we're here. We might draw attention to ourselves if we try to break out."

"Yeah, I guess. But it seems weird that they'd come here." I was tired, and struggling to find the words to say what I meant. To my right Kevin was making scraping noises with something that sounded dangerously loud, but I didn't want to stop him because I assumed he was working on getting a window open. We had to take some risks. I tried to concentrate on what I wanted to say to Homer. "Unless they've got a million soldiers, they wouldn't be searching every building in town. Plus they'd have to search the bush. They wouldn't come here especially, unless they knew we were here."

Homer didn't say anything.

"It might just be a kid playing around," I said hopefully.

Homer shook his head. "I only saw his shadow, but he was too tall for a kid."

There was a crunching noise from Kevin's window. I couldn't help myself. "Shut up," I hissed savagely.

Kevin wriggled over to where we were whispering. He ignored my comment. "I've opened it," he said. "I'll go out if you want."

Every so often Kevin amazed me with these acts of courage. I had to keep reminding myself not to sell him short. Just when I thought he was a bit of a wanker he'd do something like this.

Perhaps I should have volunteered to go out there instead of Kevin. But I didn't. The truth is, I got sick of having to do so much. Cobbler's Bay, that nearly killed me. I think it affected me in ways I hadn't even realised yet. Like, it changed me deep inside. And that's why I was struggling with so much stuff now. I know the prison was the worst thing, and affected me the most, and the deaths of Robyn and Chris, and what happened to Corrie, and the invasion itself... oh, I'll go on forever if I start. But staying in that container, then thinking I was going to be killed after the explosion, then seeing the soldiers at Baloney Creek with my friends, and what I had to do to them: somehow that seemed to get me in a terrible horrible way that had a bad bad impact on me.

So when Kevin volunteered, no, I didn't say a word.

We went over to the window he'd opened. It didn't seem quite so dark outside after all.

"I can't see anyone," Fi whispered.

The window still wasn't open enough. It would have been a tight fit for Fi, and Kevin had no hope. I touched the frame. The timber was pretty rotten. I could see and feel where he had splintered the wood in levering it open. Gingerly I pushed it up another thirty or forty

149

centimetres. I was doing it from underneath, and it creaked and squeaked as it went.

"Careful, can't you," Kevin muttered, echoing the way I'd told him to shut up a couple of minutes earlier. Still, once I'd got it up enough, he didn't hesitate. Right away he started crawling over the sill, then at the finish he took a quick dive and disappeared under the window. For one horrible moment I thought he might have been shot, he went so quickly, but there'd been no sound of a gun, so I guessed he was OK. Sure enough, a few seconds later I saw him running swiftly into the darkness, crouched over and zigzagging.

It was a brave thing he did there, a really brave thing.

Then followed six or eight minutes of silence. We were straining every nerve, watching, listening, sniffing the air, trying for any clue that would help us work out what was happening.

Finally Homer whispered: "I've had enough of this. I'm going after him."

Fi and I spoke at the same time. "No, Homer, please don't."

"Wait a while," I added. "If something's happened to him, it'll happen to you, too."

They knew what I meant.

So we waited. Another five minutes I'd say. Then I heard the sound I least expected to hear; a sound so unlikely that I thought I had finally flipped my lid. Or if I hadn't, Kevin definitely had. Because either I was imagining things, or else Kevin, somewhere out there in the darkness, had just laughed.

I gazed at Homer in astonishment. Kevin had one of those laughs that once heard you never forget. If you crossed a donkey with a machine-gun you'd get close to it. It's not the kind of laugh you can easily imitate. It was definitely laughter that I'd heard, and it was definitely Kevin's.

I risked standing a little higher, so I could get a wider view of the school grounds. It was so frustrating not being able to see. But only a moment later I saw two people coming towards the building from the black gloom of the trees. One of them was Kevin.

And the other was Lee.

Forgetting everything we'd ever told ourselves about security I wriggled through the window and ran towards him. I wanted to have one of those great reunion hugs, like you see in the movies and like I'd once had with Kevin, but as I ran up to him I realised he was in poor shape. He smiled at me, but it was more a contortion of his face muscles than a smile. His chin was trembling and his head hung low. He was walking very slowly. Kevin on the other hand was grinning like a kid who's won pass-the-parcel at three birthday parties in a row. I guess having risked his life by going out into the night he couldn't believe how lucky he'd been, how well it had ended up.

"Are you OK?" I said to Lee, in one of those dumb questions you ask when you can't think of anything better.

"I could use a good meal," he said.

We arrived at the window. Homer was hanging out of it beaming at Lee, but I said to him, "Get some food."

His smile disappeared quickly, and so did he. A moment later I heard the swing doors of the staff room open and shut.

Fi and I helped Lee through the window. He was very weak. When we got him inside he sat on a stool, then changed his mind and lay on the floor. I ran down the corridor to find Homer. He was still pulling stuff out of his pack. We had New Zealand army food these days, freeze-dried stuff mostly, that was in little foil packets. It was incredibly light and actually cooked up into a decent meal. Savoury Rice was my favourite. But you had to soak it then cook it, and I didn't know if we could cook it here. I didn't even know if the power was on. So instead of waiting to find all that out I grabbed some muesli from Homer, got the last of Kevin's orange juice powder from his pack, and took it to the sink in the staff room. The water was still running so it was easy to mix some OJ to pour on the muesli.

I'd heard somewhere, vaguely, that it's not good to eat heaps if you haven't eaten for ages. Actually I've just remembered where I heard that. It was one of those World War Two stories about prisoners on the Burma-Thai railway. Apparently when the war ended and the Americans arrived to save them, some of the prisoners died from overeating.

I mean, how unfair can life get?

Well, I didn't remember that story at the time but I had a feeling it wouldn't be a good idea to give Lee heaps of food. So I shovelled a few spoonfuls into him, then told him he'd have to wait an hour for some more. He wasn't too amused but I stuck to my guns, and Homer and Fi backed me up.

While I was feeding Lee, Kevin shut the window and locked it again. But he didn't use the security lock. It made me feel a little safer to know we at least had an escape route now. Then at last we could ask Lee the questions we'd been sweating to ask.

"What happened, Lee?" Homer asked, crouching beside him. "Where are Iain and Ursula and the others?"

Lee shrugged. "I don't know," he said. He spoke very slowly, like talking was a big effort. "I haven't got the foggiest. After they'd finished their recce they got me to hide in the bush outside town, past the church, you know, Church of Christ. They told me they'd pick me up after the attack and we'd go back to Hell flat out. So I waited and waited and they just never came."

We waited, too, for Lee to go on, but he didn't.

"So what happened?" I asked finally.

Lee shrugged again. "That's just it. Nothing happened."

"Nothing?"

"I waited there all night. I wasn't too worried because they said if there was a problem, they'd either come back and get me, or they'd hole up in town for the day. They told me to go bush and meet them the next night. But the next night was exactly the same. Nothing."

"And that's it?" Homer asked. "Do you mean you don't know a single thing about what happened to them?"

He sounded angry, like it was Lee's fault.

Lee just nodded and closed his eyes. He kept talking with his eyes shut. "There wasn't even a hint," he said. He took about a minute between each word. He sounded old and tired. After all, he'd been on his own in Wirrawee for six days. "Not the faintest clue," he said. "No noise from the airport, no soldiers racing around, no gunfire. I don't know what's going on. All I know is, something's gone wrong. Ellie, can I have some more to eat?"

I gave him half-a-dozen spoonfuls of muesli. "You'd better get some rest," I said. "If you can struggle down to the sick bay, there's a nice bed in there."

"I'm OK here," he said. "I do want to sleep, that's true. I haven't had much of it lately. But I've got some more news for you yet."

"Come down to the sick bay," I said, "and you can tell us then."

Even though he didn't want to, we made him move. He got there under his own steam, then we helped him to lie down and I pulled off his shoes. "Pooh," I said, "what a stink."

I was trying to make him laugh, but it was a waste of breath. He was already asleep.

Fifteen

Trust Kevin. And trust Mrs. Gilchrist. You never know what Principals get up to. Kevin took it into his head to have a little look around her office, and surprise surprise, what does he find in the bottom drawer of the filing cabinet but her own private grog supply. There was half a bottle of brandy, three-quarters of a bottle of dry sherry and a couple of cans of dry ginger.

"Jackpot!" Kevin yelled, coming back into the staff

room grinning, and holding his trophies above his head.

We'd established ourselves in the staff room because it had the most comfortable chairs. Trust teachers for that.

Fi was on sentry duty, but we decided she could have one glass without any serious risk. Lee was sound asleep. We realised that we'd have to keep some for him, and maybe another glass or two for Fi, and we started getting worried about what would be left for us.

Still, it seemed we'd be able to have a little party. Homer got some glasses from the staff kitchen area. It's amazing how good the boys were at catering when there was grog involved.

Kevin poured us all a sherry, then leaned back in his chair and raised his glass in a toast. "Underage drinking in the staff room," he said. "All my dreams come true."

"And it's Mrs. Gilchrist's shout," Homer added. "Makes it even better."

"Here's to happy endings," I said. "May we all live happily ever after."

"That's looking less and less likely," Homer said. But he didn't say it like he was incredibly depressed, he said it with a laugh, like he was coping OK.

It was funny, that's how we were all reacting, I think. The news Lee brought — or the lack of news — should have depressed us, because it was now very obvious that something had gone badly wrong for the Kiwis.

But we'd already known that. Well, we hadn't known it, but we'd guessed it. So Lee confirming it didn't depress us any further; instead we were rapt to find that he was alive and in fairly good shape. We were rapt that we'd found him at all. We cared deeply about the New Zealanders, of course, but the five of us had a bond that went beyond anything.

There were two dark thoughts that lurked in the bottom of my mind, in the murkiest depths. I could never bear to take them out and look at them but occasionally, when I was mega-depressed, they'd sneak out for a moment or two. One was the thought that I might never see my parents again. The other was the thought that another member of our group might get killed.

Either way, that would have been the end of me. It would have been the absolute end. I'd never contemplated suicide, even in the worst times in Stratton Prison, but if either of those things happened it would have been the end of my life, no mistake about that.

So, with Lee returned, we did have something to celebrate, we did have an excuse for a party. And although it wasn't the wildest or happiest party I've ever been to, it was a lot better than my last one, back in Wellington. This time it was with friends, true friends.

We wiped out the sherry pretty quickly, then Homer and Kevin took care of the brandy and dry. Without ice I didn't like the idea of it and, besides, the sherry was already doing funny things to my head. I decided I'd better stop, especially as I was taking over sentry in an hour's time. I figured I'd already be blowing .05 or worse, and I didn't want to do sentry duty if every tree looked like a Martian, and the moon floated in the sky like a helium balloon.

Plus, the last time I'd had too much to drink had ended so badly that I wasn't keen to do it again.

Lee slept on and on. It was like he was heading for a

record. Somehow I got through my sentry duty, but it wasn't helped by Homer and Kevin getting totally wasted and making more noise than a kindergarten at lunchtime. They had a mad game of table tennis in the staff room, which wasn't easy in the dark, then they went chasing through the building trying to tackle and wrestle each other. I kept telling them to shut up, and they weren't too bad I suppose, but compared to the noise we normally made it was way out of control.

Then Kevin crashed on the other bed in sick bay and dropped asleep as fast as Lee had done, and all Homer's efforts to wake him failed. So Homer was left with no playmate. He came and talked to me for a while but he was pretty wiped out so he wasn't making much sense. Then he suddenly fell asleep in the chair and lolled there looking disgusting and making gross snoring noises.

He wasn't very good company after that.

Kevin was meant to be on sentry and I had a weak go at waking him up, but he wouldn't move, and I couldn't be bothered making an issue of it. I left him there, vowing that he could pay me back tomorrow night. He slept for twelve hours but the moment he woke I dragged him out to do a shift. He looked awful and smelt worse, and I'm not sure how much he could see through his bloodshot eyes.

Lee slept for fifteen hours. None of us thought about the comment he'd made before he passed out, about having more news for us. Homer and Kevin were too hungover to think about it, and it just slipped my mind. Maybe I was immune to dramatic pieces of news these days. I figured I'd heard them all.

It was around noon when I heard him stirring in the sick bay bed. I went in.

"Have you got some food?" he asked. "I'm starving."

This time he was able to spoon it to his mouth himself, but again I made sure he only got a small amount. He complained a bit, like before, but he seemed distracted, eating the food quickly.

"When can I have some more?" he asked.

"In an hour or so."

But he seemed almost to ignore my answer.

"Ellie," he said, "can you get the others in here?"

The tone of his voice frightened me; his manner was so quiet and serious.

"Is something wrong?" I asked.

"Just get them, please."

"Kevin's on sentry."

"Where is he exactly?"

"In that big reception area. You know, out the front. You can see three ways from there, and the fourth way with a bit of trouble. The only problem is that the sentry can't risk moving a lot in daylight. You're pretty visible if you do."

I was talking too much, but Lee had made me nervous.

"Well, I'll go into the office. Kevin'll be able to hear me from there. Tell the others to go there, too."

He struggled to his feet and limped off towards the office. I wanted to help him but he seemed determined to get there on his own. I guess the sleep had done him good. I hurried to get the others. I felt that whatever Lee had to say would make a big difference, maybe change everything.

158

I got frustrated that it took a full minute to find Homer and Fi. They were just talking in the corridor between A Block and B Block. But when they saw my face they stopped talking and followed me quickly back to the office.

"What's it all about?" Homer asked me.

"I haven't got a clue."

"Oh, come on, Lee tells you everything. You must know."

"I don't, I swear. And there's no way Lee tells me everything. Where'd you get that idea?"

In the office Lee was sitting on a brown swivel chair, behind Mrs. Myers' desk. Kevin was leaning against the counter where he could both hear Lee and see any movement outside. He still looked pale and sorry for himself. Fi and Homer and I found places to sit: I ended up on a spare desk that was covered with dust. I sat on top of it with my arms around my knees, gazing at Lee. Quite a lot of light came in through the windows, but Lee seemed to be in the deepest shadow. It was hard to see his dark face. I wanted to see his expression. As far as I could tell he looked calm.

When he started talking he did something that surprised me. He reached out and took Fi's hand. I hadn't expected that. I felt a pang of jealousy as I looked at his long brown fingers over Fi's pale skin. I even wondered whether they'd formed a relationship without me knowing. But I realised straightaway how ridiculous that was. And as soon as Lee started talking I forgot that he was holding Fi's hand. Instead I was instantly mesmerised by the grimness of his tone.

"I told you before that I had something else to tell

you. I'm not sure what happened after I said it—I guess I went to sleep, did I? So I'm sorry I didn't get to say this last night. But here it is."

He leaned forward a little and cleared his throat. His voice, already quiet, became much quieter.

"I know pretty much what's happened to everyone's families."

There was a gasp, a cry, a groan. I'm not sure which came from where. I felt some wall break inside me. It was like a physical thing. Kevin turned around quickly, forgetting about sentry duty. He had seen his parents more recently than the rest of us, but that was still a long time ago. It didn't mean his family were OK now. Anything could have happened to them. And the same applied to all of us.

Lee looked at Homer. "Your parents are somewhere between Wirrawee and Stratton," he said. "They're pretty OK. They're on work parties; I'm not sure where exactly. But the last anyone heard, they were cool. They're on separate parties, so I don't think they'd see much of each other. And George is in Stratton. They've put him to work in one of the factories."

"George in a factory," Homer said. "He won't think much of that. And Mum and Dad, they haven't been separated since they were married."

But his broad brown face was alive with relief. He looked around the room as though he were seeing it for the first time.

"They used to send out only one member of a family and keep the others hostage in the Showground," Lee said. "Now they do the same thing by sending them out in different groups, so if someone escapes from one group they can punish their relatives in the other groups. It's a clever system."

He turned to Kevin.

"Kevin, your father's on a farm somewhere to the north. He's going fine apparently. Your mother's still at the Showground. There's not a lot of people there any more, but she and some other women are running a creche. Your brothers are there too." Lee paused. "I think your mother gets kind of depressed, you know what I mean? I don't think she's too well, as far as that goes. She's fine physically, but I guess she's struggling with the mental stuff."

Kevin grimaced and turned away again. It was impossible to know what he thought of that news. I had the feeling he didn't want to know about psychological problems. Like a lot of country guys he thought you should be tough enough to cope with anything. He thought guys should have their tear ducts surgically removed at birth. He hadn't been too keen on seeing a shrink in New Zealand. In fact Homer and Lee had accepted it better than Kevin, which is something I wouldn't have predicted.

"Ellie," Lee said.

I tensed, and felt sick. Why had Lee talked to the two boys first? Was there a problem with my parents?

"Ellie, your father's being held at the Showground, in a pavilion there. It's a special area for people who haven't been too co-operative. A sort of prison I guess, but nothing like what we were in. I think he's been pretty difficult, Ellie, fighting with the guards and stuff like that. There's a small group of them, men and women, all there for the same reason. He's copped a bit of extra punishment, though, because they say he tried to sabotage a tank that he was meant to be fixing. Not a water tank, an army tank. A million dollars or so of hardware."

I nodded, trying to stay calm.

"But he's OK?"

"Look, he's had some bruises, there's no doubt about that. But yes, he's pretty fair apparently, all things considered."

"What about Mum?"

"Well, she's been assigned to a house in Holloway, as a servant."

"As a what?"

Lee looked embarrassed. "Sorry! I knew you wouldn't be too impressed. But that's what they're doing, using women as servants in towns and farms. Having them do washing and ironing and cleaning and cooking. Stuff like that. They're pretty well organised now, as you can see."

I had steam coming out of my ears. "Mum would love that. My God, she'd go mad. She hates doing our washing and ironing, let alone anyone else's. How dare they!"

Lee didn't answer, just turned to Fi.

"Fi, I think you might be able to see your parents."

Fi went white, so white and so suddenly I thought she might pass out. I've never seen the colour drain from someone's face as quickly as that. Her hand tightened on Lee's. I could see her nails digging into the back of his hand. She opened her mouth as if to say something, but just left it open and did not speak.

"They're both working in the District Headquarters," Lee explained. "Sometimes when people have special skills they keep them together. And besides, they've got your sister at the Showground as a hostage. So your parents work there each day from 8 a.m. till 7 p.m., on computers and paperwork and stuff like that. Administration stuff."

It figured. Fi's parents were both solicitors, so they were pretty smart.

"The new Headquarters is the tech," Lee continued. "Since we blew up Turner Street they've had to find a new place to run their operation, and the tech's got everything they need. Six prisoners work there, and security's pretty slack. Partly because they're holding hostages for all of them, partly because, if you don't mind my saying so, Fi, your parents aren't exactly cut out to be guerillas or terrorists."

Fi tried to grin but failed.

"So," Lee went on, "at lunchtime they're allowed out for half an hour. They usually go for a walk in the park. You could see them if you wanted."

"If she wanted!" I said.

I was at the same time happy for Fi and jealous of her. She was going to see her parents. She was going to see her parents and I wasn't. It was wonderful for her, the kind of moment we'd all dreamed about and longed for, and I was torn apart by my happiness for her and my sense of guilt that I should have been happier.

Fi sat there as though she'd been snap-frozen. It was impossible to tell what she was thinking. She was as pale as before, and for a moment I thought of Snow White, needing love to escape her cold and lonely sleep. I moved over to her and gave her a hug, knowing as I did so that sometimes even friends aren't enough.

"Ellie," she whispered, "I don't know what they'll say when they see my face."

I was so shocked I couldn't speak. Fi's scar ran from under her chin to up past her mouth on the right-hand side. It faded as it got higher, so the most conspicuous part was under her chin, and by the time it got past her mouth there wasn't much of it left. I was used to it now, so I didn't notice it any more, but it infuriated me a few times in New Zealand when I saw that it did affect some people. And when I say people, I mean boys.

Her comment there in the high school office did horrify me, though. Her parents were pretty big on the Wirrawee social scene, and her mother was heavily into expensive dresses, pearls, classical music, all that stuff. She would have spent more on one dress than my mother spent on ten. If we had spare money we spent it on a new tray for the one-tonner, or a computer programme that kept track of stock prices, or a set of portable sheep yards.

I just couldn't understand Fi's reaction. I think she was too blown away by it all. It had happened too unexpectedly. So she grabbed hold of the first thought that went spinning past, and she spoke it.

I didn't say anything. I held her while the others asked Lee a thousand different excited questions about their families, and I just sat there and listened.

"How'd you find all this out?" Homer asked the obvious question.

"There was a big fire started up by the lookout. I guess you must have seen it..."

Lee couldn't work out why we laughed. Even Fi smiled a bit.

"We lit it," Kevin explained. "To get away from a bunch of soldiers."

"Really? Playing with matches? You sure burned up a bit of country. Nearly burned up the whole of Wirrawee, from what I could see. Well, while that was going on, heaps of soldiers went past in their fire-fighting gear, and I thought it'd be a good chance for me to move. I'd been hiding in the cemetery, and I didn't want to stay there any longer. You know how Iain said never to stay in the same hiding place for too long? So when the streets seemed empty I started sneaking along towards the school. That was where I'd decided I should go. And I was about halfway here when I took a shortcut across the park, and I saw Dr. Krishnananthan. So I started talking to him from out of a rhododendron bush. He got quite a shock, I think. But it turned out he's doing what your parents are doing, Fi, and he told me all about it, and about everyone else. He's actually working on a computer programme that keeps track of all the prisoners' movements, so I'd found the right person to ask. But he's not allowed to know anyone's exact location, just the region they're in. Security's still pretty tight."

"Did you ask him about the New Zealanders?" Kevin asked.

"Yes, of course. He didn't know anything about them. He hadn't heard of any disturbances like that. But he said the airfield's a law unto itself, so if something happened they mightn't tell the town authorities about it."

"What else did he tell you?" I asked.

Lee looked away into the distance for a minute. I couldn't quite work out what was going on. Finally he said: "Not much. The fire distracted us. Dr. K. was getting really worried. He was scared of the soldiers, of course, plus he thought Wirrawee was about to burn up. I think that was actually his biggest fear. We had ash raining on us the whole time we were talking. Anyway, I wasn't in good shape by then. I was so hungry, and tired. I didn't know whether to try and get back to Hell on my own, or what. I didn't know if you guys would still be there, or if you'd called Colonel Finley and got the helicopter back to New Zealand, or if you'd be coming into town looking for us. I thought if I couldn't get some food I wouldn't have the energy to get to Hell, and I didn't know where to get food. Dr. K. was no help with that. He said they controlled food so strictly for prisoners that they couldn't smuggle anything out."

A thought struck me and I asked: "Where were you going to hide at the school?"

He looked surprised. "I was hiding in the bike shed. I didn't think anyone would look there."

I laughed with delight. "I'm psychic! I always knew it!"

I told them about the message I'd written in the Hermit's hut. They weren't very impressed, but I thought it was great. I love weird things like that. But we were all so off our heads with excitement and nerves and hangovers and lack of sleep that the talk was crazy, jumping all over the place like a plague of locusts.

Gradually, though, it developed into a very intense serious conversation. It turned out there were three big decisions to make. How to arrange for Fi to see her parents was the first one. How to get ourselves to safety was the second. Stupidly I had thought that we could stop at those two, but it was Lee who hit us with the third.

How to attack the airfield.

Luckily he didn't mention it until we'd dealt with the first two. And they were fairly easy. Dr. K. was going to break the news to Fi's parents that she might be around, so they would look out for her. We'd have to get Fi in position during the night and she'd hide in the park until her parents were allowed out for lunch. It would be a long day for Fi but, of course, who cared about that? It'd be worth the wait.

It would be a long day for me, too, because Fi whispered that she wanted me to come with her, and you can't refuse a request like that, not that I'd want to.

The second decision wasn't so hard, either. We had to call Colonel Finley on Wednesday, and we all thought if the Kiwis hadn't turned up by then we'd return to New Zealand alone. There was nothing much more we could do to find them.

Then came the third topic, out of the blue. I think it took us all by surprise, not only me.

"We have to have a go at the airbase," Lee said.

He said it just like that, calmly and unemotionally. But very firmly. There was a stunned silence.

"We can't do that," Kevin said at last.

"Yes, we can."

"But a dozen Kiwis, with all the training and equipment they've got, if they couldn't do it, what hope do we have? None, that's how much. You've got to be bloody joking. No way, José. No way in the world."

"We can and we have to," Lee replied. "We can't go back to New Zealand with our tails between our legs. We can't go back without making an effort. For all we know the Kiwis might be dead. We have to do it for their sake. We have to work out some simple way, something we can manage."

"Do you know what their plan was?" I asked.

"More or less," Lee answered. "They had explosive charges to put on the planes."

As he had been all the time, Lee was talking without looking at us. It was like he was miles away. It was strange. Sure he was still exhausted, still recovering from the lack of food, and the loneliness and fear he would have felt during the days and nights on his own, but there was something more happening, something I didn't understand.

Homer joined in the argument.

"I wish you'd never suggested it in the first place," he said, quite bitterly. "God knows, I'm sick of hero games. But now that you have suggested it ... well, you've landed us in it, haven't you? It makes it pretty hard for us to walk away."

"Let's take a vote," Fi said. She was still very quiet, like she was in shock.

I was about to agree, but Lee beat me to it.

"Take a vote if you want," he said. "But it won't make any difference to me. I'll attack the airfield on my own if I have to. You can come or not, whatever you like."

We all protested. It was unfair of Lee to put us in that position. If we let him go on his own and he didn't come back, where did that leave us? If we went with him and we were all killed, well, that wasn't too good either. He was trying to impose his will on us, and none of us liked it.

Lee just couldn't see it, though. Or wouldn't. He kept saying: "It's my decision and it's my life. It doesn't concern anyone else. If you don't want to come, that's fine."

Lee was back in one of his revenge and honour moods, and I knew he wouldn't listen to us. The crazy thing was that he had no idea how to attack the airfield. Just a vague belief that he should do it.

The discussion broke up at about four o'clock with no result. Instead of being elated and excited about the news of our parents we were tired and angry. I went and had a sleep to make up for all that I'd missed the night before when I was on sentry. But again I couldn't sleep. I wriggled and twisted around on the narrow hard bed, thinking about it all — my parents, my father locked up and my mother having to wash other people's clothes, Fi's parents and the reunion she and she alone could look forward to, Lee's stubbornness, his mad ambition to kill himself and anyone who went with him.

And suddenly, in horror and guilt, I thought of the two questions that none of us had asked him. It seemed incredible then and it seems even more incredible now. I can only explain it by saying that we had too many things to think about: our brains were in overload. But that's really no excuse. I was mortified, disgusted, incredulous, ashamed.

But I realised.

I realised everything.

Sixteen

I found him after a long search. I'd gone through every room in every block: offices, classrooms, staff rooms, even the toilets.

Then I thought, "Oh, of course, stupid, how could it take me so long to work it out?"

I found the window unlocked. I went straight through it to the bike shed.

By then it was some time after nine o'clock and very dark, too dark to see anything. But I had no doubt. I knew he was there.

I stood in the doorway and asked the first question.

"Lee, what happened to your family?"

There was no answer. I stepped forward, three steps, trying to see in the darkness, trying to see where he might be sitting. It was impossibly dark. I tried again.

"Lee? Are they all dead?"

There was a kind of spasm away to my left, in the darkest corner of the shed. I turned towards it and using my hands in front of me to feel for obstacles I groped my way over there. The last few metres I was doing a kind of shuffle. It was his knee I at last bumped into. I put my hand on it. I felt a shudder run through him. I found his shoulder and made him turn a little towards me. He kind of fell against me. He started shaking so severely I could hear his teeth rattle. I got my arms around him and held him tightly. I had the feeling that this was the most important thing I had ever done in my life, that if I didn't hold him with enough love he would fall apart, or he would slip away and never return, not just to me, but to anyone, to life itself. I prayed to God, to Robyn's God again, to give me enough love to keep him with us. I thought I'd hold him for as long as it took, even if it took forever. I was devastated by my sense of guilt: all the time we'd been talking about our parents and the airfield we hadn't thought to ask Lee about his own family. But gradually that feeling went. I started to realise that it didn't really matter, that love could over-come all those stupid misunderstandings; that if some-one really loved you, they knew what was in your heart and it didn't matter if you made mistakes. They looked past your words and read your heart. If they liked what they saw there, if they recognised it as good, they'd for-give just about anything.

So that was what I thought sitting there in the dark, with my leg and left arm going to sleep under me as Lee and I hugged and tried together to hold off the forces of fear and loneliness and sadness.

It took a while, too. I suppose it's one of those battles that you never win. You have to keep fighting it forever. Maybe the best you can hope for is that you don't lose too much ground, that as long as you keep fighting you can at least hold your own, most of the time. You might have to call that a victory.

We were there for probably two hours before he quite suddenly started telling me the story. How his parents had been killed when his father attacked a guard at the Showground, and the man fired just as Lee's mother ran in to try to stop him. The same bullet killed them both. And it happened in front of Lee's little brothers and sisters. They were still at the Showground, being looked after by the women who ran the creche.

About an hour after that I asked him the other question that had been plaguing me.

Lee answered me straightaway, to my surprise. But he didn't answer in the way I expected. He didn't use words. Instead he stood and took my hand and led me out of the shed, into the dry hot air of the night. After the bike shed it seemed quite light, quite easy to see. The smell of burnt trees and grass still lingered, and as we walked across the playground I caught a glimpse of trees glowing red on the hill that overlooked the town. They would take days to burn; each of them a mass of hot red coals that would have to be watched carefully for a long time. I hoped someone was up there doing just that. Bushfires aren't only dangerous while they're blazing.

I think we both felt bulletproof as we walked away from the school. I don't know why; no idea. But for about the only time since the invasion we didn't bother looking around or taking any special precautions.

We also didn't tell the others we were going, which was pretty rough. I can't make any excuses for that. We just didn't think of it.

Out in the streets we did get careful again. We didn't talk to each other. I guess I knew where we were going. We did all the usual things, sticking to shadows, going from garden to garden rather than along the street, taking special care at intersections. There was plenty of activity. I wasn't surprised: they knew we were in the district somewhere, and they might have started to realise we were in the town, not the bush. When we got back to school I'd tell the others we had to move. It was too dangerous to stay there any longer.

But the activity was mainly vehicles, and they were fairly easy to avoid. Cars and trucks went by at different times, some obviously in a hurry to get somewhere, others obviously patrolling. We saw a foot patrol too, but we hid in bushes until they had gone. I had no real fear now that I would fall apart when I saw them. Things had changed again since then.

It was about two o'clock when we got to the cemetery. Two o'clock's a cold time to visit a cemetery, even on a dry warm night like this one. Lee didn't hesitate though. He knew exactly where we were going. We walked down the centre path to near the end, then turned left. I was starting to cry already, and I took Lee's hand and held it tightly. We turned left again and came to the newest row of graves. They were just piles of raw caramel-coloured earth, seven or eight of them, and a little white cross stuck in each. A bit different to the ornate grey and white marble tombs in the next row. They were from before the war. Some of them were two metres high, and a couple had crosses twice my height.

Corrie's grave was the third of the little mounds of dirt. It had her name and the date of her death on the white cross, nothing else. Tears kept running down my face, but it was just water out of my eyes; I didn't feel I was crying in the way that people normally do. Like, sobbing. It's lucky Lee was holding me though, because I would have just folded into a heap on the ground if he hadn't been. And if I'd gone down, like a sheep in a drought, I don't think I'd have got up again. That's what war does to you. Either kills you in one go or destroys you bit by bit. One way or the other, it gets you.

In the end we didn't stay there long. I think we'd both had enough grief for one night, enough emotion. I pulled some flowers off a tree, reddish blossoms they were, and I said a little prayer and promised her I'd come back and spend more time there, and then we moved away a little, and sat on a tombstone in the next row.

And then the horror of it hit me. Corrie was my age, my friend, my best, best friend who I'd shared my childhood with. This was Corrie, whose mother found her crying in her bedroom when she was four and when she asked her what was wrong Corrie sobbed, "Ellie told me to go to my room, and I haven't even done anything wrong!" Corrie, who played school with me, when we used poddy lambs as the students and tried to make the poor stupid things stand in straight lines for their lessons. Corrie, who had conspired with me to be naughty one day in Grade 1, and we threw Eleanor's lunch in the rubbish tin and filled her lunch box with sheep droppings. We got in so much trouble that we were shocked. We hadn't realised how naughty we were being. But only a week later we threw our undies on the overhead fan when we were getting changed for swimming and one pair flew off into Mrs. Mercer's face.

We played dentists when we were seven and I actually pulled out one of Corrie's teeth. It was loose anyway, of course, and she didn't mind, but Mrs. Mackenzie was a bit flabbergasted. We'd put on puppet shows and magic shows for our families and charged them twenty cents to enter. We shared a bag of sherbet that Corrie knocked off from her Mum's shopping bag, then somehow convinced ourselves that it was Ratsak and we panicked and rushed to the tap and tried to wash it all out of our mouths. We lay in our tent on our first campout, sucking on tubes of toothpaste. Another time in the same tent we pretended we were married, and we kissed and felt each other the way we imagined married people did. And on another campout we managed to persuade ourselves that there was a boogie-monster outside the tent, until we got so scared we rushed into the house screaming and refused to go out there again.

We were mates, that's all there was to it. It was always Corrie's hand I held as we walked in a crocodile to the library or the pool or the art room. Like Fi, we went through the usual list of things that kids try: jazz ballet, swimming lessons, piano, pony club. Unlike Fi, we didn't last too long at any of them. There was too much to do at home, and our parents complained at all the driving. We went through the grades: 1, 2, 3, 4. We wrote love letters to boys, and decided the next day that we didn't like them after all. We played softball for the Wirrawee Under 10's but when Corrie got dropped for being rude to Narelle, our coach, I quit the team in protest. We tried to peep at the shearers through a little hole in the wall of their dunny. We had a competition to see who could last the longest without going to the toilet and nearly bust ourselves in the process. We dared the other girls in Grade 5 camp to run topless to the flagpole and back, and I actually did it, but Corrie, who by then was getting something worth covering, chickened out. Grade 6, Year 7, Year 8. We read in a magazine that sometimes girls who were close friends would menstruate at the same time, so we tried to synchronise ours but failed. For more than a term we kept a list of the colour of Andrew Matthewson's undies each day, because he wore wide shorts and always sat slumped down with his legs apart. It was a joke, but there was something I never admitted even to Corrie, and that was how I used to wish he'd forget to wear undies at all one day.

Corrie, who made herself sick worrying about tests. Corrie, who spent a whole lesson typing groups of A's — just the letter A — into a computer, then blocked it, copied and pasted it, and did that over and over until she'd created a file eight megabytes long. Then we did a word count. It took twelve and a half minutes.

Corrie, who broke her collarbone when she fell off the back of the trailer as we picked up the posts from the old fenceline. Corrie, who talked me into following her on a crawl through the little gaps between the bales in their hayshed, then suddenly panicked and thought she wouldn't be able to get out and got total claustrophobia. Corrie, who fell so madly in love with Kevin, and so suddenly, that I was jealous and had to make myself like him. At first I'd even tried to talk her out of going with him but for once she was not going to be talked out of something: she had her heart set on him, and she got him, and in the end I had to resign myself to the fact that our relationship had changed forever.

We would have to bring Kevin here too, to the cemetery, because he had as much right as I did, maybe more after the sacrifices he'd made to get Corrie to hospital.

But no, I thought, I had a right to be here too. Corrie and I were mates. We were mates for life.

And now my best mate was under the earth, under six feet of cold heavy soil, separated from me by six feet and by eternity. How could it be possible? All those futures we discussed, all those plans to share a flat and go to uni, to travel the world together, to get jobs as pilots or jillaroos or teachers or doctors or governesses: in none of those plans did we ever consider for a moment that it might end like this. Death wasn't on our agenda. We never mentioned the word. We thought we were indestructible. And what would happen to me now? Our plans had always been for two, but Corrie had left me and I was on my own. I felt like a Siamese twin who'd been amputated from her other half. Sure I had Fi, and sure I loved her dearly, but I hadn't grown up with her the way I had with Corrie.

The last time I'd seen Corrie was at the hospital and I thought I'd said goodbye to her then and I'd sort of known I wouldn't see her again, but now I realised I hadn't accepted that at all. There were so many more things I should have said, wanted to say, had forgotten to say. Now, how would I say them? If I lived for a hundred years I would never get the chance to say them.

"How did you know she was here?" I asked Lee.

He shrugged and put his arm around me.

I welcomed that, I wanted it, and I snuggled into him.

"I didn't know. I was just browsing. It got so boring hanging round here. I saw the new graves and thought they might be people who'd died since the invasion."

"Where are your parents?"

"They're buried at the Showground."

I sat up a little, and drew away from him and looked at him. "The Showground? Why? Why not here?"

"Anyone who's been executed—that's what they call it when they murder someone—gets buried at the Showground. I don't know why. I guess they figure they're too naughty to get a proper grave."

"How'd you find that out?"

"Dr. Krishnananthan told me."

"So that's how you found out they'd died? You haven't seen their graves?"

"That's right."

"Oh, Lee. It's all so sad."

We hugged for, I don't know, an hour or so, trying to comfort each other.

Finally I said, "We'd better go back."

"I don't want to."

"Yeah, I know."

And I knew why. When we went back we would have to break the news to the other three.

In a way I would rather have faced the enemy again than face that.

Seventeen

Sometimes friendship has quite a price. I loved Fi and I liked her parents, but when Fi asked me to hide with her in the park while she waited to meet them I agreed, then realised later I didn't really want to do it.

Why? I'm not sure. I think it was too much to cope with. One night I find that three people who were so very important in our lives are dead, I go through more grief than I knew I could feel (I'd been thinking I could never feel anything again), and I realise that I'm still fairly rapt in Lee. And that was all just after Fi asked me if I would go to the park with her.

Fi reacted kind of strangely to the deaths of Lee's parents and Corrie. It didn't seem to sink in somehow. She didn't react with grief, like Homer did, or rage and despair, like Kevin. Maybe she was numb to it all. The shock of finding out about her parents seemed to leave her like a robot. It was like she had shut down.

I'd done the same thing myself a few times, that's how come I recognised it in her.

But I went to the park at four-thirty in the morning, with her and Lee, and Lee showed us where to hide in the middle of the tree ferns. It was cool and damp there. Unlike the ferns at the high school, they had survived the neglect while the invasion was happening. Someone was looking after them now because their fronds were a fresh green and their trunks a strong brown.

Not that we could see that until the sun came up. We moved the garden seat, which was the signal to Fi's parents that Dr. Krishnananthan suggested, then, after Lee left, I spent all my time trying to find a comfortable spot. It was so damp that I soon had a wet bottom. It was pretty cold in among the ferns. The next thing I gave a series of sneezes, about seven I think. That startled Fi out of her coma. She peeped out of the ferns nervously in case hundreds of soldiers were running towards us with boxes of tissues. Or something else.

I was hanging out for dawn, so it would warm up, but even long after the sun rose no heat reached the fernery. It was designed that way, of course. I felt that I would die of hypothermia soon. When my teeth started chattering uncontrollably, and no amount of rubbing would warm my arms and legs, I said to Fi, "I'll have to go out in the sun for a minute, or it'll be the end of me."

She was too nervous to do the same but she kept lookout while I did a quick two minutes in the early heat of the morning.

The day dragged on. Fi and I didn't talk for a long time. There was so much to say that we couldn't even start. I took to looking at my watch every few minutes: 7.50, 8.05, 8.15, 8.35. We'd hoped to see them arriving for work, but we didn't. They probably came by car or truck from the Showground, and the carpark was on the other side of the building.

Gradually I got into the spirit of things. At last I was getting excited on Fi's behalf. The only problem was that once I started sneezing, I couldn't stop. Every time I sneezed Fi jumped a metre, then looked out fearfully to see if anyone was coming. I tried to bottle up the sneezes but I couldn't stop them all. I've always had a theory that it's bad for you to suffocate your sneezes and, sure enough, I soon found myself getting a headache, so that proved my theory.

10.35, 11.00, 11.15, 11.45. The hands of my watch moved so slowly I kept putting it to my ear to make sure it still worked. We didn't know what time Fi's parents would come out, but any time after noon seemed possible. Neither of us could stand still. Fi was almost spinning, she was so excited. She was talking now. She kept fingering her scar, and starting sentences, then changing to new ones and forgetting what she'd been talking about.

"Do you think this bracken is . . . it reminds me of the botanical gardens at Stratton . . . I wonder if they got bombed . . . do you remember the church there? They sure . . . oh look, there's a pigeon on the hand of the statue . . . did you ever see Mr. Morrison's parrots, the way they used to . . ."

All of this would be in bits and pieces, like she wasn't really listening herself, stuttering and stammering and switching topics, and taking five minutes to get a few words out.

I didn't blame her, though. If all went well she was about to have one of the most powerful moments of her life, the moment that we'd all dreamed about and longed for, and that for at least one of us could now never happen. I kept wondering how it felt for Lee to break the news to Fi that she could see her parents. No one would ever break that news to him now. Not in this lifetime, anyway.

But side by side with my grief for Lee was my happiness for Fi. I just wished there was more room in my little body to accommodate all these violent wild feelings that kept screaming around inside me. I already had so much stuff squashed in there — liver and appendix and intestines and heart and all that junk. There was absolutely no room for feelings. But they still managed to squeeze in somewhere. Most of them lived in my stomach — a whole huge mess of them in there — but some kept crawling over my hands, and some stuck in my throat like I'd swallowed a doorknob.

While I thought about all that, half an hour more sneaked past. And suddenly Fi grabbed my left wrist so hard she nearly broke the bone. Just like she'd held Lee's hand back at the school. I had no idea she could be so strong. I looked up at the tech building. There they were, sauntering across the grass, trying to look casual. They did look pretty good, too. They were both very thin, although they always had been, but before the war they were slim and now they were skinny. They both wore jeans and T-shirts, which was funny, because their style used to be corduroy and tweed. Mr. Maxwell looked naked without a tie.

Fi gave a little sob. If I hadn't pulled her back by the shirt I think she would have run straight out there. But I wasn't much better because I sneezed, three times, very loudly. Mr. and Mrs. Maxwell looked over towards us like they'd heard gun-shots. Then they both glanced around guiltily. They were walking about five metres apart but it was as though a string connected them, because their movements were so co-ordinated.

I hoped desperately that no one was watching. I scanned the park, searching for any sign of movement.

Mr. and Mrs. Maxwell went past the ferns, one on

each side, then Mr. Maxwell pretended to see something in there worth looking at. He called to his wife and pointed to it and they both came walking in, as though they were botanists in the jungle.

I grinned at them and Mr. Maxwell gave me a nervous smile and patted my arm but, of course, they only had eyes for one person.

"Oh my poor darling, look at your face," I heard Mrs. Maxwell say, as she put an arm around Fi and sort of folded Fi into her.

I left them to it and eased my way to the edge of the fernery. The pretend reason was to look out for soldiers, but if any appeared I wouldn't be able to do much. We could run away but Mr. and Mrs. Maxwell couldn't, because Fi's little sister was at the Showground as a hostage. And if we ran away and the soldiers saw us they would know we were the ones they'd been searching for in the bush, the ones who lit the fire. So Fi's parents and her sister would be in deep sewage if that happened.

On the other hand we couldn't just stay there and let ourselves be caught. In all the time I'd spent with Fi since early morning we never got around to discussing what we'd do if we were seen. I supposed we would run — we would have to run — but the consequences would be so awful that I couldn't even imagine how we'd live with them afterwards.

For the first time I began to realise just how terribly dangerous this situation was. We should have thought it through much more. We were losing the old habits of caution that we'd had before we went to New Zealand. We were getting too casual.

I felt guilty thinking it, but I couldn't help hoping Fi wouldn't spend too much time with her parents.

Of course, the real reason I stayed away from their meeting was that I wanted Fi to have her parents to herself. It was precious time she was getting — it might be months, or even a year or two, before it happened again — and despite all the dangers I was anxious not to interrupt it.

I suppose there was another reason I kept away. And it was simple enough. It was just too painful for me to get involved in all this. It hurt too much. That's all.

So I crouched at the edge of the damp greenness and sneezed as quietly as I could and wiped my nose and sneezed some more.

From the fernery I could hear Fi's voice rising and falling. She sounded surprisingly calm, and she was doing nearly all the talking. I guess she had plenty to talk about. I heard my own name mentioned a few times, but for once in my life I was trying not to eavesdrop. I heard Mr. Maxwell's deep bass rumble as he said something about Fi's sister, Charlotte, and I nearly got the giggles suddenly as I remembered a corny magazine article I'd read in an old *New Idea* magazine back in New Zealand. It was about relationships between fathers and children and it said it didn't matter if the father was away a lot as long as when he was with his children it was "quality time."

I wondered if the editors of *New Idea* would call this quality time, and if they'd think it didn't matter that Fi hadn't seen her father for over nine months.

I checked my watch. We knew that Mr. and Mrs. Maxwell had only half an hour for lunch. The one thing

Dr. K. had been adamant about was that they got back on time. Otherwise the supervisor came looking for them and there were big punishments because the supervisor's job depended on everybody being where they were meant to be and doing what they were meant to do. The punishments didn't necessarily matter much but the supervisor coming out looking for people mattered a lot.

It was twenty-four minutes already by my calculations and I thought I'd better say something. I called out, "I think you're meant to go back in a couple of minutes."

Before the war I'd never have dared to speak to people like the Maxwells in that way, but now I did it with no real hesitation.

Mr. Maxwell answered. "Yes, thanks, Ellie, we're coming now."

I stepped back into the ferns as I heard them saying goodbye to Fi. I turned to face them. Mrs. Maxwell had obviously been crying and Mr. Maxwell's eyes were red too. They both hugged me and said nice things, so I guess Fi gave me a good report. "Give heaps and heaps of love to my parents if you see them," I said. "Tell them I've been good. Tell them I miss them and think about them every day, and I can't wait to see them again. Tell them the Landie's still hidden up on Tailor's Stitch."

I don't know why I said that last thing, just to show I'd looked after the Landie in a responsible way or something.

They both patted me and then went out of the fernery on the side away from the tech building. What made me laugh, and what gave Fi the giggles, was the way they'd figured out to look innocent in case anyone was watching. They walked out like lovers, hand in hand, kissing and canoodling as if they were in an old movie. So it was pretty obvious what they wanted people to think they'd been doing. Fi, who was beside me by then, squealed. "Oh how embarrassing!" she said. "Oh God, I hope no one's watching."

I had to admire their guts though, and the cleverness of it. It was a good trick.

As they got back to the building a soldier came a-round the corner and said something to them, but it didn't look too serious.

It reminded me, though, that we were right in the middle of the enemy's nest.

Now Fi and I were faced with another long wait. We'd decided before we arrived that we'd have to stay there till dark. But it was I—normally the patient careful one—who persuaded Fi we should leave.

"Even if we take an hour to move a hundred metres, it'd still be more interesting than sitting here all day," I argued.

Fi agreed after a bit of hesitation. She was in a different mood. It was fascinating to see how much she'd changed in that little time. She seemed to be floating, making irrelevant comments, leaving me to do the worrying, the watching out. All she wanted was to chatter nonstop about her parents. Fair enough, of course, but we were still in an incredibly dangerous situation.

We withdrew gradually from the fernery and kept on retreating through clumps of bushes and trees. At one point Fi was so distracted she leaned over and pulled out a weed from the garden bed next to us. "Oh, for Christ's sake, Fi," I said irritably, "concentrate on what's happening, will you?"

She looked away, but didn't say anything. I felt guilty, and angry with myself.

The boys were going to wait at the school, so that's where we headed. There wasn't anything very interesting about the trip, except that from one point, near the vet clinic, we could see the airfield. I was amazed at how Wirrawee's little airfield, which before the war had been a dirt strip for Cessnas and Cherokees, for cropdusters and rich graziers, was now transformed into a big busy place, with a dozen brown and green jets parked outside a big new terminal building. There was a huge new hangar too, and a highwire cyclone fence around the entire base, and the runway was all concrete, and much much longer. And there were people everywhere. We counted eighteen, just in the short time we were watching.

No wonder the Kiwis wanted to attack it. This was a major part of the enemy's plans.

I noticed they were improving the road into the airfield, too. They had a bunch of graders and bulldozers and trucks, just like in peacetime. I was surprised and sad that everything was going on with no sign that they were scared of opposition.

As for evidence of an attack by the Kiwis or anyone else — there was nothing. Not a single hole in the fence, not a damaged plane anywhere, not even a broken window. The twelve New Zealanders had vanished without a trace.

That reminded me to check with Fi to see if she'd

187

asked her parents about them, but she hadn't. She'd forgotten. Which made me mad all over again, although this time I had enough self-control not to snap at her.

We couldn't stand there watching for too long. The sun was still bright in the sky and we were in cover that was very thin. So we slipped away and continued our slow journey back to the school.

When we got there the boys were much nicer to Fi than I had been. But then they hadn't spent most of the day huddled in wet ferns with her and getting no thanks for it. They crowded around asking a million questions, laughing with her. I felt very out of things. I stood there and sneezed.

Of course, I was just jealous, and missing my own parents. But that's no excuse. I could have been more generous. If anyone had a reason to feel rotten right then it was Lee. But he acted like he was really happy for Fi. Knowing Lee, I thought he was faking it. He might have been pleased for her, but underneath that, he was just plain desperate.

When things were more normal again the boys started telling us how they'd spent the time. I should have guessed what they'd do. From early morning till now they'd been discussing the airfield. They'd even done what we'd done: snuck up to a good lookout point and checked the action from there. They'd made notes of what we could do.

The first thing I told them was to get rid of the notes. If we were found with them we'd be executed on the spot as spies or saboteurs. We'd have no hope of talking our way out of that one.

Still, I listened to their ideas. Lee did most of the talking. With a few decent meals in him he'd got back a bit of energy and health but the main fuel he was running on was the thought of revenge.

I made a mental resolution to keep a close eye on him. Lee didn't care much any more if he lived or died. The rest of us still did care. We'd have to watch that Lee didn't get us in trouble by doing something crazy or gung-ho. I figured I should try to get him on his own and remind him about his little brothers and sisters. Maybe that would help him to realise that he had responsibilities.

Anyway, the boys did have two main ideas. I was kind of reluctant to listen, but I already knew I wasn't going to get much choice in the big question of whether we'd try an attack. If I didn't have a choice in that, I could at least make sure I had some choices in the smaller questions: how and when and where, and how much we attempted. I didn't want to get stuck with another rotten job, like being inside a pitch-dark container full of anfo, and taken down to Cobbler's Bay on the back of a truck. Thank you, but no thanks.

One of their ideas was quite clever, quite cute. Lee had gone past Curr's, the fuel depot in Back Street, three nights before. We all knew it because ages ago we'd taken a truck from there and used it to blow up the old Wirrawee bridge.

"Now," Lee said, looking at Fi and me like he was a teacher and we were a couple of new students. I wondered how long it'd be before I saw him smile again. Would he ever smile again? "Now, they've improved the security since then. There's a cyclone fence around it, higher than the old one: in fact it's the same as the one at the airfield, about two-and-a-half metres tall. There are two sentries, and they walk around the inside of the fence every half hour or so. They don't look too excited about it, I must say."

"Neither would I," said Homer, "if I had to spend years of my life walking around a fuel depot."

"Then they go back into their little shed," Lee said. "It's a galvanised iron one near the main gate. It used to be the office, I suppose."

"That's right," I said. "There was a book in there. When we had to get fuel in town we'd write our names in it and how much fuel we'd taken. And the night we blew up the bridge Fi and I got the keys for the tanker from that hut."

Lee continued. "The point is that that's the fuel depot for the airfield. I saw the whole thing. These trucks marked 'Aviation Fuel' come in from the Stratton Road and connect their hoses to an underground tank and empty their loads into it. It must hold heaps."

"It'd be a security thing," Kevin said. "They wouldn't want millions of litres of fuel in a tank at the airfield."

"Well, I'm not blowing it up, I'll tell you now," I said. "It's not worth it. All they'd do is put new tanks in and bring in another million litres."

"I know that," Lee said impatiently. "You're not the only one with brains here, Ellie. What I want to do is something more long term, something that'll wreck the delicate engines of their beautiful jets for weeks, maybe forever. Maybe cause them to crash just after they take off."

I guessed then what he was thinking. "Sabotage the fuel?"

"Yeah. Exactly."

"What with?"

"Sugar."

"Where would we get the sugar?"

"We'd break into Tozer's."

"How do you know there's sugar in Tozer's?"

"I've seen that too. During the daytime they have the delivery dock open at the back of Tozer's, just like in the old days, and there's plenty of sugar there. Pallets of it."

"But the sugar's not the only thing," Homer broke in. "We want two different points of attack. Supposing you and Fi do that, lace their fuel. At the same time we could start another bushfire, at the bottom of that hill behind the airfield. If the wind is right, like it was the other day, it'd go right through the place in five minutes, before they got their planes in the air. They'd never get them all up in time. We could wipe out half of them."

"So if one plan failed, the other should work," Lee said. "And if they both work, so much the better. The next lot of planes they bring in, to replace the burnt ones, would get a nice load of sugar in their fuel tanks."

"But by then we'd be back in New Zealand," Kevin said.

Obviously that was the part of the plan he liked best. Fair enough, too.

We sat there going through it all. It had a lot of attractions. One was that we could return to New Zealand

191

with our honour intact. Although we'd lost contact with Iain and Ursula and the Kiwis, we had to recognise that there was nothing we could do about them. They might be a thousand k's away. If they'd been caught they wouldn't still be in Wirrawee. They could have been carted off in ten different directions. Anywhere that had a maximum security prison.

And, of course, they might be dead. Dr. K. knew nothing about them, and I assumed Fi's parents knew nothing about them either, or else surely they'd have said. But if we could carry out their mission at least something would be salvaged from the wreckage. We could call Colonel Finley and order up the chopper and get out of here. I could talk to Andrea again.

Our rush to leave Hell and save the Kiwis seemed pretty naive now. For a while we'd thought we were heroes on white horses, saving the people in distress. Well, we'd ended up on horses, that part came true, but nothing else from the dream had. And our rush, throwing away our normal care and caution, had caused us the trouble we were now in. Stumbling into those kids: that had messed things up badly.

So as far as saving something from the wreckage, the boys' plan did have a lot of attractions. It had a lot of problems too, of course. The first was to get access to the sugar. Lee had made a number of little trips around Wirrawee in the middle of the night when he was sick of the cemetery, and he thought there were no guards at Tozer's. There were patrols through the town at random times, on average about half an hour apart, but Tozer's itself was just locked up the way it was in peacetime.

Assuming we could get in there, the next big problem was to get all the sugar to Curr's, the fuel depot. Getting through Curr's fence would be another risk. We could get wirecutters, from the Technology Room. They'd cut the wire OK, once they'd been cleaned and oiled. Then if Fi put the panel of wire back into place behind me when I went in, the guards shouldn't notice it.

But so many little problems worried me. If just one thing went wrong the whole plan failed. I suppose that was the case with everything we did, but it seemed even more so this time. And the same with what the boys were planning. Lighting a fire mightn't be so easy now. The long spell of hot dry weather, so early in the season, was certainly helping, and so were the dewless nights, but on the other hand the enemy knew we were loose in the district so they would be more vigilant than ever.

The petrol plan actually appealed to me more because it was kind of lateral thinking or whatever they call it. It was using brains, imagination, which seemed like a good start.

Homer quite seriously wanted us to use a golf cart, from the golf club, to carry the sugar. He wouldn't give up on it. He figured it'd be quiet, which was true, of course, because they're battery operated. But they're also slow, conspicuous, and probably hadn't been charged up since the war began. The batteries would be as dead as bricks. Homer still didn't agree. "Are you kidding me?" he said. "Are you telling me that the officers wouldn't be down at the golf club every day having a round or two? I bet you, in every army in the world the officers manage to find themselves a golf course."

I had to admit it was possible. "But you can see them

a mile off," I argued. "They're always white, and they have little flags on them. And they do make some noise."

"At three o'clock in the morning, who's going to hear them?" Homer pointed out.

He was quite obsessed with it. I couldn't help wondering if he just wanted another good story to tell when we got back to New Zealand. But sometimes when people argue long enough and hard enough you can end up losing your sense of reality and agreeing with them. They wear you down, even if it's ridiculous. So at one stage I nearly did give in.

"Look," I said, "if you can have a golf cart sitting outside Tozer's at 3.01 a.m., we'll use it. Just make sure you wipe your blood off the seat though. I don't want any mess."

I regretted that comment the moment I'd said it, of course. Homer looked a bit shaken and Lee looked like I'd hit him. We didn't normally make jokes like that. They'd stopped being funny ages ago.

"Sorry," I said. "Bad joke."

There was an awkward pause, then we went on with the plans. How were we going to break into a department store? There might be burglar alarms, although the ones at school hadn't worked. We couldn't rely on that, though. If we made a noise getting in we might alert someone. If we broke a window the patrols would notice and we'd be more busted than the window. The more I thought about it, the more I thought that could be our biggest problem.

"There is one way we could do it," Fi said. "It's a big risk, but it might work."

"Yeah?"

"Well, you know how sometimes you see an open window and you can't tell if it's open or not?"

"Like it could be glass or it could be nothing? Yeah."

"We're assuming that we'll break a window and the soldiers will see the broken glass. If there was no broken glass, though, if we cleared all the glass from the window and from the ground, then how would they know it was broken?"

"Most of the patrols are in cars and trucks now," Lee said, after we'd sat for a minute or so thinking about it.

He meant that it'd be harder for a soldier in a car to see that a window was broken.

What we did then was just about the most fun we'd had since the invasion. With the deaths of Lee's parents and Corrie hanging over us, we needed something else to think about. There was a teatowel I'd seen at Corrie's place ages ago, before the house was destroyed by bombing. Somewhere in the ruins that teatowel was probably slowly rotting away now. It had been one of Mrs. Mackenzie's favourites. She loved all those corny things. It said something like, "When this is all over I'm going to have my nervous breakdown. I've worked for it, I'm entitled to it, I deserve it, and I'm going to have it." I thought it was mildly funny the first time I'd seen it, and after that I hardly noticed it. But it seemed to sum up our attitude to life now. My attitude, anyway. I just wanted to get back to New Zealand and have my nervous breakdown. By God, I deserved it and, by God, I was going to have it.

But before I had it, there was work to be done. It

was just like life on the farm. "Hate it but do it." I want to watch TV. I want to ring Corrie. I want to take a motorbike and go over to Homer's. I want to play on the computer, E-mail Robyn, go for a swim, eat, sleep, listen to music.

Preserving pan could do with a good scour if we want any jam this year. Finished that seed grading yet? Chain on the chainsaw needs sharpening. Time to get out and chip a few burrs, Ellie. Ashtray in the Aga's full. Ellie, can you check that mob of wethers in Bailey's for footrot? Rock-picking, stick-picking, blackberry-spraying. Hate it, but do it.

I hated what we were doing now, but I knew it had to be done.

I didn't hate what we did that evening at school though. We got to vandalise the place and no one was ever going to get mad at us for it. No one except the enemy, of course. But what we did was try different ways of breaking windows without making any noise. We only broke inside ones along the corridor in A Block, and we didn't break them all, although Homer would have if we'd let him.

We soon found the best way: put a blanket over it then tap it with something hard, like a hammer. We'd have to make sure the glass all fell on the inside, then we'd knock out any glass left in the frame so a patrol wouldn't see the jagged broken pieces.

Fi and I decided we'd turn down Homer's kind offer of a golf cart and use a wheelbarrow instead. We'd have to steal one beforehand and have it close by.

As for security systems — well, there was nothing we

could do. If they had one we'd just have to run away again. If we didn't hear anything go off, we'd take the risk and continue.

Eighteen

"Towel."

"Check."

"Hammer."

"Check."

"Wirecutters."

"Check."

"Wheelbarrow."

"Oh no, Ellie, what do you think this bloody great thing is?"

"OK, OK, just making sure."

Fi swearing: one of life's rarest moments.

The familiar tension was with me again. God, would we ever reach a stage where we could stop doing this? And how many more times could we get away with it? "Well," I thought, "no sleazing out now. Let's get it over and done with."

I was feeling a bit stunned actually, and upset. After we'd made our plans we wandered off in different directions. I suppose we each had to get ready for what was ahead, and we each did it in our different ways. Everyone except me that is—I had sentry duty for three hours.

But after I'd finished and handed over to Homer, I did what I badly wanted to do. I went looking for Lee.

He took a bit of finding but eventually I tracked him down. He was in the Technology area, gazing moodily at a dusty jigsaw. Most of the big stuff in there was gone—plundered, probably—and I guessed that the jigsaw would one day follow it.

"What are you doing?" I asked Lee.

I felt quite nervous.

"Getting some fuel."

"What for?"

"To help this fire off to a good start."

"Find any?"

He nodded without speaking at a twenty-litre drum that stood at the foot of the jigsaw.

"Is it full?"

"No, only half. But it's better than nothing."

I didn't really want to talk about fuel, of course, and I assumed neither did he. I put my hand on his arm.

"Lee, I just want to say it again. I'm so sorry about your parents."

"Did you ever meet them?"

"Not really. We went to the restaurant a few times. And I saw your mother at school stuff every now and then."

He sighed and looked at the window. It was dark out there but he seemed to be seeing something.

"They'd put up with so much already. It doesn't seem fair."

I didn't say anything.

"My mother got out of Vietnam when she was eleven."

"Was she like, a refugee?"

I was pretty hazy about all this stuff, how people emigrated.

"Her father paid a fishing boat captain to take them."

"So was it illegal?"

"Oh, yes. It cost a lot of money, too. Luckily they were quite wealthy—my grandfather was a trader in cloth and furniture. But by the time he arranged their escape there wasn't much left. He brought some gold with him, that's all." Lee sighed again. "There were more than fifty people on the boat, but it was a sound one and the captain was a friend of my grandfather, so it should have gone OK. And they did get away without any major problems. But, somewhere in the South China Sea, they were boarded by pirates. It was a common thing then, and the captain was ready for them. He handed out rifles and they tried to fight them off. But they lost. Too many pirates, and they had better weapons.

"So they boarded the boat. They searched everyone and found my grandfather's gold. All the men who were still alive they chucked overboard. The women they took in their boat. The children they left. I guess they thought they'd die soon enough anyway. So the last my mother saw of her father was when the current carried him away, and the last she saw of her mother was her face as the pirates' boat disappeared in the distance."

Lee paused for a moment. I was still holding his hand but I'd forgotten that I had it. I was mesmerised, frozen with the horror of this story that he told so calmly, seemingly so unemotionally.

He continued. "The children survived. A day and a

half later a patrol ship from the Singapore navy found them and took them in tow. It became quite a famous case. 'The boat of orphans' the newspapers called it. My mother came to this country after eighteen months in an internment camp. She boarded with a Vietnamese family who'd known my grandfather back in Nha Trang. Eventually they adopted her and they became the only grandparents I've known. That scroll I told you about, that's the one thing I have of my mother's father. My mother kept it even through everything that happened on the boat."

"How did your parents meet?"

"Oh, in high school. They were friends briefly but they didn't see each other again for three years, then they met by accident on a train. They started talking, decided they liked each other, and it grew from there."

"And..." My throat was croaky and I had to clear it and start again. "And your father? How did he come here?"

"It was a bit different. His father was working for an American company in Bangkok, as a computer programmer, and they transferred him here. He liked it, and ended up getting citizenship. But he was angry when my father married a Vietnamese woman, and one who didn't have what he considered to be a real family. And when they came to Wirrawee and started the restaurant he cut them off completely. He felt that my father should have aspired to something better. I don't know where my father's family are now. I guess I'll probably never track them down."

He paused again. "You see, that's why it seems so unfair. My mother especially. She survived so much, only to be killed by some gun-happy little shit in the Wirrawee Showground."

"Are . . . are you angry with your father for getting in a fight with the guards?"

"No, of course not. I was brought up to have more respect for my parents than you Anglos. I would never criticise my parents in the way you guys do. Anyway how can I say what they should or shouldn't do? I wasn't there to see."

That was the first time I'd heard Lee comment on the differences between our families. It showed how much the death of his parents had affected him.

I think I did the wrong thing then. I leaned over and took Lee's face in my hands and kissed him. I was embarrassed and disappointed when I realised he was not responding. I sat back again. I suddenly wondered, "Did he think I was trying to crack on to him?" I hoped not. I thought not. It was more complicated than that. But I was still upset, the way he just sat there. Then, to make matters worse, he got up and without a word to me, or a look, left the room.

So that's why I felt a bit shaken. I'd realised lately how strong my feelings for Lee still were. His story had held me in total fascination. I felt such an agony of grief, not just for him but for his parents, and for people I'd never met, like his Vietnamese grandparents. I felt it for every refugee, every orphan, every victim of war and cruelty. When I went to kiss him it was because of all those feelings. But to him, I don't know what it seemed like, just some immature reaction, I guess.

That's why I couldn't concentrate on what Fi and I were meant to be doing. Of course I knew that she was holding a wheelbarrow. It'd be strange if I didn't, seeing we'd gone and got it ourselves.

We'd said goodbye to the boys. One of our usual sentimental scenes where we made weak jokes and said moving things like, "See you," "Good luck," and romantic stuff like that. I'd thought I wouldn't be able to look at Lee, but he gazed at me calmly, with his grave eyes, and even kissed me on the cheek.

Sometimes, especially since we'd met up again, I felt like he was about twenty years older than me, which was very annoying. This had been one of those moments. Maybe people suddenly grow older when their parents die.

Getting the wheelbarrow had been so nerve-racking that I wondered how I'd go when it came to the tough moments, like breaking into Tozer's or wheeling bags of sugar through the streets of Wirrawee, or sneaking into the fuel depot. At least three o'clock in the morning should be pretty quiet. But still in my mind was the knowledge of how I'd cracked up when I'd been with the New Zealanders and seen the enemy soldier. I was sure it wouldn't happen again, but it did take the edge off my confidence sometimes.

We went from backyard to backyard looking for a wheelbarrow and found one in the fourth place. Well, that's not totally accurate. We found one in the second place and another in the third place, but the first was too small and the second had flat tyres. The one we chose was good. Big deep tray and well pumped up. The thing that worried me though was how nervous I'd been getting. The risks were fairly small, after all. We only went into the yards that were easy, with houses a good distance away from each other and no big fences to get over. We took our time and moved quietly. So why did I have the shakes?

We moved the barrow to Jubilee Park and hid it in the bushes. There was still plenty of time. We'd deliberately left early so as not to put more pressure on ourselves. This whole operation was relying heavily on times being right. The boys had to light their fire when we were ready to break into Curr's so the soldiers at the depot would be distracted. We'd then have to move fast to meet up with the boys and get out of town. We needed to be well away by dawn. The plan was to go back to Hell, call Colonel Finley, and arrange the pickup.

From Jubilee Park, Tozer's was within view. We climbed a big old oak tree and sat in the lower branches looking at Wirrawee. The tree was beautiful. I love people who plant trees that take centuries to grow. It means they're thinking of others: not being selfish, but thinking about people in future generations who might enjoy their work. Farming, good farming, is a bit like that, I suppose. "Live as though you'll die tomorrow but farm as though you'll live forever." Dad was always quoting that.

This tree must have been planted when the British settlers arrived in the district. It would have stood here all its life, coping with what came along. It didn't show fear. It didn't hide or run away. It didn't call for help when things went wrong.

"Ellie, are you still thinking about when you screamed at that man in Warrigle Road?" Fi suddenly asked me.

I nearly fell straight out of the tree. How did she know?

I waited a long time before answering.

"Yes," I finally admitted.

I thought she'd launch into a big speech about how I shouldn't blame myself and so on, but she surprised me yet again. She didn't say anything. Then I started panicking that maybe she thought I should blame myself; maybe she was wishing she wasn't with someone so unreliable. So I blurted out:

"Do you think I've lost it?"

Again she wouldn't follow the script that I kept writing for her in my mind.

"I guess you won't know until you get tested again." She paused. "You were good when you were waiting at the tech with me, but that wasn't so dangerous. Out there in the bush, and at the lookout, you were fantastic, but it was different there too, wasn't it?"

"Yeah," I said. "Because it was in the bush, and because we didn't have a choice, and because it was a matter of survival..."

"It was in hot blood," Fi said, "and this is in cold blood."

She'd said it. That was the big difference.

"Are you getting more scared or less scared?" I asked her.

"You mean each time we do something like this?"

"Yeah."

"Oh more, of course."

"But shouldn't we get less scared? Because we're getting more experienced all the time. It should get easier."

Fi shivered. We were very close together and I could almost feel the goosebumps on her skin.

"Stratton Prison," she whispered. "I have nightmares about that, thousands of them. I can't get it out of my head. Every time we start doing things like this, it's all I can think of. Robyn's face..."

"Don't think about it," I said, quite brutally. Suddenly I had to be the strong one again. "Don't think about it. If you do you'll paralyse yourself. Think about it afterwards if you want, but not now."

She bowed her head. "Yes, I know you're right."

I thought I'd better change the subject, fast. But for a full minute I couldn't think of a single topic that wasn't painful. Corrie, Fi's parents, Lee's parents, everyone's parents, the New Zealand soldier who Fi had a crush on, everything in our lives now was related to war. In desperation I searched the past for something safe.

"I wonder how Courtney's going at the Showground."

She knew what I was doing, of course — I wasn't being very subtle — but she played along. Courtney was the ultimate airhead of Wirrawee High School. Without her makeup, accessories, CD player, she'd be lost.

"She'll be cruising round to all the soldiers, going, 'Oh hi, my name's Courtney, what's yours?' Every time we got a new student she said that. It drove me crazy."

"Homer always said she took an hour and a half to watch 'Sixty Minutes.'"

Fi giggled. "Her bra size matches her IQ. Do you remember what she said when her mother messed up her date with Ryan by getting the times wrong?"

"No, what?"

"She said, 'My mum blew my date.'"

We both nearly fell out of the tree. "Shh," I said, "we've got to be quieter." I was starting to enjoy myself at last, though. We hadn't had a good goss for ages. Well, it felt like ages. I think it was actually the first night hiding in the high school.

"You know who else I can't stand?" I said. "Celia Smith."

"Oh, she's nice. Why don't you like her?"

"She's such a liar. Everything she tells you, you have to halve it, halve it again, take away the number you first thought of, then you might be getting close to the truth."

"She was so popular in Year 8. You remember how we all flocked around her?"

"Well, she's funny, I guess. But she'll say anything to make herself sound cool. You know Bernard's party? She told me she was invited to it, and half an hour before that Bernard told me she was the last person in the world he'd invite. He said if it came to a choice between her and Mrs. Gilchrist he'd invite Mrs. Gilchrist. And then remember that time when Mrs. Kawolski asked her if she'd copied off me in the English assignment, and she just stood there and lied through her teeth? She was the same in primary school. I wouldn't trust her one iota."

We suddenly had to stop talking as the rumble of a vehicle in the distance frightened us into silence. We peered anxiously from the tree. It was a four-wheel drive—I'm not sure what type—and it went slowly along Barker Street, slowing even more at the main buildings. A spotlight on the roof swept the front of each building, looking for trouble. Then it turned the corner and was gone. We both sighed and settled back into our positions.

"What's the worst lie you've ever told?" Fi asked me.

I laughed. "Telling my parents that I didn't put a ding in the Landie. I wasn't meant to drive it when they weren't home, but I took it down to the river to meet Homer for a swim. And I backed it into a tree. I told Mum and Dad it wasn't me, but I confessed half an hour later. They knew it had to be me, of course. There weren't many other suspects."

"I don't think I've ever lied to my parents," Fi said. "But in Grade 3 I owned up to something I hadn't done, so that was a lie."

"Why on earth did you do that?"

"Well, she was putting so much pressure on us. Someone had gone into the classroom during lunch-time and written rude words on Jodie's folder. Cos everyone hated her. And Miss Edelstein was giving us such a hard time, saying we wouldn't be allowed to go home after school until the person owned up. We had to sit there in silence, no moving, nothing. And eventually it got to me, I just couldn't take the pressure any more, so I put my hand up and said I'd done it."

"God," I said in awe, "I'd never do that."

"My parents were so mad at me when I told them."

"What, mad that you'd written on Jodie's folder? But you hadn't."

"No, mad that I'd confessed to something I hadn't done. My father went to the school the next day and yelled at Miss Edelstein. So then the inquiry had to be opened again, of course, and it was even worse than the day before. But no one ever owned up."

"I think I remember it, vaguely" I said. "But I was in the combined 2/3 that year. It's the only time we weren't in the same class in primary school." I pulled a leaf off the tree and picked at it with my fingernail. "Your parents are so different to mine," I said. "My father never came to any school stuff. I think he thought education was women's business." I sighed. "Was it good seeing them today?"

"Oh yes, of course. It was . . . I don't know, everything. I felt guilty that you guys couldn't be in the same position. It seemed so unfair. And I thought my parents might be angry at some of the stuff we've done. I mean, I go along with all the things we've done, of course, but sometimes you think, 'Oh, I wish adults were here to tell us what to do.' It's very confusing. And I knew my mother would be upset about my scar." She felt it as she talked. "She was too. Did you hear her?"

"Only the first bit." I was uncomfortable with this conversation.

"Well, I'm stuck with it now. I don't mind it, really. I'm heaps better off than a lot of people. It was just a shock to my mother, that was all."

It struck me for the first time that Fi often said "my mother" instead of "Mum."

But there was no time to think about all this. We heard another vehicle coming, and we stopped talking. The same four-wheel drive went slowly past again. As soon as it had gone I put my hand on Fi's knee, gently.

"Time to go."

"Oh yes. OK."

We got down and dragged out the wheelbarrow. Fi pushed it to the edge of the park then hid it in the shadows again. We'd worked out a rough plan. I'd go over to Tozer's and get in through a window. If I could open a door from the inside I'd do that and Fi would bring the barrow in. If I couldn't, I'd wave a piece of cloth and Fi would bring the barrow there while I lifted the sacks of sugar out through the window. Speed was the main thing. I assumed the soldiers in the four-wheel drive wouldn't be stupid enough to come past at the same intervals all through the night. On the other hand they might be very stupid. It probably didn't matter much. A stupid soldier with a gun was as dangerous as an intelligent soldier with a gun.

I ran across the road and down to Tozer's. There was a small side window we'd agreed to try. With my heart thumping I held the towel to it and hit it with the hammer. But I was too scared to hit it properly, so nothing happened. "Come on, Ellie," I urged myself, and hit it again. There was a satisfying crack and my hands felt the weakness of the broken glass. It seemed like two or three big pieces. I pushed them into the dark interior of the shop and heard them crash and break on the floor.

I'd heard no burglar alarms, so I kept going. I glanced around at Fi and she gave me a wave. Our agreement was that if she was out of sight when I looked for her, it meant something was wrong. I put my fist in the towel and hit out all the fragments of glass left in the window. Again I checked with Fi, again she waved, so I made my dive through the window, hoping I wouldn't get more than superficial lacerations.

The window was only two metres from the ground, so I was able to land quite gracefully. There was glass everywhere, and a few bits of it stuck to my hands, but they didn't cut me and I was able to brush them off.

Then I went prowling through the darkened shop.

When I was a little tacker I'd dreamed of being accidentally locked in Tozer's for the night. I had fantasies of getting into the toy department, the sweet department, the pet shop, and spending the whole night doing whatever I wanted, without adults saying "Don't touch," "Come away from there," "No, you can't, you've had enough already."

Well, the dream had come to life, but too late, like most dreams. I thought of it, though, as I groped through the different departments, and gave a little smile, a smile that no one saw, not even me.

It was so dark in the middle of Tozer's where the streetlights couldn't reach, but gradually I got some night sight. Everything was very different. The counters were mostly bare and there were vast empty spaces that in the old days would have been filled with heaps of clothes and electrical goods and shop dummies. I think it was still being used as a shop, though, which would fit with what Lee had seen through the door of the loading dock. There were little piles of stuff here and there, with rough signs on them that looked like price tags. Just handwritten scraps of paper. For instance, in the old menswear section there were big stacks of garden tools: hoes and rakes and spades.

I knew where I wanted to go. We didn't come into town too often for shopping, and when we did we bought up big. I'm talking four trolleys full. Mum didn't like shopping, so she did as much as she could in one hit. To pick it all up we'd drive the car into the loading dock. So I knew my way around there quite well. It was the invisible side of Tozer's, where the bulk stuff was kept on pallets, and where Lee was sure he'd seen the sacks of sugar.

That's where I went. And that's where they were. Pallet after pallet. There seemed to be nothing but sugar in the place. If there'd been time I would have torn a bag open and shouted myself to a spoonful or two. But I was worried about how long I'd taken already.

I had no idea how many bags we'd need, but I figured the wheelbarrow would only hold half-a-dozen. And that should be enough. I was beginning to get a little excited. If we could do this, then tell Colonel Finley about it, the Kiwis might be able to bomb any targets in this district without aerial opposition. It'd be a great break for them.

But that was still a long way in the future. A lot of stuff had to happen first. I got a shopping trolley from the main part of the store and quickly filled it. The bags I took hardly made a dent in the pallet. With a bit of luck they'd never miss them. The trolley groaned under the weight, though, and wanted to steer sideways all the time. But I forced it back to the door that we'd a-greed was our first choice. It had bolts top and bottom, a Yale lock, and a bar across it, but none of those looked a problem. When I tried them the only one that proved difficult was the bottom bolt, which was stiff and squeaky. I moaned a little in frustration as I wrestled with it. Things like this always infuriated me. And, of course, I was scared of the noise. At last, though, it came up, with a quick slide that cost me a bit of skin from my knuckle.

I eased the door open. The street seemed quiet. I looked at once for Fi and saw her watching anxiously from the trees. I waved; she grabbed the wheelbarrow and rushed it across the street.

"You took so long!" she gasped.

I didn't answer, just grabbed the barrow and brought it in, then shut the door.

"What do you think?" I asked Fi. "Should we wait for the patrol to go past? Or take the risk and go now?"

I was loading the bags as I asked her.

She gaped at me. "I don't know. Oh golly, what a choice."

I felt stronger with every passing minute. "Let's go for it," I said. "We've been able to hear them coming each time. If we wait for them we might be waiting an hour, and we can't afford that."

The wheelbarrow was full. I grabbed the handles. "Sneak out and have a listen," I said to Fi. "If there's nothing coming, give me a holler."

I watched her as she slipped through the door. She crossed the footpath and stood beside a telegraph pole. I realised it was not much wider than her. Was she eating enough? Our meals sure were getting irregular. Fi had always been slim but now she was thinner than slim. I sighed. We'd all lost weight. Robyn used to make jokes about having anorexia. There were just too many things to worry about. I couldn't stand here in the middle of a war zone trying to decide if Fi was eating properly.

She gave me a little wave. I took a deep breath, lifted the handles of the barrow, and started to follow her across the road. It was heavy, but once I got it going and balanced it wasn't too bad.

Until I heard a vehicle coming. And trust my luck, it came at the worst time. I was in the halfway zone. Too far across the street to turn back, too far to go to reach safety. The point of no return. Suddenly the park looked a million k's away. I forgot about being strong and in control. I looked at Fi frantically, helplessly. I didn't want to abandon the barrow, because that would mean we had failed already, so early in the trip. But I sure didn't want to die for a barrow full of sugar. Fi was no help. Just looked back at me as wildly as I was looking at her. I swivelled around to see if there was anything behind me that would save us. But the street was bare. The only tiny bit of cover was a telephone box side by side with a mailbox. It would have to do. I swerved the handles of the barrow around, and with my little legs pumping away ran hard straight at it. Fi followed, which wasn't very clever of her because she would have been much safer in the park. I skidded the barrow in beside the phone box just as the headlights came round the corner. I was crouched between the handles of the barrow and Fi was on top of me. I felt every tremble in her body, and there were plenty of them. The car came along slowly. I could see the dark getting driven back by the headlights.

Then the car stopped.

For a split second I hoped it had stopped for some innocent reason. I started desperately trying to think of some nice possible reasons so I could feel better, comfort myself. But I only had a split second to enjoy that luxury. I heard the doors of the car being ripped open, and shouts and running feet. Fi's trembling increased a hundred fold. I glanced down the footpath and saw the biggest mistake I'd made since this war started. An unbelievably stupid mistake. Something so horrifyingly stupid that I actually shut my eyes for a moment in horror.

Nineteen

I'd left the bloody door of Tozer's open.

All that trouble about breaking the window so carefully. It had all been wasted.

I saw the soldiers go inside, rifles ready, covering each other. Because the door was in the part of Tozer's that sticks out into the street the soldiers had their backs to us. That was the only break we got, and we didn't even deserve that.

We had about half a minute, I guessed, before they would think to come out again. I felt a sick lurch in my stomach as I realised what our only option was. The park was so bare that we couldn't go there now—not enough cover. But the four-wheel drive was sitting in the middle of the street, rumbling away quietly. It seemed empty. We'd have to hope to God it was. I started out for it, then made the crazy decision to take the sugar. I spun around, grabbed the barrow and, with Fi sticking to me like a shadow, ran madly to the car. I nearly capsized the barrow about six times in that short trip. We ran round to the back and threw open the door. I felt sick doing it, but there was no one in there. With Fi trying to help, but getting in the way more than anything, I started chucking the bags in the back. One burst and sugar went everywhere, but that didn't bother me a lot. We got them in and Fi tried to shut the doors again. "No, wait," I said. I grabbed the barrow and lifted the whole thing. It was heavy but I was in no mood to let anything get in my way: soldiers, sugar, Fi, and definitely not a wheelbarrow. I swung it with all my strength and hoisted it in on top of the bags. Then I let Fi shut the doors while I raced around to the driver's side.

One good thing about diesels is that people can always be relied on to leave them running. I jumped in, slipped it into gear and took off the handbrake.

Fi was watching the door of Tozer's and just as we started forward she gasped, "Here they come!"

Our aim was to get to the end of the street as fast as possible. I dropped the clutch and we took off. I heard the screech of the tyres even from the driver's seat, and you have to spin them pretty hard to do that. There would have been a nice smell of burning rubber and a good black skidmark on the road for the soldiers to enjoy, no worries. The car rocked from side to side with the reaction. I had my eyes fixed on the street corner, hoping it would take the soldiers a moment or two to lift their rifles and take aim and squeeze the triggers...

We were maybe seventy or eighty metres from the corner when Fi, who was looking behind the whole time, said quite calmly, "They're firing." I knew she was telling the truth when I heard a terrible clatter, as though someone was bashing the side of the four-wheel drive with a power-hammer. I think there was one round of that, then a pause, then it started again. I was trying to zigzag the vehicle, but it was dangerous with the corner coming so fast. And even with my zigzagging their aim was improving. All the windows along my side, the driver's side, went. Fi and I cowered in our seats. We were practically down on the floor. I took the corner completely blind. If another car had been coming we would have had the greatest head-on of all time. As it was we had to cope with trees and footpaths and telegraph poles. There was a lurch as we went over the footpath and a thump as we swiped something on Fi's side. I looked up just in time to see a tree coming. I hauled the wheel down hard to the right-hand side. We were still going really fast, so I knew it was a choice between rolling or smashing into the tree at ninety k's.

Somehow we didn't roll. I still don't know what make of four-wheel drive it was. I wish I did know—it was a good one. Handled well. We went into a skid that took us halfway down the block but we ended up facing the right way, engine still running. I gunned it again.

As soon as we turned the next corner I slowed down, deliberately. My mind was still working. I knew that if we went hooning around town at these speeds, crashing into things, we'd wake every soldier in Wirrawee. They were used to patrols going past all night, at a nice quiet speed. So we had to make like a patrol.

I think Fi realised too, because she didn't say anything, just sat there, eyes searching to the left and right while I concentrated on what was ahead. The last time

I'd been in a situation like this was with Robyn. She'd been great and it felt weird not having her with me now, but I was fine about Fi. I'd actually raided the same fuel depot with her, a long time back.

And maybe Robyn was with us, anyway.

We went round another corner. I was still determined to do what we'd set out to do, to get to Curr's, the fuel depot. I was thinking as quickly as I could of how we should handle it. I was driving more or less directly there. Our plan to synchronise with the boys' bushfire had to be scrapped. We didn't have the time to sit a-round waiting for them now. A lot depended on the quality of the communications systems that these people had. If they were well equipped Wirrawee could be swarming with soldiers in no time.

I parked a block and a half from the fuel depot. We both jumped out and ran round to the back of the car. I pulled the barrow out and we chucked in the bags of sugar. Fi went to shut the doors again, leaving the split bag in the back. But I took it out and added it to the barrow. I even did a quick sweep of the fallen sugar with my hands. I didn't want it too obvious what we'd been doing because I knew these people weren't stupid. They might guess why we wanted sugar and that could ruin the whole thing. Sure they might realise some sugar had gone from Tozer's, but they might not realise, too. There were so many bags on those pallets and the ones I took weren't obvious.

Then I said to Fi, "Can you drive the car a few blocks away?"

She looked horrified.

217

"Why?"

"Because the further away from here the better. I don't want them connecting sugar with the fuel depot."

"Is it an automatic?"

"No, this is a serious four-wheel drive."

"Well, I don't think... I don't know..."

"Oh, come on, Fi, just do it." I grabbed the barrow and started off with it. I knew Fi wasn't strong enough to wheel the barrow, so she'd have to drive the car. I couldn't do everything.

But before I'd got a hundred metres I had to stop. Fi had stalled the four-wheel drive three times. I was scared the noise would wake anyone in the houses nearby. I ran back to her. "Don't worry about it," I whispered. "Leave it here. Let's go."

She was looking really stressed, almost crying I think. I realised I'd done the wrong thing, asking her to have her first go at driving in these conditions. As we ran back to the barrow I gave her arm a squeeze.

"Sorry," I said.

"It's OK," she whispered back. "I'm OK."

As worried as I was about her, I was more worried about getting to the fuel depot before we had ourselves a bigger mess. I was still cursing my stupidity in leaving the door of Tozer's open. I couldn't believe how badly things had gone so far. What a shambles.

There's nothing like anger for fuelling you up though. Better than Premium Unleaded even. My rage at our mistake gave me new energy. I got hold of the barrow again and we moved pretty fast down the little lane that was a shortcut to the back of Curr's. We didn't need to be too stealthy there and we didn't have time anyway.

As we got close to the depot I did slow down again, though. I didn't want to commit suicide.

Fi whispered in my ear, "I'll go ahead and check it out." I nodded and stopped the barrow and leant against someone's back fence. I even closed my eyes. If Fi wanted to do something brave to make herself feel better, that was fine by me. My short burst of energy was giving out already.

I opened my eyes again and watched her. She was slipping through the shadows from the trees that lined the lane and was now at the rear corner of the depot. I tried to remember what the back part of the place looked like. There was grass, I thought, and a bunch of old abandoned stuff: fuel tanks and vehicles. Then there was the neat part, all gravel and shiny new tanks. Out the front was the little galvanized-iron building. There wasn't anything very interesting in there: it was just a shed with a calendar on the wall, and a bulletin board with lists of phone numbers and notices about safety rules. The calendar always had photos of girls in the nick, which as a kid I thought was very rude. Half the time I looked the other way; the other half I sneaked fascinated looks at them, wondering if I'd ever look like that. I knew now I never would.

Fi gave me a little wave. I glanced around. The coast seemed clear, so I pushed the barrow up there. When I was ten metres from the corner I put it down again. Fi came to meet me. She put her mouth to my ear and whispered, "I don't think we need to cut the wire. I think we can lift it from the bottom."

I cheered up a lot at this news. If she was right, it reduced the danger quite a lot. Cutting wire might sound easy, but it's not. It takes time, and it's noisy.

"Have the soldiers done a round of the fence yet?"

"No."

"I think we'll have to wait till they do. It's too dangerous otherwise."

"It's dangerous either way."

I knew that was true, but I didn't see that we had much choice. We'd tried doing it the other way at Tozer's, and look what a disaster that had been. On the other hand, although we'd put the four-wheel drive in a quiet corner, it wouldn't stay hidden for long. I wished Fi had been able to move it.

We waited and waited. I kept looking behind me, expecting at any moment to see soldiers rushing into the lane with guns blazing. The lane stayed empty but there was action not far away. I could see occasional flashes of light in the sky, from spotlights I guessed. And after a while I thought I could hear vehicles, first one, then maybe two or three more.

"Can you hear cars?" I asked Fi.

She nodded.

I began to realise how precarious this situation was getting. Smuggling the bags under the fence and carrying them to the aviation fuel, pouring them in one by one, that was going to take quite some time. And while I was doing it, the searching soldiers would be getting closer and closer. I broke into a sweat thinking about it and in my imagination felt a cold and hostile hand clutching me by the back of the neck. Somehow that brought back the sneezes I'd had in the park with Fi, and I snapped out three quick ones, all in a row. Fi just about gave birth to a litter of kittens right there on the spot. She put her hand over my mouth, and kept it there. I don't blame her. I would have done the same. I didn't mean to sneeze, of course; it just happened too fast for me.

But I still didn't realise how serious it was until Fi breathed in my ear: "The guards."

I froze then, not the freezing that comes from being cold, but the freezing of an animal under threat. I'd seen it a million times when we were spotlighting at home: foxes, rabbits, roos, even sheep when we accidentally turned the spotlight on them. They all froze. It's one of Nature's great reflexes. Unfortunately it's no defence against a hunter with a rifle and spotlight, and unfortunately it would be no defence for Fi and me against armed soldiers. But it was all we had. I remembered how so long ago when all this started I encouraged the others to think about using firearms. Very quickly I'd decided it wasn't a good idea after all, mainly because I thought we'd be executed on the spot if we were caught with weapons. But at times like these a rifle or a shotgun might have helped. Or it might have made things a lot worse.

Fi was a little closer to the fuel depot than I was but soon enough I heard the men on their patrol. Men or women, you could never be sure in this war. They were doing what Lee said they would, going round the perimeter of the fence checking for problems. I hoped with every fibre of my being that they wouldn't realise how big a problem was lurking just metres away. They were so close that I could see their shadows as they turned the corner and went along the back fence.

Then, just five metres along, they stopped. I watched

the shadows anxiously. What on earth could they be doing? One put something to his mouth, and I suddenly realised. They were having a smoke!

I'd always been taught that smoking kills, and here was the proof. Their smoking was about to kill us. We were neatly trapped. Anyone coming along the lane now would see us and start shooting and our only escape route had just been perfectly cut off.

I cast an anxious look at the fences around us. Could we get up and over them in an emergency? Sure, if we had five minutes. None of them were easy. By the time we got to the top we would have been cut to shreds by bullets.

I could understand why these turkeys were having their smoke here. All around the depot were signs warning of the dangers of smoking, telling people not to smoke anywhere near the tanks. These guys were doing the right thing in every way. It just happened to be the wrong thing for us.

Fi and I were flat against the fence of the house next to the depot. That wouldn't help us much either, because the barrow was out in the open, although a few metres further back along the lane. It was just another reflex, flattening ourselves like that. The way rabbits did when a bird of prey hovered over them. Sometimes it worked for them. Sometimes it didn't.

Those cigarettes, I've never known people take so long over a smoke. I felt like marching up to them, grabbing the smokes out of their mouths and saying, "Come on, that's enough, get back to work." The worst thing, the almost unbearable thing, was that the lights in the distance were getting closer all the time. I'd say they were maybe three blocks away. It was like they were conducting a very thorough search this time. I think they were probably getting a bit sick of us.

So much of war seemed to be this way: sick fear while you waited for people to do very ordinary things before you went in and risked your life.

I didn't breathe any easier until first one glowing butt and then the other curved through the air, hit the ground and rolled away, little sparks falling off them. The shadows at last peeled themselves off the fence where they'd been leaning, and slowly resumed their monotonous walk. You could tell even from the way their shadows moved how bored they were by their job.

Well, speaking for myself, I hoped they stayed bored. I didn't want them to get excited.

We edged closer to the fenceline and peeped around the corner. We could see the backs of the soldiers disappearing towards the hut. Behind us an engine sounded a little louder than the ones we'd heard before. I glanced around apprehensively. The lane was still clear but I felt the hunt was closing in. If only we'd hidden that four-wheel drive properly.

I looked down at the bottom of the fence. Fi was right. It could be lifted quite easily. It was the sloppiest bit of fencing I'd ever seen. Dad would have had a fit if any of the fencing contractors—or me—had done a job as bad as that.

The soldiers went into the hut. It was now or never. I brought the barrow up and lifted out the bags.

"I'll go in and you push the sugar through to me," I

whispered to Fi. "Then you wait at the end of the lane." I pointed to the other end, the opposite end to where we'd left the four-wheel drive.

But Fi shook her head furiously. "No! I'm coming in with you. You're always taking the risks."

I was surprised, deeply surprised, but this was no time to argue. I was moved, too. Sometimes I thought that no one appreciated the risks I ran. It would have made more sense to leave someone on guard in the lane—I'm sure that's what Iain and Ursula would have done—but I desperately wanted company in the yard of the depot, so I was grateful to Fi.

We brought the bags even closer and Fi lifted the bottom of the fence. I squeezed under it without too much trouble. We were committed now. Fi lifted the first bag, with some difficulty, and slid it in. Again the sensible thing would have been to take it straight to the tank while Fi kept pushing other bags in, but now that Fi had made her offer, I suddenly felt incapable of going on my own. I really wanted her with me. So we got every bag into the depot, then Fi pushed the wheelbarrow back into the shadows. And in she came, under the fence.

I have to admit, she slipped through the gap more gracefully than I had.

We picked up a bag each. Fi staggered under the weight but got it on her shoulder. We needed both hands to hold and balance them. They were an awkward shape.

From somewhere not far away, maybe Nicholas Street, came a single shot, loud and terrifying. We waited a moment but there seemed to be no more, so we had to assume it wasn't anything to do with us. Crouching as best we could, we made the little run across the grass to the tanks.

That first part wasn't too bad. Just like I'd remembered, there was lots of old junk lying around. So we were able to use those for cover. It was the next part where we'd have problems. Noisy gravel on the ground, crunchy gravel, and nothing but space between us and the big underground tank. The tank was even marked "Aviation," so Lee was right about that, too. Less than fifty metres from it was the glow of light from the little shed. "We're running a hell of a risk here," I thought grimly. But we'd gone too far to back out. Simple human bloody-mindedness, the feeling that you're pathetic if you give up. The marathon runner at the Olympics who risked death to finish the race when her whole body was in a state of collapse. The last wild sheep in Nellie's paddock that defied every attempt to muster it, but you kept chasing it anyway. The guy who climbed Everest even though he knew his toes were freezing off. I've seen a photo of his toes in a book, and they weren't pretty.

It's stupid, but there's a lot to admire in it, too. And there in the fuel depot, that's the stage I'd reached.

I looked at Fi, she looked at me. I made a face at her, shrugged, and wrinkled my nose. That was meant to say, "Can you believe we're doing something this mad?"

She grinned, so maybe she understood. We started across the gravel.

Crunch, crunch, crunch, I've never known anything as noisy as that gravel. It was like the noise your mouth makes when you're eating celery. We went slowly, but that was the problem: we couldn't go too slowly, because there were two more of these trips to be taken yet. If we'd gone as slowly as I wanted we'd have been on our second trip when the sun came up.

I hardly looked at where we were going because all my attention was focused on the shed. It's a pity neither of us looked at the tank, because we might have saved ourselves some trouble. The first time I looked at the tank was when we were standing in front of it.

It was padlocked.

There was a dirty great padlock on it, about the size of my fist and made of hardened steel.

My skin burned. It was like on beach holidays: that first evening when you have sunburn and your skin prickles and burns all over. Then I felt angry, wildly angry. If Fi hadn't been there I think I would have smashed my head into the tank, or tried to rip the padlock apart with my bare hands. I knew right away there was nothing we could do. I looked at Fi again. It was almost funny. She was standing gazing at it with her mouth open, blinking like she'd just been asked a question in Cantonese or Bulgarian or Pitjantjatjara. When she realised I was looking at her she whispered frantically: "The wirecutters?"

I shook my head. "You'd be better using your teeth."

"But there must be something . . ."

"There's nothing. Let's go."

I thought it'd be better to take the sugar. I don't know why, partly the feeling that it'd be good if we could deny that we were saboteurs or guerillas. Partly because I still hoped we could come back and try again later. I thought briefly of that sixteen-year-old in Western Australia, before the war. The one who'd set off to sail single-handedly around the world and had the guts to return after a week when his radio stopped working. I remembered seeing him on TV leaving for the second time.

Patience and persistence. The opposite of bloody-mindedness, and a lot smarter.

When I picked up my bag, Fi followed suit. We started to retreat.

We were just at the edge of the gravel when I felt it coming on. Again it came quickly, too quickly for me to drop the sugar and grab my nose. So the sneeze, only one this time, echoed across the quiet of the depot like a fart at a funeral.

A moment later the light in the hut went off.

Twenty

That was the end of my attempts to save the sugar. The whole night had been a complete failure from start to finish. The only thing left to save now was our own lives.

Here dead we lie because we did not choose
To live and shame the land from which we sprung.
Life, to be sure, is nothing much to lose;
But young men think it is, and we were young.

Millions, hundreds of millions of people, have died in wars. And some of them died in the stupidest ways. Another poem from World War One that the Dunedin teacher gave me was about a soldier who didn't want to use the same toilet as everyone else. He stepped aside to take a leak away from his mates and he was seen and shot dead by a sniper. The guy who wrote the poem said this was nothing to laugh about: the soldier paid his price to live with himself according to his own standards.

> *How is this matter for mirth?*
> *Let each man be judged by his deeds.*
> *I have paid my price to live with myself on the terms*
> *that I willed.*

Mind you, the teacher had to explain it to me. I didn't get it at the time.

Sometimes I think there's a poem for everything.

So, a lot of people had died in wars, and some of them over little things. Why should we be any different? If Fi and I were killed by a sneeze, or a couple of bags of sugar, would that be anything special? We'd just join the hundreds of millions of others.

We ran like hell. We'd already frozen like rabbits that night, and flattened ourselves like rabbits, now we ran the way rabbits do when they get a sniff of the warren and think maybe they can just make it. We put our ears back, kept close to the ground and went for it. We heard nothing behind us at first. That surprised me. I'd expected shouts, running feet. But then I thought, "They don't know who or what's out there. They won't come rushing out into the dangerous darkness." I ran even harder.

The fence loomed up at me. I dived to go under it. Still like a rabbit. Beside me Fi did the same. As we went down, the first shot wailed above our heads. If I've timed one thing perfectly in my life, that was it.

As we wriggled under the fence the sharp ends of the wire scratched me painfully. I could feel the deep gouges in my back, but I didn't care a damn. For a moment there were no more shots: I think they were unsighted by our being down so low, and by all the junk in their way.

Then we were through the wire and still alive. Which way to go? Either way there was a long stretch of lane with no protection. Fi went to go right, I suddenly decided left was better. It meant going back the way we'd come, which seems crazy, but with the search closing in we only had one real hope now, and that was the four-wheel drive. I'd never thought when we casually dumped it that it might figure in our lives again, but we had to get out of this area fast. Things were getting very hot. I could see lights everywhere. Not just the white lights of spots or torches but house lights too. Seemed like we were waking up half of Wirrawee.

Fi followed my lead, although she must have thought it was madness. We belted down the lane, our feet clattering on the rough surface. The sound was amplified by the high fences on both sides. It was a race between us and the soldiers back in the fuel depot. We had to get to the end of the lane before they got to the fence. But what might be waiting for us? Funny sort of race where the guy at the finish line shoots you. Normally it's the starter who has the gun.

The end of the lane was fifty metres away, then forty, then thirty. I began to let myself think the impossible, that we might make it. It's always dangerous to think that. Only a second later the unmistakeable fast "brrr" of a bullet flashed past my ear. "We're dead," I thought. "The end of this alley'll be the last thing I see in this world."

But not for the first time that night, instinct cut in. And for the final time that night it was rabbits who inspired me. I dropped to the ground and did a fast crawl towards the corner of the lane. I realised Fi, on my left, was doing the same. Suddenly we'd become a really difficult target. The final ten metres I zigzagged as well. Bullets were flying. The other soldiers looking for us would have no trouble now. The noise was terrible. It was like the air was full of insects; the most dangerous insects ever invented, fast, loud and deadly. They were hitting the cobbles of the lane, or the fences either side of us, or simply flying away into the distance. A sharp sting in my leg let me know one had hit me. Again I thought that I'd never reach the end of the alley.

Then suddenly we were there. Fi swerved to the left and I followed. I was content to let her lead now. The lane seemed to disappear behind us as though it had never been. I heard a few more shots, then silence. About a hundred and fifty metres ahead I could see the dark shadow of the four-wheel drive. I was limping a bit and my leg hurt, but worse than the pain was my fear: the fear that at last I'd been shot and maybe I'd bleed to death. Fi was five metres in front of me now.

"The car!" I gasped, in case she didn't realise that's where I was heading. She just nodded without looking round. I'd underestimated her again; I was always doing that.

But we didn't even get close to the car. The shooting from the fuel depot had done exactly what I'd feared. Attracted soldiers the way a dead lamb attracts crows. At the end of the street three or four soldiers suddenly appeared, spread out across the street and looking like they knew what they were doing. I turned fast, getting a sharp stab of pain in my leg as I did so. Down the street, in the other direction, was a line of soldiers running towards us, in single file. They were still a block away.

I had the same fear of Stratton Prison that Fi described in the tree outside Tozer's. I had the same nightmares. I could never go back to a place like that. I was desperately—desperately—determined to do whatever was necessary to get away. Not that we had many options by this stage. Without any need to discuss it we both turned left and ran straight through the open gate of the house next to us. I just hoped the soldiers hadn't seen us.

I don't know who lived there before the invasion. Someone rich, though. It was a big enough place, one storey but very classy: a deep verandah that ran the whole way around it with lots of plants hanging from its roof, and a fountain in the garden. As far as I could tell the house was all dark colours but nice, probably dating back to the 1800s. Everything solid and conservative. There'd be no plastic outdoor furniture or aluminium window frames here.

We ran straight up onto the verandah. Fi hesitated. I sure didn't. I grabbed the door handle and turned it and pushed. The door wasn't locked. It opened quietly and smoothly. Now I did hesitate. We might be going into a trap. There might be no way out. But the soldiers were too close to give us any choice. I shrugged to myself and limped in, Fi following.

My senses were so alert that I seemed to notice everything. There were polished floors, an entrance hall, an umbrella stand, a coat stand, a tall cupboard, more pot plants. The hall was large, as big as our sitting room at home, and lit by a softly glowing lamp in the corner, probably only twenty-five watts. On the coat stand was a uniform tunic loaded with gold braid and shiny buttons. Someone rich had lived there before the war; someone important was living there now.

I'd looked around the room so quickly that I thought the black stick next to the umbrella stand was actually an umbrella. I'm sure glad I took a second look. When I did I realised it was a rifle. Near it, on a table that held a pot plant and an overflowing ashtray, was a small, black hand gun. I remembered Colonel Finley saying that officers got hand guns, as well as rifles. This house had been taken over by an officer. But I didn't spend a lot of time thinking about that. I took three quick steps to the table, picked up the gun, loaded a bullet into the chamber, flicked off the safety, and gave it to Fi. I grabbed the rifle for myself.

Fi's eyes were popping. "I...I can't...," she started saying, then stopped.

Not because she'd run out of words but because, like me, she'd heard someone coming.

The door opened quite slowly and, as it did, I lifted the rifle. A man appeared. The whole thing reminded me of those games at Timezone where you shoot hundreds of baddies but every so often a good guy appears, with his hands above his head. As someone pops up you wait a split second to see: goodie or baddie? Shoot, or hold your fire?

This guy didn't have his hands above his head though. I suppose the only reason I thought of Timezone was that the innocent guys on those games are dressed in light colours and the baddies are always in black. And here was this man, in white boxers and nothing else, yawning and scratching his chest.

I've got to say, though, he had dignity. Even in his boxers. When he saw us he didn't fall apart or go into some wild reaction. He straightened up quite slowly and stopped scratching himself. He was a tall man, young, with black hair and a watchful expression, cautious, like he was thinking, "What's going on here, how do I take control of this situation?"

To be that young and such a big-time hotshot officer he'd have to be pretty good.

I didn't trust him one millimetre.

I'd flicked the safety off as I lifted the rifle, and now I pulled the bolt backwards and forwards, really fast, feeling the satisfying clunk of a round entering the chamber.

"Get your hands up," I screamed. He gave a little smile and started lifting his hands, but slowly. I didn't like the smile. I think he figured we were just teenagers, we weren't going to be a big problem for him. Sure they had teenagers in their army, but I guess by now they didn't have much respect for our fighting abilities, compared to theirs. I knew I had to get his respect, fast. I was so scared that the rifle was shaking like crazy in my hands, but I swung it fractionally to the right and pulled the trigger.

Christ, the noise. It deafened all of us in that confined space. The damage to the wall wasn't as severe as I'd thought it might be. A hole suddenly appeared in it, and a couple of cracks spread quickly from the hole, that was all. It was the noise that was dramatic. Fi gave a scream behind me; probably a loud scream, except I was so deafened it didn't sound too loud to me. But the shot did have an effect on the man. He went very pale and staggered a little at the knees. I saw sweat appear suddenly on his face, above his eyebrows. I'm not surprised. The shot sure had an effect on me and I wasn't the one facing the barrel of the rifle. I thought, "I've got to take advantage of this, keep him on the back foot." I already knew what we had to do. It would be our biggest gamble ever, our most dangerous throw of the dice, but we had to make it work or we were dead. Really dead this time; they wouldn't let us get away from them again, especially after I'd just shot at one of their senior officers. I used the rifle to motion to the man: "Out the door." My ears were still ringing with the noise. It made my head hurt, badly, and my leg was still burning. I didn't dare look down at that. I hadn't even mentioned it to Fi.

The man paused for only a moment, then started walking to the door with his hands up.

"Wait!" I heard Fi call.

"What?" I asked, without looking around at her. I wasn't taking my eyes off this guy.

"Make him put his tunic on," she said.

I thought immediately, "Yes, yes, of course. Fi, you're a genius." The soldiers out there mightn't recognise him in his boxers, but they'd recognise his uniform.

I yelled at him, "Put your tunic on."

I hoped he understood English. He stopped but he shrugged his shoulders and said, in perfect English, "Are you going to shoot me if I don't?"

For once in my life I lost my temper completely. Without caring too much whether I shot him I pressed the trigger. If I'd had it on automatic I'd have emptied the magazine. As it was I fired either three or four rounds. From then on we were all deaf I think and this time the damage to the house was fairly serious. Half the front wall came down. There was plaster and dust and splintered wood and smoke and broken glass.

But he put his tunic on.

We marched out of the house. Straight down the front path. Fi and I both had our guns trained on him and we kept as close to him as we safely could. Fi wouldn't have had much chance of hitting him, even at this range, and even assuming she knew where the trigger was, but I was hoping no one would realise that. By now he had his hands on his head instead of up in the air but I didn't mind him changing the script that much. The important part of my script for him was yet to come.

As we came down the path, half-a-dozen torches were trained on us but we used the man as cover. We got into the street. I checked the other way, to the right. No one was there. All the torches were coming from the left. So the two groups of soldiers had met at the four-wheel drive and were, as far as I could tell, bunched there now. That was good. It meant we could keep using the officer as a shield.

But I felt we had to move really quickly, before they had time to think of a strategy. It wouldn't take them long to put two snipers in positions where they could shoot us both. We had to be gone before they did it. We had to hustle.

I yelled at the officer, "Left."

Still walking at the same pace he turned and we went towards the four-wheel drive. We walked ten metres then I yelled, "Stop!"

I took my biggest risk of all, then. I made Fi move a little more behind the officer, so they knew her gun was pointing right at his head. Then I came out in the open. It was necessary. I had to move them all away from the vehicle. I stood there completely exposed in the hot night air and I screamed at them, "Five seconds to get away from the car!" Again I didn't know if they spoke English, but I figured they'd know a few numbers. At the top of my voice I started counting, "Five, four, three..."

I pointed my rifle more firmly at the bunch of them as I counted and I could have smiled as they scattered. I didn't smile, though. I had to convince them I was super-tough, super-ruthless. But I'd created a new problem for us. With them quickly moving away in both directions I had no control over where they might go. We had to get to the car before they used the darkness to get around behind us. "Hurry," I said to Fi. I jabbed the officer with the rifle. In twenty rushed steps we were at the vehicle. Some torches followed us all the way, and I heard a man shouting, but still no one seemed to be doing anything.

There was a big problem, though, when we got to the car. Fi couldn't drive, and I was scared the officer would realise how hopeless she was with a gun. I couldn't expect her to control him while I drove. You only had to watch her for a minute to realise that. There was only one solution. I yelled at the man, as loudly as I could, knowing his ears were probably still ringing as much as mine. "Get in the front."

He opened the door as I quickly opened the rear one on his side. We got in together and I shuffled across to the left. Fi got in beside me.

"Start it," I called.

There was a short wait while we stared at the glow plug, willing it to come on. When it did, he started the ignition.

"Go, go," I shouted. "Turn right, go to the end of the street. Then right again."

I felt like cheering as the big vehicle slowly moved forward and began to turn. But I wasn't going to let the man know how pleased I was. "Faster!" I yelled at him. I fired another shot past his head, which took out the windscreen, and blasted away into the darkness. I was so pumped up. I'd never been so close to out of control before. Normally I'd be embarrassed to be so full-on. Some of it was fear, but most of it was anger. Stronger than anger: rage.

If anyone had asked me, I think I would have said I was angry at our failure with the sugar and the aviation fuel, but the real anger went further than that. It was focused that night, like it never had been before. And it was at these people. Fair and square, right at them, right in their guts. The way they'd taken over our town, our district and our country, and denied me everything in life I cared about. In particular, they'd denied me the right to grow up in the company of my parents. Unlike Fi I hadn't even had the chance to see my parents since the invasion. I was still jealous of Fi, but happy for her, too. I just wanted what she'd had. I wanted it for all of us.

Well, I wasn't thinking about that as we drove along, going a lot faster since I blew the windscreen out, but it was somewhere in the back of my mind.

I saw a couple of people running after us as we accelerated down the street, but in a kind of uncertain way. It seemed like our speed had worked for us. I'd say that no more than six minutes had passed from the time we went into that house, to the time we reached the intersection in the car and turned right. And less than three minutes from the time we'd come out of the house.

We were going in the direction of the airfield because our meeting place with the boys was on that side of town. We said we'd meet them at the racecourse, which was down a dirt road that didn't get used much. It was safe from the fire that we hoped would be raging across the airfield because the wind was in the opposite direction, and it was fairly safe from the enemy because we figured they'd have their minds on other things than scouring remote corners of Wirrawee in the dark. Or horse-racing, for that matter.

The total distance we needed to travel with the officer driving was four k's, I guessed. It shouldn't have been a problem now that he was co-operating but he tried to be smart. We went past the back of the airfield OK, except that there were no blazing planes or buildings. There was no sign of fire anywhere. I tried to be optimistic. The boys could have been delayed — all the commotion we'd caused might have made things harder for them. I glanced at Fi anxiously. It was impossible to tell what she was thinking.

I couldn't look at her again because I dared not take my eyes or my rifle off the man in front.

We came towards the turn-off to the racecourse. In the other direction the road went to the Showground. I'd like to have gone there to rescue the prisoners but now wasn't the time. No time for even thinking about it. I yelled at the officer: "Turn left."

He started to swing the wheel, then kept swinging it and accelerated hard. I was taken by surprise. The car seemed to leap forward, straight at a patch of trees and at the same time, it fishtailed. He swung the wheel violently back the other way. The car tipped sideways. I thought it was certain to roll. Neither Fi nor I had safety belts on and I was thrown across onto Fi. At the same moment the car hit the first clump of trees, and hit them hard. We started to go over. The inevitable happened. The rifle I held still clutched in my hands went off. I guess my hand had gripped tighter, by reflex, and my finger kept squeezing the trigger. It was kicking around everywhere for a couple of seconds, lurching hard against me, until I could unlock my fingers. More violent bangs, more smoke, more terror in my heart and my guts as I thought, "We're going to die." I meant Fi and me, of course, I didn't care a lot about the guy in the front seat. The four-wheel drive kept tipping until it reached a point where I thought it couldn't come back. It seemed to hang there for a minute as though making up its mind: to tip or not to tip. Second time that night it had nearly rolled. But this time it didn't recover. It went over. Fi and I were piled up against the left-hand door. We were both reaching up trying to find something to hang on to, but not succeeding. The driver didn't slide down though and I realised he had put on his seat-belt. Bastard, he must have been planning this all along.

There was a tremendous crashing smashing clanging noise as the car slid to a stop against another tree. Then there was the hiss of steam escaping from the radiator and creaks and groans from tortured metal, and bangs and rattles from behind us. I was scrabbling around trying to get my hands on the rifle again because I'd lost it in the last second of the crash. I was all the time watching the head of the man at the wheel. But he wasn't moving.

Then I saw the blood.

It was running everywhere. Down the backs of the seats, dripping onto the fragments of glass left in the shattered windscreen, leaking through the back of his seat. Trickles of it flowed past Fi and me and onto the side window. Big heavy globules of it, really thick, fell slowly from the left-hand side of the front seats. Some of it splashed on me and some went right through to the back of the vehicle. I looked at the man. His head was gradually tilting to one side. I saw for the first time the hole in the back of his seat. I felt sick but I admit I also felt savage pleasure that we had won. He'd tried to beat us but he'd failed. We had survived for a few more minutes of precious life. He had not. Tough.

"Fi, are you all right?"

"I...I don't know. How do you tell?"

I laughed. Strange time to laugh, but that's what I did. "If you can make jokes you're all right."

"I thought that was your blood for a minute."

"I did cop a wound back in town but nothing here."

"Is he dead?"

"Very, I think. But we'll check."

I crawled up to what was now the roof. The door seemed undamaged. Pushing it open was hard because it was so much heavier when you tried to lift it from underneath. The funny thing, the amazing thing, was that the inside light came on when I opened the door. That was a tough little light. Before that, all we'd had was the moon, which wasn't bad, but not as good as this light.

I put my shoulder to the door but it was still difficult, because I couldn't get my feet on anything to push against. I climbed a bit higher and at last was able to lock my feet in an uncomfortable position between the two front seats.

"You're getting so much blood on you," Fi said.

The funny thing was that she was serious. I collapsed completely. I suppose it was more hysteria than anything. I got the giggles. Only Fi could worry about things being messy at a time like this. She'd never make a farmer. By the time I recovered I had more blood on me from falling against the seat as I laughed. Fi sort of joined in, but not very enthusiastically. The way people do when they realise the joke's on them.

But finally I got the door open. I hoisted myself up by whatever little strength I still had and crawled onto the top of the car. Then I helped Fi up and out. I took a look inside, at the young officer. His career was over. I think the bullet had gone through the back of his seat and come out through his chest, because his chest had been ripped open like giant hands had grabbed each side of it and pulled it apart. It was all blood and bone and minced red stuff. His head had now flopped completely to the side, his eyes were wide open and staring and his face was without colour. Fi took one glance and turned away. I didn't look at it too much myself. It was pretty terrible.

Until that moment I hadn't been sure whether it was the car crash or the rifle that killed him.

Now I wonder what would have happened if he'd survived the crash. I didn't wonder that at the time, though.

"Come on, Fi," I said, "we've got to find the others."

I wanted to get her moving because she was starting to look so ill.

We stumbled along the road. My leg stung like hell. I was really worried about it now. I remembered a story the New Zealand soldiers told me about a guy being mortally wounded but not having any reaction for half an hour, then keeling over dead. For the first time Fi noticed I was limping. She hadn't commented at all when I told her I'd been hit. Now I realised she hadn't registered I'd said it, because she suddenly asked, "Did you hurt your leg?"

"I told you."

"No, you didn't."

"Yes, I did. I got hit by a bullet when we were running down the lane."

"Oh my God. Let me see."

"We haven't got time. Anyway I think it's all right."

"No Ellie, stop. Let me look."

A little reluctantly, but pleased to be fussed over, I did stop. She kneeled to inspect it. After a moment she stood again and gave me a disgusted look.

"Ellie, you've got a bit of gravel or stone in there, that's all."

So my bullet wound had been a fragment of flying rock, caused by a bullet, but not quite as directly as I'd thought. I was mortified. We started running. After a minute I said to Fi, "Promise you won't tell the boys about my bullet wound."

"If you promise not to tell them what I said about you getting blood on you."

"Deal."

And suddenly my leg hardly hurt at all. Guess I'm a bigger hypo than I'd realised.

Twenty-one

By one of those rare coincidences that hadn't happened often enough in this war we arrived at the racecourse at the same time as the boys. We came in from the south-east as they came in from the north-west.

Things were pretty tense by then. I think someone back in Wirrawee had found time to do some serious thinking because we could hear the unmistakable sounds of another hunt. There were even sirens, just like when the Wirrawee cops were chasing someone in peacetime. Not that we had many high-speed police chases. Carving your name on the seat at the bus stop was a big crime in Wirrawee.

I could see headlights too, and they were getting awfully close. I'd say they found the wreck of the four-wheel drive at about the same time as we found the boys. I can imagine how the car looked to the soldiers: like I'd shot the guy in cold blood and he'd then crashed the vehicle. Not a good scene for me if they caught me. I was fast getting into one of those "They'll never take me alive" states of mind that they talk about in movies. Instead of being a cliché it was beginning to sound like a smart idea.

We met at the grandstand. It was certainly quiet, certainly deserted, which was a relief. Not many places in Wirrawee would have been safe for us at that moment. Our meeting was kind of funny, though. Everyone panting, everyone crazy with fear, everyone wrecked.

Homer looked at me in horror. "Are you hurt?" he demanded. "What happened?"

For a moment I thought Fi had somehow already told him about the bit of gravel in my leg. Then I realised he could see the blood all over me.

"It's nothing," I said. "Someone else's blood. Did you get the fire going?"

There was no time for this talk, of course. We were in the most terrible danger still. I was hoping against hope that the sirens I'd heard were for a fire at the airfield, not for us. But Homer shook his head and I knew not to ask any more.

We were all completely whacked. Like, completely. Like, hardly able to stand. And things weren't helped by the fact that we felt such a sense of failure. Well, I know I did anyway. But there was no help for our exhaustion or our frustration. No help for us, except what we were able to give each other.

And for once I did do something to be proud of. I reached deep inside to find something extra. I knew that if someone didn't rev up the five of us, then this was the end of the road. We were finished.

"OK guys," I said to them. "Forget the being tired crap. Lee, can you get us to the packs?"

"Yes," he said. But his voice was dead, like he'd had enough.

"Lee!" I yelled at him. I ran at him and turned him round and pushed him hard in the back, pushed him along the road for twenty metres. That was all. It wasn't very much. But I got them moving, and only I know how utterly and hopelessly exhausted I was at the time.

Lee led us to the packs. I think we struggled even to find the strength to get them on. But we helped each other and we did it.

I was trying to think where we should go, what we should do. Hell was the place to go, of course, but we had to be so careful not to lead the enemy there. If we ever lost that sanctuary we would be in more trouble than a Mars Bar in a school canteen. At first I thought we had to go bush again. That was where I felt safe. I still had faith in the bush, as the place where we were still better than them. I could live in the bush the way an alligator can live in a swamp. There was a kind of comfort about the bush for me.

245

But there were problems in going bush right now. The main one being that around Wirrawee was mainly light scrub. And less of that since our bushfire. Sure there was enough to hide us for a day or two. But a major search lasting a week or more, possibly using dogs again, that was a different matter. If we stayed in the bush around Wirrawee they'd find us eventually. And if we did the other thing, headed out into the real bush, the serious bush, that was like saying to them, "Look, we're hanging out around Mt. Martin, OK? Try Tailor's Stitch or Wombegonoo." Not quite that obvious maybe, but if we went in that direction, and they knew it, they'd work it out sooner or later.

Then a little image floated into my brain. It was the entrance hall of the house in Wirrawee where we'd met the officer wearing the boxer shorts. The image was of the overflowing ashtray in the entrance hall. And the one tunic hanging on the coat stand, and the one pair of guns, and the one officer's cap. Those images said something loud and clear to me: that here was a man who lived alone. Not even a housekeeper to come and clean his ashtrays. In these days of free labour, slave labour, that was surprising, but maybe he just didn't like to have someone tidy up after him. My father, who never touched a vacuum cleaner in his life, who probably wouldn't know which end of it to use, was like that. Even the noise of the vacuum enraged him. He'd always tell me to come back another time.

"Do you have to do that now? Can't it wait?"

Loading the dishwasher was the extent of his domestic effort.

I tried to put myself in the mind of the enemy. To

imagine how they'd think. They'd expect us to go bush. That was the first thing, the obvious thing. To go back into Wirrawee would seem suicidal. They'd credit us with more intelligence. They must know that we were creatures of the bush. And the place in Wirrawee where we were least likely to go was the house of the dead officer. We would have no reason to go there, and because it was the centre of the night's action it would seem too dangerous for us to even contemplate. The only people who might go there in the next little while were his friends, to clean up his things.

I didn't tell the others what I thought. Even though Homer had used the same argument when we were at the lookout—that we should go into Wirrawee because that's what they wouldn't expect—I decided this time to get them moving first. Otherwise I'd have a rebellion on my hands. Things were tougher now than they had been at the lookout even. I wouldn't have blamed them for rebelling—the thought of voluntarily walking back into the hotbed of soldiers and blood and death that we'd just stirred up horrified me enough. Might as well paint jam all over yourself and walk into a nest of European wasps. But I felt strongly that it was our best chance.

I got them going again. "Come on, I know a good place, let's move. Come on, Kev, sure you're tired, but just do it. Hate it if you want, but do it. Come on Fi, I'll give you a push start too."

I'm sure it made them mad, my carrying on like that. I felt like a kindergarten teacher. "Now children, have you all been to the toilet? Tim, you take Jodie's hand. Charlotte, you take Rick's. Simon, where's your jumper?"

But I got them going. And what's more, once they started they moved fairly well. That was more than I'd dared hope for. We had a few big hours ahead. We had no hope of getting into Wirrawee from this side, with the noises we could hear through the trees. Noises and lights. This was building up into something bigger than a Grand Final. We had to get away fast and do almost a complete circumnavigation of Wirrawee. I figured if we came in from, say, the other end of Warrigle Road, past the Mathers' place, Robyn's house, we'd be fairly safe. But that meant a hell of a hike, through rough bush, in darkness, in a state of terror and depression and exhaustion.

The only advantage we had now was that the soldiers knew we were armed. They'd seen Fi and me with the officer's weapons, and they'd think, having found his body, that we were happy to use them. Lucky they didn't know what we were really like. I hoped they wouldn't know how much ammunition we had. I hadn't checked the hand gun but the rifle had only one more round. But they would be less than thrilled about plunging into the bush in the middle of the night to confront a gang of trigger-happy half-crazed teenagers. I was as certain as I could be that they'd wait till daylight.

So I led the gang of trigger-happy half-crazed teenagers in a big circle around Wirrawee. As we walked I gradually broke the news to them. I took my time, because the longer I talked the longer they'd have something to think about besides their own exhaustion and sense of failure. It gave me something to think about, too. So I went through all the options, chucking in any joke I could think of, no matter how weak or sad or downright tragic. I told the boys how Fi and I had been forced to run into this house and how I thought only one man lived there, and now he was dead. Until finally I got to the point where I could say: "Our best chance is to go right back into that house. I know you're not going to like it, but we've got to keep doing the unexpected, the unpredictable, or we're dead meat."

Lee said, "I agree."

Homer said, "It wasn't half-obvious that's what you were going to say."

Fi said, "OK."

Kevin said, "Oh God, not more days hiding in Wirrawee."

But he was the only one to complain. And I did have some sympathy with him. The boredom, the solid hour upon hour of doing absolutely nothing, of waiting for the clock to tick away another day, of feeling that each day consisted of 120 hours, of playing stupid meaningless card games, of arguing over trivia, of having to do sentry duty where you'd stare out into the street with nothing to look at but knowing that if you took your eyes away for a second it might mean the death of your friends, the sense that you had all this energy but you couldn't find anything to do with it...I hated, Kevin hated, we all hated these terrible days holed up in little corners like scared rats.

But we still wanted to stay alive. When all was said and done, that was the ultimate motivation. And so we trudged on, with nothing much to look forward to but the right to stay alive a little longer. Lee came up beside me as we walked along and, although he didn't say anything, I felt a little better that he was there.

Walk, walk, walk, that was all we seemed to do. And towards dawn I had to get everyone to speed up even further, because I realised we were getting short of time. So we had to half-jog to reach Warrigle Street.

The last stretch, through Wirrawee itself, was surprisingly easy. After all our problems it seemed a bit of a joke that this part went so smoothly. But we hurried along the streets, doing our usual things like leapfrogging and keeping to shadows. We heard a couple of vehicles and saw a couple of headlights in the distance, but nothing that really threatened us.

Maybe it wasn't all that surprising. They'd had an exciting night, but after that they'd want their sleep. The ones who were still up, searching for us, would be concentrating their energies on the other side of town and out around the racecourse. Our whole strategy was based on that belief. I suppose my real surprise came from the fact that something I'd thought through in my head actually worked in practise. Life would be a big shock if that happened too often.

So, we got there, without a lot of drama. The drama was in the fear and exhaustion along the way. It was in the anticipation, the expectation. It was in the fear that every step could bring danger. The air crackled with tension, the hot night sweated as much as we did. But the drama was all in my mind.

The house was as still and silent as the cemetery. We tiptoed through each room. Homer and I carried the weapons—he the hand gun, me the rifle. There was nothing but the smell of the man who'd lived there, the smell and the little signs of his stay. He'd more or less camped in the place, it looked like: a couple of kitbags were scattered across the bedroom floor and there were socks everywhere. Two opened cans on the kitchen bench. A load of washing still in the machine. It was kind of sad, to see how little trace of his life was left already.

I still felt, and the others agreed, that the only immediate danger would be from people coming to clean up the house and pack his stuff. And that would only happen during normal hours. We were safe from, say, ten o'clock at night to eight each morning.

The later danger would be from new people moving into the house. But I knew that probably wouldn't happen for a while. There were still plenty of empty places around, and I didn't think people would want to move straight into the house of a dead man. I mean, it was a good house, sure, but not that good.

Once Homer and I proved to ourselves that the place was empty there was a rush to the kitchen. We were all so hungry, and keen to get a bit of variety in our diet. And the kitchen was quite well stocked. Nothing like an officer for having the best of everything. Mr. Kassar told us in Drama about an American convoy in Vietnam that was going north, being escorted by soldiers, and some of the soldiers died in a big ambush. And when they finally got the convoy to its destination they found they'd been escorting caviar and champagne for the officers. People had died for that.

Well, this guy didn't have any caviar and champagne but he did have a nice assortment of chips and bikkies and fresh bread, and lots of food that I didn't know and had never seen before. It was a weird time to be eating, with the sun just appearing, but that didn't worry anyone. The only interruption was when Kevin paused between mouthfuls to say, "Good idea coming here, Ellie."

I made a face at him and kept eating.

We sussed out the backyard. It was well protected, lots of big trees to stop the neighbours peering over the fence. And in one tree, a nice old jacaranda, there was quite a big tree house. We made it our choice for a day-time hiding place. If the only people who came here were cleaning up after their mate they wouldn't bother checking that out.

I was feeling a bit better about myself. I knew — or, at least, I thought — that we wouldn't have made it this far without me. Just so long as there were no disasters while we were here. But now I really did them a favour. I volunteered to take the first sentry duty. Fi looked at me in disbelief, but no one waited around to see if I was serious. They grabbed pillows from a linen press in the hallway and headed out to the tree with their packs and sleeping bags. I settled myself in the entrance hall where I could see the street.

I actually did the unforgivable while I was there. I think — no, I know — that I went to sleep for a short time. Probably half an hour or even forty minutes. I was disgusted with myself when I woke; when Chris did the same thing once I went sick at him. For the rest of the morning I made myself get up and walk around every time I felt tired.

I wanted to give them as long as possible to sleep. I was really into martyrdom that day. Must have been Robyn's influence.

In the street the traffic flowed backwards and forwards. Wirrawee was a lot more alive again these days. Not the life I would have chosen for it, but in a strange way I almost preferred this to when it was dead and blacked out in the early stages of the war.

I didn't feel that there was any particular search in Wirrawee for us. There was no urgency about the traffic going past. Why would there be? They'd be searching the bush, and it'd be a full-on hunt there. But in town they had to get on with their other business, their normal business. There was no way in the world they'd expect us to come back here. And if they did we now had both the hand gun and the rifle.

By lunchtime I'd had enough. Even walking around didn't help. I knew it'd take half an hour to wake Homer but I had to do it. I toddled out to the tree, almost zigzagging in my weariness, and climbed to the tree house, one slow step at a time. I was right — it did take about half an hour to wake Homer, and even then he didn't want to move. But I just wouldn't let him go back to sleep. I couldn't. They say fatigue kills, and it sure was killing me. Once I'd evicted Homer from the tree house I slept till after sunset.

Twenty-two

I woke around ten. There was some light from the house next door, not much, but enough to see that no one was left in the tree except Lee and me. He was asleep beside me, breathing softly and quietly. But even in sleep his face looked troubled. Too many lines, too dark. He moved restlessly as I watched him. He drew his arm in closer to his body and turned a little.

I couldn't help leaning over and kissing him on the mouth. I think he woke instantly, because as I straightened up again I saw his eyes open. I didn't know my kisses were that powerful. He didn't smile, but neither did I. I was remembering the last time I kissed him. We just looked at each other for a while without blinking. When I kissed him again he put his arm around me and pulled me closer. After we kissed I rested my head on his chest. Glancing down I could see that my kisses were even more powerful than I'd realised.

I smiled and said, "I thought boys only woke up like that in the mornings."

"What?" he asked.

He hadn't heard me.

"Nothing," I said. I didn't even know if what I'd said was right and I didn't want to look ignorant. I was just going on what I'd picked up from jokes at school.

We kissed again, gradually getting more and more passionate. I felt so warm. Everything seemed to slow down and feel soft and close and private. There's nothing like the feeling of someone's hands on your skin. His hands were inside my shirt and I liked it a lot. I was rubbing the back of his neck. I was getting more and more excited. But I also realised, suddenly, a bit to my own surprise, that I didn't want to go all the way with him. I knew we were both heading fast into a zone where it might be difficult to stop. So when he slipped his hand into my jeans I fished it out again. And reluctantly, hating it, I started drawing back, disentangling myself.

"What?" he asked, scowling at me. He reached out for me again.

"Sorry," I said, "I don't know why. I just don't want to. Not for a while."

"Now you tell me," he said, sulkily.

I buttoned myself up, already feeling the warmth go. My clothes weren't enough to keep it in.

"Sorry," I said again. "You looked so cute lying there. I couldn't help myself."

"Thanks for nothing," he said.

I was determined I wasn't going to get angry, so I ignored that. I didn't blame him in a way. If only I could have understood what was going on in my own mind... but I found that difficult at the best of times. And this wasn't the best of times.

I put my boots on and went down the ladder. I was still wondering why I'd backed off like that. It was nothing to do with Lee. I still liked him a lot. I'd got over the feelings I'd had ages ago, the negative feelings towards him. So it wasn't that. I thought maybe it was something to do with the boy in New Zealand, whose name I realised with a shock I'd forgotten. It would come back to me, no doubt about that, but for the moment I couldn't think of it at all. And I thought it was probably also to do with the dead man whose house we had sneaked into — not that it was his house anyway — but the fact that we were living in a dead man's house.

And, of course, the fact that I'd killed him. I didn't know his name either. Weird: two guys who figured prominently in my life, and they were both nameless to me.

Instead of going into the house right away I stood in the backyard for a few minutes thinking about all this. I saw Fi's shadow, briefly, through the kitchen window, but I was pleased there was no other evidence of people being in the place. We were getting pretty good at this stuff, hiding out, living rough and tough. It seemed a funny skill to be proud of, but it was a skill. I admired the fox his craftiness, the way he could get into the chookyard and out again, leaving nothing but blood behind. Blood and feathers and a few squawks from the chooks. We were getting more like foxes all the time.

That made me think of Lee again, for some reason. Why didn't I want to have him in me, to lie naked with him and do the things that excited us both so much?

A slow awareness came over me, a kind of burning, as I realised. Yes, it was because of the boy in New Zealand and the man who'd lived in this house. And because I'd screamed at the soldier in the street. And because I'd left the door open at Tozer's. And because the fuel tank had been padlocked. And because I'd sneezed. It was something like: "I don't deserve to enjoy the loving feelings of Lee embracing me and making love to me. I don't deserve that."

I still felt cheapened by what had happened at that Wellington party, and disgusted and horrified by the blood that had spread through the four-wheel drive. Blood shed by my finger on a rifle trigger. Blood from a man who one moment had been living and the next was dead because of my hands. I felt embarrassed and ashamed that I'd screamed at the soldier. I knew that scream might have cost twelve New Zealanders their lives.

Not for the first time I wished I was back in Andrea's office, talking to someone who seemed to understand.

I saw Fi's shadow again through the kitchen window and felt another of those rushes of affection and admiration for her that I'd been feeling since I was about five years old. I thought, "At least I can talk to Fi."

Maybe one day I'd be able to talk to Lee about all this stuff. I hoped he'd understand. I felt like until we had that conversation our relationship would struggle. It was hard having any kind of relationship in the middle of a war. We'd both have to work at it.

I sighed and went inside. While I'd been getting Lee turned on, Fi had been turning on the electric stove. We knew we couldn't risk cooking anything that might give out a smell to alert the neighbours, but she had boiled some eggs. Hot food is one of the greatest luxuries in life, I think, and I ate three eggs without pausing. Then I grabbed some junk from the cupboards—dried seaweed and Twisties and a bit of cheese—and took over from Kevin in the entrance hall.

I spent three hours watching the stupid street. Nothing happened. There had been plenty of times doing sentry when I'd almost wished something would happen to break the boredom, but this wasn't one of them. I knew we weren't in any condition to cope with another crisis. But in the last hour of my shift Homer came out to talk to me, which was really nice. We seemed to talk so seldom these days. And for the first time I heard the story of what happened at the airfield. Homer actually laughed when he started telling me

257

about it. "It was such a mess," he said. "I'm embarrassed. Or I would be if you guys had done any better. But the way Fi described your trip to the fuel depot, I'd say there's not much to pick between us. It wasn't too professional, compared to Cobbler's Bay, for example."

I wasn't yet at a point where I could laugh about the fuel depot. So I ignored Homer's comments.

"So tell me, tell me."

"Well, I think they've got some kind of super-duper security system there. Fair dinkum, I can't see how they could have busted us without some special gadget to do it. We were so bloody careful. We walked about fifty k's around the airfield with the packs, you know, to give it a wide berth so we wouldn't set off any alarms. Then after we dumped the packs we walked all the way back, being just as careful. We got up into the bush, still no problems. We had plenty of time — for a while we thought we were running late so we belted along pretty fast and ended up getting there early. So we chose the best spot, agreed the wind was good and coming from the right direction, and sat there with Lee's little can of fuel, telling ourselves that we were soon going to be heroes. Then the next thing we hear is this uproar from town — vehicles and guns, the whole bit, and we thought 'Bloody Ellie and Fi, causing trouble again. Can't leave them alone for five minutes.' But we also thought, 'Maybe we'd better bring our bonfire forward, cause a distraction for anyone having a go at you guys.' It took us about one and a half seconds to make that decision. Lee jumped up and started pouring the petrol and I got the matches, which I'd cleverly remembered to bring. And just as I'm ready to strike the match Kevin says, 'Get a load of the soldiers.' And I look down at the airfield and there's three jeeps, all loaded with guys, screaming out of the main gate. I thought they'd turn right and go into town, to join the shooting party there, and that's what I was hoping, of course, because I'd rather they chased you than me, any day. But the next thing they turned left and came straight up the road towards us. Kevin yelled, 'They're coming after us!' and I thought, 'He's right.' I struck the match, chucked it on the ground and we all took off. There was a good little whoosh behind us and I thought, 'Beauty, it's caught, should go well with this breeze,' but I didn't look back. There wasn't time. I could hear the jeeps coming flat-chat up the hill, and there were a couple of shots just as we went over the ridge. It was all action, I promise you."

"How long had you been up there before the jeeps came out of the gate?" I asked.

"About five minutes. That's the weird thing. It's like they knew we were there. We thought you guys must have dobbed us in."

I sure must have been tired, because I looked so horrified that Homer had to quickly add: "Just kidding."

"Oh, right, OK. So how do you think they knew?"

"Well, like I said, I think they've got some gadget. Maybe radar or something. I didn't know. But that could explain what happened to the Kiwis. Because when I was talking to Iain, he never thought there'd be any problems like that. He thought it'd be a bit of a snack actually."

"Yeah, I got that impression." Privately I was feeling enormous relief. Maybe I hadn't sabotaged the Kiwis after all. "So what did you do then?"

"Circled around, yet again. I got to know that patch of bush pretty well, I tell you. We came back over the ridge about three-quarters of a k along. Mainly we wanted to enjoy the sight of the fire roaring down onto the airfield and the planes bursting into flames before they could get off the ground."

"But...?"

"Exactly. But. The bloody fire was completely out. We could see a few red bits smouldering, but no flame at all. And the worst thing was I don't think the soldiers even had to put it out. I think it just didn't catch in the first place. Wouldn't it wreck you? At home, you're desperate never to start a bushfire and every time you turn around you've set off another one."

This was only a slight exaggeration because to my certain knowledge Homer, as a little boy, had started at least three fires. But I held my tongue and he went on.

"So here we were doing our best to start one, even using petrol, and we get absolutely nowhere. It's like the song says: 'Isn't it ironic?'"

I grinned. Didn't matter what mood I was in, Homer could always make me laugh. It occurred to me that maybe that was why he'd come into the entrance hall, because he sensed that I was depressed and needed cheering up. It wouldn't be the first time. I hated to accuse Homer of being a warm sensitive guy, but deep down inside he did have a trace of it at times.

Only a little trace mind you.

"So what happened then?" I asked.

"Well, we hadn't realised that the soldiers were spreading through the bush. And fast. These guys were professionals. I suppose they'd have their crack troops

260

guarding the airfield. Suddenly one of them popped up about fifty metres away. We saw him before he saw us, which was fairly lucky. We just turned and sprinted. We were into the trees before he started firing but a couple of bullets went so close to me." He shivered. "I reckon I could have put my hand out and caught one of them. What do they call that in Australian Rules, a mark or something?"

That was Homer being funny again. He hated football; in fact, he hated nearly all sports, and he often tried to pretend he didn't know anything about them.

"They'd call it committing suicide, I think," I said. "So what happened? You got away OK?"

"No, the next bullet went straight through my heart and I was killed. Chuck us the rest of those Twisties, will you? Thanks. Seeing you've been so generous with them I'll admit I was lying about being killed. No, we just kept running. We took a roundabout route to the racecourse, and got there at the same time as you guys. And then another roundabout route to here. Lucky you're such a bully, Ellie, because we were stuffed. If we'd tried to come the direct way, like we would have if you hadn't driven us along, we might have walked into those soldiers. They were smart. I reckon they'd have been sniffing around a lot longer than some of the idiots we've seen in action in the past. But last night I wasn't thinking of that. I was just cursing you for nipping at our heels all the way here."

Homer said all this while casually tipping Twisties into his mouth but I sat there burning with pleasure. Homer simply didn't pay people compliments. If God appeared in front of us Homer would say, "Listen mate, you've done a lousy job on my belly button. And what'd you give us toenails for? I mean what's the good of them? They're a bloody nuisance."

So although I didn't give him the slightest clue that I was pleased, I sure was.

"Well," I said casually, "in my last life I guess I must have been a blue heeler."

Twenty-three

We stayed there four days. We had only one real moment of fear, and that was when a couple of soldiers came to pack the man's stuff. It was at eight o'clock on our last night, Sunday. Fi was on sentry and the rest of us were up the tree, waiting impatiently for the time when it'd be safe to re-enter the house. Ten o'clock was usually the earliest we went inside.

Fi saw them coming and did what we'd agreed. She ran through to the back door and out of the house. As she crossed the backyard she pulled on a string which we'd hung from the tree house. This was the warning to us. Then she hid in the passionfruit vines that formed a huge mass of leaves and flowers on the back fence.

The men were only there for half an hour. I guess they wouldn't have enjoyed the job. After the sounds from the house had finished, and the lights had gone out, we waited a full three hours, till nearly midnight, before going to the back door. Then we found they'd locked the house.

We weren't too keen on breaking a window. We could've done it without much noise, but anyone visiting the next day would have known something was wrong. We looked at each other, trying to decide our next move.

"It's time we were out of here, anyway," Homer said. "It should be safe enough by now. There's no real point in even going inside. We ate nearly all his food and these guys probably took the rest. I vote we go back to Hell, call up Colonel Finley, and get ourselves a ticket to New Zealand, business class."

We agreed quickly, and with relief. We were all ready to go. We felt there was nothing we could achieve in Wirrawee for the time being. Maybe Colonel Finley would suggest something when we reported to him again, but the airfield seemed beyond anything we could manage, and the fate of the Kiwi soldiers was a complete mystery. I couldn't speak for the others but for myself I had such a longing to get to safe New Zealand that I thought I might faint when Homer mentioned the word. I'd changed my views again since we'd first come back.

And so we started on that familiar journey. Again we became shadows in the night, dark dingoes slinking home to our lair. We didn't flinch when we heard the strange cackling noise that foxes make when they feed together, nor when we heard the *oooooom* of the tawny frogmouths or the clatter of bark falling from a gum or the sharp ripping and crack of a branch suddenly breaking. We slipped silently through the dry scrub when we could and at other times moved quickly and quietly across the bare paddocks. Cattle followed us curiously, sheep baaed and bolted when we startled them with our approach.

Occasionally a bird, as startled as the sheep, would fly away with a wild shocked whirr of wings. We ignored them all and hurried on.

The sun was well up and the land and air getting rapidly hotter when we climbed to the top of Tailor's Stitch. As was usual for us nowadays we had made a big detour around my own house. I didn't know who lived there now and I didn't want to know. I felt more comfortable in Hell than around home.

We did the same as we had such a short time ago with the Kiwis: waited off the side of Tailor's Stitch until dark. Another of those delays that at times I thought would make me scream with boredom, but which at other times I spent quite happily, talking or thinking or daydreaming.

This day passed at the pace of a day on a tractor, when you know at the end of it you'll still have three paddocks to go and each one will feel the same as the one you're in.

I think it seemed all the longer because for once there was something to look forward to. If we could contact Colonel Finley from the top of Wombegonoo that night, we could maybe be out of there within three or four days. It was nearly a week — five days to be exact — since we were meant to have called him, so I figured he'd be keen to hear from us. And although we had no good news for him it would be a relief to hear his voice. It would make me feel I was back in New Zealand already. I longed for the moment when we could make the call, and hungrily counted the hours, the minutes, before we switched on the little transmitter.

At nine o'clock we eagerly trekked to the highest point of Wombegonoo, to the spot where we could be sure of getting the best conditions for our broadcast.

Epilogue

I wouldn't say I'd ever trusted Colonel Finley. I quite liked him in some ways. He was so English, like an actor out of those old black-and-white British movies. He had a moustache, smoked a pipe, and worked in a study with tonnes of books in oak bookcases and nice pictures of things like horses and farmlands and oceans.

Maybe it was all a bit too good to be true, a bit too much like an English gentleman in a film.

I don't know. Fi and I argue about this. She says I'm too hard on him. She may be right. I still feel he's doublecrossed us though. Sure, I know times are hard, there's a war on, the New Zealanders can't afford to waste their resources, but I do think he should have sent the helicopter. I feel we've done enough to be given a bit of consideration. OK, maybe not on this trip, where we failed at just about everything. But we did quite a bit in the past, especially at Cobbler's Bay.

They might come for us yet, of course. He didn't say they were dumping us here forever. He's not that ruthless. It was just the shock, I suppose. Or the disappointment. Being so keyed up to make our escape. Being so happy at the thought that we could be safe again, live normally again, eat and sleep and talk openly to people. Hot food and hot showers and clean sheets. That was all I wanted, all I looked forward to. It doesn't seem much to hope for, does it? Not much compared to what we once had, and what we took for granted.

So I can't make up my mind about the Colonel. Is he a good man, trying to make the best of a bad situation? Allocating his resources without fear or favour? Sticking to his principle of "cost-effectiveness," no matter what? Or is he a cynical cold-blooded cold-hearted mongrel who used us and then dumped us?

Maybe time will give me the answers to those questions and maybe it won't.

I guess our fate is up to us now. And we've been there before, of course. There's something quite comforting about it in a strange way. We've learnt a few things. We know we've got a few things going for us. A bit of imagination, a bit of guts sometimes, a bit of spark. I remember our old dog, Millie, getting run over by a tractor then struggling up again and trying to keep mustering. That's us, I reckon. Some of the things that have happened to us were like being run over by a convoy of tanks.

But we're still here, we're still alive, we're not giving up yet.

It's like Homer said this morning when I was talking to him about our next call to Colonel Finley, on Tuesday, "Well, tell him, stuff him, we'll do it on our own."

From the first day of the invasion I knew that if we were going to live with ourselves on the terms that we wanted, we'd have to pay a price. Like the man in the poem. And we've paid a price every day since. It's expensive. The man in the poem found that out. But I don't want to live cheap, or live for nothing. I never have wanted that and I've never liked it. That's one lesson my parents taught me. That's why I don't like what I did with the boy in New Zealand. That's why I do like my friendship with Fi and Lee and Homer and Kevin. It's why I love and respect the memory of Corrie and Robyn. It's why I feel sad that Chris never learned that lesson.

When I think about it, I realise it was the same before the war. I was never so aware of it then though. Pity I needed a war to learn it properly. Believe me, I'd do a few things differently if we had those days back again. Even in peacetime it's expensive to be the kind of person you want, to live the kind of life you know is right.

Well, I've learnt this much: it doesn't matter what it costs, it's worth paying the price. You can't live cheap and you can't live for nothing. Pay the price and be proud you've paid it, that's what I reckon.

Poems Appearing in the Text

Page 228, "The Refined Man," by Rudyard Kipling, from A *Choice of Kipling's Verse*, T.S. Eliot ed., Faber and Faber, London, 1963.

Pages 2 and 227, "Here Dead We Lie," by A.E. Housman, from *Up the Line to Death*, Brian Gardner ed., Methuen and Co., London, 1976.

Page 100, "Smoke curls up around the old gum tree trunk," Australian traditional.

Page 45, "The Man from Snowy River," by Banjo Paterson.